Mark Powell was born in 1967. He teaches literacy part-time and lives in Bethnal Green, London. *Box* is his second novel.

By Mark Powell

Box
Snap

BOX

MARK POWELL

PHOENIX

A PHOENIX PAPERBACK

First published in Great Britain in 2003
by Weidenfeld & Nicolson
This paperback edition published in 2003
by Phoenix,
an imprint of Orion Books Ltd,
Orion House, 5 Upper Saint Martin's Lane,
London WC2H 9EA

A CIP catalogue record for this book
is available from the British Library.

ISBN 0 75381 701 2

Printed and bound in Great Britain by
Clays Ltd, St Ives plc

To my parents

The Sons of Arsenal

1

The jazz-funk days are long gone. The days of the Lyceum on the Strand and the Goldmine on Canvey Island, when thousands descended in Cortina, Escort and Granada from all over London and the South-East to dance to Lonnie Liston-Smith, Donald Byrd, Light of the World, Ramsey Lewis, Bob James, Roy Ayers and the rest of the legends. Sporting wedges, ski jackets, loafers, Farahs, garishly striped tees. When the ghetto came to Guildford and Manhattan met Manor Park. When Studio 54 surfaced in Stapleford Abbots. And Somers Town, NW1.

Somers Town lies south of Camden, wedged between Euston and King's Cross stations. Wide streets in straight lines running between twenty housing blocks. Identical in shape and the colour of milky tea. Cars slowly clambering over speed bumps. Children staring out of high-rise glass. Black stains of sewage from ruptured overflow pipes paint the block walls. A blot of inner city within a throw of the exclusive Bloomsbury, Regent's Park, Primrose Hill and Marylebone. Somers Town: home to an intimidating hum rather than the noisy harmlessness south of the Ring Road. Somers Town: home to Clive and Stanley.

The jazz-funk days are long gone, but still the two thirty-six-year-olds wear market-stall jewellery and spin vinyl on turntables and nod heads to Earth Wind and Fire as if 1980 had stretched for twenty years. They still live on the home patch and await the break.

The air smells of dustbins and the wind blows coughs and sneezes from the bus queue into the faces of the two friends as they march past.

They don't like Mondays: their seriousness; their loneliness.

– What do all rich people have in common? Stanley asks.

Clive pushes out his bottom lip.

– Think about it, Clivey-boy.

– I d-d-don't know.

Stanley throws a bewildered stare at Clive. – Think about it, for Christ's sake. Don't just say you don't know when you haven't even thought about it.

Clive pulls the lip back in and pretends to concentrate on a question to which he knows he does not have an answer.

– I r-r-r-really don't know.

Stanley hurls his head to one side in disgust. He mumbles to himself before turning back and locking eyes with Clive.

– OK, OK, Stanley says, his hand flapping in front of him. – What do all successful people have in common? Forget the money bit, just think success.

The friends walk the street under a sky of pigeon grey. To the Employment Service for the fortnightly signature and 'How's the job-search going?' enquiry.

It is mid-June yet the sun has not shone all year.

– I just don't kn-kn-know, Clive shrugs.

Stanley folds his eyes into a squint. – I've been thinking about it.

– Well? Clive asks.

A quick cough. A wipe of the mouth. A hand shaped into a point and prodded towards Clive.

– Bollocks.

Clive creases his eyebrows and continues to walk, saying nothing.

– Bollocks, Clivey-boy. Balls, nerve, front. You know, bottle.

Clive's expression opens and he breaks into a nod. – Yeah, yeah, I g-g-guess.

– That's been our problem in the past. We haven't pushed ourselves out of the comfort zone. We've buckled when things got rough.

– M-m-m-maybe.

– We haven't been fearless.

– Maybe.

2

The friends have spent years looking for opportunities, seeking the idea that will make the loot and retire them before forty.

They've had a go at most things.

Windows

The second week out of school and Stanley is traipsing around Camden Town (too many flats in Somers Town, not enough money) in baggy shorts knocking on doors. Clive lugs the ladder and bucket.

– Do your windows, love? Stanley asks at the first house.

A tiny woman, even smaller than Stanley – who stands little over five foot – peers from behind a door. – I'm afraid I've got a regular.

– We'll undercut him, Stanley blurts.

– I couldn't do that. Sorry.

Next house.

– Do your windows, love?

– How much? a woman with cropped hair enquires.

– Ten.

– No, ta, she says, pushing the door shut.

– Eight? Stanley says to the door-knocker.

Tenth house.

– Do your windows, love?

The woman occupant just stares at Stanley, disdainfully. – How can I afford someone to clean my windows? she says. – I've got four kids to look after on my own, there's water dripping down my living-room wall, the council don't answer the phone, and you want me to pay for window-cleaning?

– Calm down, love. Only asking.

– Well ask elsewhere.

Fifteenth house.

– Do your windows, love?

– Who are you calling 'love'? a man in a Spurs shirt sneers.

They managed to create a round of twenty houses throughout Camden and parts of Islington but the money wasn't enough, it was hard work, and none of the women wanted to know. The window-cleaning game was all over within six months.

Hot Dogs

Stanley knows a friend of a friend of a friend who is off-loading a frying wagon with an attached steamer. Perfect for the tourists in town willing to pay over the odds for food.

Stanley and Clive save a few cheques, take a little loan off Sylvia (Stanley's mum) and buy the dream; as well as the sausages, rolls and onions.

They push the cart all the way from Eversholt Road to Leicester Square.

Following a series of near-misses with cars, buses, taxis, and a shower of verbal abuse from pedestrians, they arrive in town and start frying.

Even before the first sausage is cooked and the tangy scent of onions can entice the hordes, two policemen are standing large in front of the wagon.

– See your licence?

Clive looks to Stanley, Stanley looks to the browning sausage.

– Licence, please, the policeman repeats.

– What do you mean licence? Stanley replies.

They receive a warning and decide to lie low for the rest of the day.

The next day they try Buckingham Palace. Before they make their first sale the police are at the cart. This time they take names and addresses.

The next day they try Madame Tussaud's on Marylebone Road. Tumbled by the old bill before the hot plate becomes hot.

The following night they change tack and decide to steer clear of town and head for outdoor events. They try the travelling circus in Clissold Park in Stoke Newington.

The sausages crisp, the onions melt into mushy brown, the rolls are buttered.

A black man with dreadlocks stacked beneath a hat approaches.
– You can't sell here, he says.
– What's that, mate? Stanley replies.
The man stares down his nose at Stanley, throws a fist into his palm, then nods towards another hot-dog stall at the other side of the park. A guy behind the wagon is pointing a spatula straight at Clive.
Clive's black skin turns pale. – L-l-l-l-let's pack up.

On the way home they decide to tip the cart into Regent's canal and collect the insurance.

Disc Jockey

Stanley dreams of being a DJ, making it big and playing the all-dayers, the all-nighters, the all-weekenders. Sees some of the guys from school making a packet spinning at clubs and parties. Sees the guys walking out with different girls every week.

Clive carries the equipment and the record bags while Stanley, a.k.a. Stan Francisco the Man with the Disco, ingratiates himself with the crowd at the wedding. Got the job through an ad in the local paper.
– Ah, this is what it's all about, he sighs to Clive, lining up the first record of the night.
– Looks like a n-n-nice crowd.
Stanley runs through the regular set that includes 'Celebrate' – Kool and the Gang; 'Good Times' – Chic; 'I Will Survive' – Gloria Gaynor; 'Night Fever' – Bee Gees.
Stanley is enjoying the evening, standing like a king behind the decks looking down on the dancing throng as Clive passes up the next disc on the playlist. He even winks at one of the bridesmaids.
– She's after me, Stanley shouts over the sound, using his eyes to push Clive's stare towards the bridesmaid. – This DJ lark is great. The girls just go for it.
The next moment Stanley is being hauled over the turntables by the bridesmaid's husband. Stanley squirms on the dance floor under a barrage of kicks.

Stanley, despite his DJ dreams, never quite got his confidence back to go public again with his sound system. Stan Francisco retired from disco.

2

The signing is swift and Stanley and Clive are soon back outside under cloud. Stanley's dark eyebrows twitch at the impending rain. He throws his side-parting across his forehead with a flick of the neck.

    – Let's hit some shelter.

    – Where do you w-w-want to go?

    – A drink?

    – I'm easy.

    – What about the Brewers?

Clive suddenly looks exhausted. – What about s-somewhere different?

The Sons of Arsenal are squeezed into the Two Brewers. Dressed in Arsenal shirts, sweatshirts; others in suits. White faces, a few black, all flushed with hooch. Most went to school with Stanley and Clive.

    The two friends slip into the half-light and make their way to the bar.

    – How's tricks, Clive? a face asks.

    – Not so b-bad, Dean, Clive replies. – Yourself?

    – Well happy, just got me bonus.

Stanley edges through a gap of red jerseys, his head brushing against shoulders.

    – Hello, Stan, says someone else.

    – All right, Craig. How's things?

    – Just selling up the old man's firm.

    – What you going to do?

    – Get out of this dump, he says, laughing.

Stanley offers a lacklustre grin.

*

The Sons do not always drink in the Brewers. They often congregate at a private drinking house on Copenhagen Street in King's Cross where Calais booze is served at a decent price. Where there are sofas to lie back into. Where people go way back when. Where ladies are forbidden (except for the fortnightly arrival of girls from downtown to play). Where old battles are discussed (taking on the Leeds, meating up the Everton, chopping coppers at Finsbury Park in '82). Where they talk about money – for outside the Brewers, outside the house on Copenhagen Street, there are BMWs, Porsches, Mercs, Jaguars, top-of-the-range Japanese saloons. Most of the Sons have done well: in the City from barrow to broker; inside family firms; feet under the table at global corporations; setting up DTP companies, tyre-fitting franchises, painting and decorating firms, printing businesses.

South Camden Community School (SCCS) is a long time ago for a lot of the Sons. Only for Clive and Stanley does it seem recent. Not so much water under the bridge.

Stanley takes his bottle of 5 per cent lager, Clive grabs his Coke. They sit at a table towards the back of the pub, on their own – the Sons subconsciously close ranks to shoot the breeze.

– Blimey, Stanley sighs, pushing back into his seat.

– Not much for them to w-w-worry about, Clive adds, his brown eyes enlarged.

Stanley grabs his drink and slurps, licking the rim before tapping it back onto the mat.

– This is our town, Clivey. This is our city.

– W-w-well, theirs.

– School, yeah? You keep your head down, do your time, wait for the bell. We all left at sixteen but we all knew things would happen for us. We all knew people working the firms, running the show. We all did.

– S-s-sort of.

Another swig. An exaggerated swallow.

– We all went out to get it. What we saw others getting, what the pinstripes from suburbia were having, what this country fought all these wars for. Got dressed up, got stuck in, played hard, worked hard. You must remember it all, Clive? We were all meant to end up in the system somewhere. End up somebody.

Yeah, sure, some did bird, others hit the high road, some burnt, but it was ours for the taking.

– It is not always that e-e-e-easy.

– The Sons all got it. They took the opportunities whoever they were, whatever they were; ugly, handsome, black, white, all that shit didn't matter.

– Maybe there weren't enough o-o-opportunities to go round?

– Things were different a few years ago, Clivey. That sense of excitement, sense of belonging. Like going to the Goldmine.

– That p-p-place is long shut.

– Yeah, there ain't no cunt dancing there no more.

Only Child

1

Patricia combs damp hair, watching the grey merge into black, watching a line of drips ooze from the plastic teeth onto the bathrobe. She gently places her hand on her mother's cheek. The skin is fragile: a sheet of fine fabric. The skin is cool, despite a hot bath.

The steam from the bathroom has drifted into the bedroom and made a mist on the mirror. Mother sits in front of the dressing table. Patricia's cursory wipe clears a section and allows Mother to stare. Stare at her spent face. At her angry eyes.

Monday evening is a time of reflection.

The comb squeaks through the hair as it guides strands over ears and into a point on collar. The squeak is the only sound in the house now the hot-water pipes, growling with exertion during the bath-running, have settled.

A towel rubbed over head. Hair roused into frizz. Mother's ears are cold. The steam creeps back over the mirror. Patricia fiddles with the wall plug. The hair-dryer blasts into Mother's unblinking gaze. The scent of heat and shampoo gusts over Patricia. Mother's ears remain cold.

– There you go, Mother. That's better.

Mother's response is minimal: a slight twitch of fingers resting on her lap.

Patricia reaches underneath Mother's armpit and gently raises the scarecrow to her feet.

– Don't pinch! Mother hisses.

– Sorry.

Together they limp towards the bed made up with sheets and

valance and blankets and patterned coverlet. A stack of pillows rests against the headboard. A clock and a lamp stand on side-table decorated with lace cloth. Eight thirty p.m.

Patricia bends into the light, casting a shadow across Mother's body. A kiss placed carefully on forehead. Patricia doesn't see a face – the head of Mother becomes a skull. The skin tastes stale.

Mother has lived in the city all her life. Now the city closes in on her as she shuffles through each day. Dragging daughter through the relentless nursing that begins at dawn and ends around nine.

Patricia watches the skeleton struggle into daybreak, watches her hobble to toilet, leak into clothes, drip corn flakes. Watches her lips dry and shrivel, eyes close for forty winks in front of the one o'clock news, veiny hands wipe skirt for no reason, body fold into the shape of the armchair. Watches her cough spittle and limp back into downstairs bedroom at the end of day for bath and brushing and bed.

Patricia goes to the kitchen to make a hot chocolate. Unburdened, with Mother wrapped in sheets and tucked away for the night. Unhappy, with a sense of emptiness, exacerbated by the monotony of the routine.

Cheered by the rumble of boiling water in kettle and the sweet, dry scent of powdered cocoa.

Time alone to think at the close of each day, as it folds away into darkness and silence. To find a light-hearted programme on the telly and join the rest of the watching world in the flicker of blue light. And wait for Mother to interrupt. Patricia has to keep one ear tuned into the bedroom across the hallway. There will be calls for the toilet, for a reset of the sheets and blankets, for a comforting hand to wipe away the sweat of a nightmare. There will be the tap-tap-tap of the glass on table calling for a drink of water.

Patricia stirs the chocolate; the satisfying clink of teaspoon. Lifts the mug to carry to the lounge. Turns to the door and gasps. The mug falls out of her grip and crashes to the floor, spreading steaming cocoa across the linoleum.

– Mother, what are you doing up? she says, ignoring the dropped drink.

Mother stands in the doorway. Tiny and shrunken in her transparent nightie.

– You scared me, Patricia says.

– Broken a best mug, sneers Mother.

– You should be in bed.

– And look at the floor.

– Come on, let's walk you back to your room.

Patricia approaches with opening arms.

– I want to watch the telly, says Mother, looking confused.

– Don't be silly. It's far too late. Let's get you back to bed.

– Don't drop me! Mother says.

– I'll clear the cocoa afterwards.

– Clumsy girl.

– You shouldn't be out of bed.

– Can't even make a drink, can you?

Patricia leads her back to the bedroom. Feeling her fingers pressing bone as she holds Mother's arm. Into the room that has already devoured the scent of bath and returned to its customary stench of old carpet.

With Mother restored to the blankets and the kitchen floor cleaned, Patricia skips the hot drink and the telly to retire upstairs. So tired tonight. She will sleep with the door open and with the alarm set for six. Set for the weekly routine that mother and daughter share in the family house. The Victorian terrace which was once home to three but now just for two. On Sunday Patricia makes a roast, on Wednesday she shops, on Friday she does the washing, on Tuesdays and Thursdays Joan the home-help comes and Patricia goes to work. At the chemist's on Roman Road.

Eight thirty a.m. to five p.m. behind the counter, framed by medicines, dressed in white coat, telling customers to take three a day, rub it on, press it gently, use a finger, pat dry, leave on for five minutes, eat just one a day as a treat, mix it with fruit juice or milk, rinse it, bathe it, pop it, press it, wipe it, brush it, try it and see if it makes a difference. To stand next to Lorraine, thirty years her junior, and joke about the customers after they've left the shop.

The pay is minimum wage, the hours negligible, but it's a break from Mother. Time away from the biting rebukes: 'It's too hot!' 'Not like that!' 'Stop it!' 'Go away!' The thin, high-pitched voice spitting wrath.

2

With her bedroom door open to await Mother's calls and taps, Patricia also hears the moans, hisses, grunts and the creak and crack of old bone.

Mother's call for toilet prompts Patricia's tired clamber from bed to gown and slippers, to Mother and bathroom, to stare out of the window through the gap in the blinds at the flashing lights in sky from aircraft and the stillness on street lit hazy like a bonfire.

Mother was always small but now she is minute. Patricia watches Mother sit wizened on the toilet. The scowl has turned saggy, the acid eyes have rotted. Her once-taut mouth now rubbery.

– Don't stare at me! Mother squeals.

The voice is more squeaky and strained than in younger years. Like the brakes on an old car.

– With those daft eyes, Mother adds.

Patricia turns back to the gap in the blinds. Refusing to respond.

– Like you've swallowed a fly.

Mother sniggers at her own joke. The decaying teeth exposed as she laughs. Mother strokes a hand over her face and the expression returns to misery.

– Wipe me.

Patricia's left eye is skewed; it looks in at the nose. No one ever teased her about it except for Mother. It was not too much bother. She felt more sorry for the people who spoke to her and fought to find and then focus on the good eye.

Mother walks back to bed, supported by daughter. Step by step, slowly inching over carpet. The springs of the mattress make no noise as Mother is lowered back onto its softness. She closes her eyes in relief when her fragile head touches pillow.

Patricia drags the sheets over the body and returns to the bathroom to turn out the light. The cistern hisses with refilling water. Patricia transforms into silhouette, carefully moving across the room like an apparition.

Mother sleeps easily. At the flick of the light switch, or the closing of curtains. As if her conscience is clear. As if there is nothing to fear, either outside or in.

Patricia – alone in her room, flicking through magazines. Stroking her mind clear of thoughts. Emptying the head.

Bow – terraces, streetlights, the occasional tree stuck in tarmac, banks of five-storey council blocks running the length of roads from Roman Road towards Vicky Park. Bow Road. Busy with garages and bridges and traffic pulsing into city, marking the southern border. Tree-leaved corridors delineate the north, where urbanity collides with the park; now full of shadows balanced on benches.

Under a faint moon. Under a sheet of scraggy air that contains the neighbourhood miasma and the drift of smoke from burning butts held by the figures on the benches dotted along the lake's lips. Solitary shapes rush into the park, followed by clusters of slow-moving groups huddled beneath baseball caps. Arrivals and departures maintain a constant presence in the park – within screaming distance of Mother. Who sleeps under conventional covers and a blanket of memories that recall the park during childhood (when toy boats filled the pond; flowers burst from every bed; families picnicked on Sunday after church; it was always sunny; gentlemen in suits raised hats; and even the street kids stole nothing more than a dropped sweet) and during wartime (when the railings were removed for smelting; contractors built a shelter by the tea pavilion; she joined the crowds to marvel at the anti-aircraft battery and listen to the whistle of the anchoring wires at the barrage balloon sites; she walked with friends and watched dogfights overhead with a cheer as German 109 and 110s died; families and friends gathered to sing 'A

Nightingale Sang in Berkeley Square'; and everyone smiled knowing that the war would be won). A time when there was beauty (watching the London skyline as a silhouette under sunset during blackout) and horror (body parts being shovelled into wheelbarrows) but the park, 26 Fairfield Road, Bow, east London, England, the Empire, never felt more like home and never before was so much worth fighting for.

Straight outta Willesden

1

It hasn't been a good year in north-west London (NWL). It has all been too much. Too many gangstas killing gangstas; too many mural memorials being painted on walls; too many scores being settled; too many girls giving birth; too many vials of contaminated rock. And there has been no sign of the sun and summer is already here.

Pow-Wow stands by his bedroom window, toking on a stick and watching the Jubilee line rattle past. Watching the red and silver pipe slide into the station that looks old with rusty bricks. Watching the sour faces peer from the Metropolitan trains that run the fast track.

Pow-Wow likes Tuesdays. He likes their brightness even though the morning sky outside is still a shroud.

Pow-Wow knows what his house looks like from the rails – tatty, loose-tiled, sloping sideways – but he is not afraid to look passengers in the eyes as they stare up at his bare black torso.

– Tyrone! Brenda, his mum shouts.

– I know! Pow-Wow (real name Tyrone) shouts back, without taking his gaze off the trains.

He scrunches the joint into an ashtray and reaches for his crash helmet that lies on the floor.

Topless, he leaves the room and locks his door. Jumps down the stairs two at a time and pushes past a younger brother who stands in the hallway yapping on a mobile. Pow-Wow grabs the phone and cancels the call while slipping it into his trouser pocket.

– I've told you before, young blood, he says to the brother.

Outside, mopeds fill the street.

Pow-Wow high-fives a few of the nearest riders before mounting his own bike and popping the engine.

Twice a week the All-Star Chapter Pack patrols the neighbourhood for outsiders.

The Pack is for the 15–17 age group; their penultimate posting before hoping to hit the big league with the Daddy-Boy Homing Crew, who command the postcode.

Most of the All-Stars have worked their way up through the junior battalions and under-15 squads to find themselves taking orders from Mister B, All-Star Number One.

The scooters, the moped, the bikes, the peds, the rockets are the badge of belonging. Those who ride pillion dream of the day of ownership. Some under-15s steal the wheels to ride illegally. The police have little interest in the kids.

The tattoos smudged onto dark skin identify the loyalties. All-Star written in Japanese characters and/or a star covering the edge of the shoulder.

Despite the dull weather, most of the Pack go half-naked and slouch on scooters with loose jeans falling over hips as they pull back throttle and thrash along terraced streets. The roads are pot-holed and dotted with broken drain-covers. The riders swerve and bounce their way round the patrol. Cars swing into the kerb to avoid the convoy.

The peds slow down as they pass a basketball court in which a dozen youth run about in singlets and high boots. The faces on the playground are scrutinized. All locals.

A black Mercedes sounds its horn and Mister B throws his arm up to halt the patrol. He spins his scooter around the back of the car and brakes by the driver's door.

– Wha's happening, Papa? Mister B asks, offering a hand.

They shake with three components: a standard grip, a thumb grip, ended with a grasp around the wrist.

– Mister B, my mantra, Papa replies through sunglasses. – Keeping it tight, yeah?

– Damn right.

There is a stiff pause; Papa checks his mirror, Mister B checks over shoulder at the crew.

– How's business? Mister B asks.

– Nice. Real nice. Sugar and spice. We'll need some carriers later in the week.

– We're always ready, you know it.

– I know it. Things are expanding at such a rate, man. This town is booming.

Mister B smiles; he knows it will not be too long before he is enjoying some of the high life. Has been All-Star Number One for a year now. A promotion to the Daddies is due.

Papa reaches into the passenger seat's headrest. A heavy gold chain slips down the forearm.

– Slip that into the pants, Papa says, pulling out a wad of notes along with a plastic bag of weed.

Mister B stuffs the package into his trousers.

– You're running things good. You know we look out for you, Papa adds.

– That ain't no shit.

– We know you can show it.

Mister B offers an appreciating smile in reply.

The electric window purrs up and the face of Papa is gone. The Mercedes moves off the kerb and away.

Mister B's mobile rings. A lookout has spotted a stranger on Neasden Lane. The crew take off.

Neasden Lane is dusty from the works site next to the station. It is smoky from the lorries trundling in and out of the yard.

The Pack arrives at the scene to find an unknown kid strutting up the hill. They slam brakes and leap off seats to make a grab. Mister B takes the throat and pushes the boy against an advertising hoarding.

– Where you heading, brother? Mister B spits.

– I ain't done nothing, man, the kid gurgles back, trying to move his neck out of the grip.

– How old are you?

– Ten, replies the kid.

Mister B stares into the nervous face. Notices the bubbles of sweat on his eyebrows.

– Where do you live, boy?

– Wembley Cent.

– Why are you walking the hill?

– To the subway, head uptown.

– You know where you are?

– Yeah, man. I'm down seeing a blood.

– Who's your man?

– Menalic Jackson.

Mister B checks his crew's faces for recognition.

One of the riders gives a slight rock of the head.

– This is All-Star patch. You know that?

– No.

– You're young, dude. You don't want to start making foes.

– No, no, I hear you.

Mister B puts his hand into his trousers and takes the knife. The kid's face panics.

– No, man, this ain't right, he pleads.

– You seen a blade before? Mister B says, flipping the weapon from hand to hand.

– I'm easy, man.

– Oh yeah? Mister B says, suddenly pressing it against the kid's head.

The kid waves his hands in front of his face and grunts.

The watching pack snigger.

Mister B lowers the knife and grins.

– So you don't want to get plunged. Cool. So strip.

– Say what?

– I said strip.

Slowly the kid undresses, folding his trousers and T-shirt, left standing in knickers.

– And the shreddies.

The kid pulls in air from one side of his mouth, making a sucking sound, pulls down the red underwear.

– You don't come onto our fucking patch, yeah? Mister B says to the kid standing naked on the pavement.

The Pack lean back on their bikes and jeer at the kid as he jogs towards the main road, his hands clenched over his balls.

– Sucker! Mister B shouts.

2

Pow-Wow has just turned sixteen. Almost a year between him and Mister B, despite being in the same year at school. The two friends go way back, spending their youth together on the top of brick walls and stealing from the 7-Eleven. Watching the big boys roam like tigers. Fight like lions. Promised each other to do the same.

Both saw their first stabbing when they were nine, when they were sitting on the kerb flicking matches. Saw a car stop down the road. Saw a man jump from the driver's seat and rush towards a guy sitting on a garden wall. Pow-Wow and Mister B thought the knife was a torch or a mobile phone. The man seemed to press the phone to the guy's head as if he wanted him to take an urgent call. The guy was slow to react as if extremely tired. He accepted the phone to his ear, then fell backwards onto the crazy paving. He didn't get up and the man in the car drove off. Pow-Wow and Mister B went to have a look. Saw the guy lying on his back with a black handle sticking out of the side of his face. Sort of smiling. 'Mother fucker,' the guy whispered.

Pow-Wow wants the seat as All-Star Number One if, as expected, Mister B gets his upgrade to the Homing Crew.

Some voices in the Pack voice doubts. They say Pow-Wow's too quiet. Not enough of a leader.

Pow-Wow sees his reticence as thoughtfulness. His lack of dominance as quiet determination.

Ego wants the job as well. Ego has the mouth, the arrogance that gets noticed. Walks with a big limp. Enhanced by the big chip balanced on his shoulder that makes him shoulder-barge people on the street and stare at eyes on the train.

Ego is a huge guy for his age (sixteen) whereas Pow-Wow is still growing, still trying to develop some muscle.

But Pow-Wow has the closeness to Mister B in his favour. Since Mister B took charge, Pow-Wow has always been considered Deputy Sheriff. He takes control of a unit when the Pack breaks into two for rucks or missions.

*

Pow-Wow and Mister B saw their first suicide together. When they were twelve and sat on Willesden Green station throwing stones at the Underground sign on the opposite platform. Sitting on the back of a bench in the open air, away from the main part of the station. Sitting near an older women who stood on her own by the toilets. She was wearing a blue raincoat even though the weather was warm. Mister B hit the sign with a stone and made a cheer. The woman turned to look and her face was pale. And she walked further away from the boy towards the other end of the platform. The Jubilee line signboard said *1 minute* and then *Train Approaching*. The boys hopped off the bench and did not see the woman jump. The train screamed and the boys were forced to look. To stare at the woman rolled up in a blue mac being smashed along the track by black wheels. The train jolted and skidded and continued along the rail trying to rid itself of the obstruction. The woman's head crashed against the wooden posts dotted along the side. The train wouldn't go over her, it merely managed to eat half of her body and leave the rest trapped underneath its front wheels. Coming to a halt three-quarters of the way down the platform. In front of Pow-Wow and Mister B. It was the image of the blue mac that stuck in their minds.

They talked about it a week later.

– Don't you think about her? Pow-Wow asked.

– Nope, Mister B replied.

– Don't you wonder who she was?

– Nope.

– Doesn't it even make you think 'fuck'?

– Fuck her. Loony tune, Mister B said.

Pow-Wow lowered his questioning gaze. Looked back at Mister B with disbelief. – Haven't you had any nightmares?

– Take a fucking trek, man.

But Pow-Wow is no pussy. The teenage years developed him. He can do what it takes, he can mix it up with whoever. There are members of the Pack who are afraid of Pow-Wow. They have seen him turn it on against rivals and seen his fists do damage. Packs a temper beneath the surface.

Pumps weights at home with a bench, a bar and some dumb-bells. Sit-ups, press-ups and pull-ups to keep the body lean and mean. Takes good care of the hair with Vaseline, and moisturizes the skin. Has placed cucumber over the eyes for shine. Likes to look at his bright white teeth in the mirror. Winks at his reflection, knowing that he's a good-looking guy. But he's still young. Sixteen years may mean he's seen some things and got up to some tricks, but life is still overwhelming and intimidating. The past is the blue mac, the present is All-Star, the future is another planet.

Pow-Wow rides his scooter, hoping that the sun will soon begin to break through and throw some light on the ghetto.

Blitz and Pieces

1

It is morning. Mother will not get out of bed. Patricia stands impatient, shaking her head.

Mother's face is scrunched into a sneer, her greasy grey hair sticks to her skin. – I'm not well.

– What's wrong? Patricia asks.

– Bring me tea.

Patricia makes the drink and carries it through to the bedroom, where she places it on the bedside table. Mother lifts herself up and clasps the cup with bony hands.

– Joan's coming this morning. It's a Tuesday, says Patricia. – I'm off to work.

– Pah! Mother snorts.

She has always denigrated Patricia's jobs; as a shop assistant in the bakery, the shoe-shop and now the chemist's.

It was normal for an unmarried girl to leave school and start work, but Mother didn't understand. In her opinion a girl shouldn't work. A girl shouldn't be unmarried.

When Patricia pulled on her first uniform of green frock and hat Mother laughed ('You look ridiculous').

When Patricia wore her second uniform of black skirt and cream shirt Mother insulted ('I'm embarrassed to be your mother').

When she dressed in the third uniform of white coat with blue name badge, Mother just shook her head slowly and turned her attention back to the television.

Mother wanted her married. Wanted her to have children. The uniforms formalized and identified her daughter's spinsterhood.

2

Patricia never married, though there were men. There was a customer at the bakery who came in daily for a filled roll and soup. He was a lot older than Patricia – who at the time was only seventeen. But Patricia was fond of him.

The relationship began when he stopped her as she walked home from work.

A dirty March afternoon, the damp drifts. Patricia hurries home, wrapped deep in coat.

– All done for another day? a voice calls out behind her.

She turns to see the man from the shop, the man who buys the roll and soup.

– Cold, isn't it? she replies.

He breaks into a slight run to catch her up. – Walk with you?

– I'm on Fairfield Road.

The man wears a Crombie with a thick tartan scarf knotted around the neck. His cheeks are flushed from the wind.

– You didn't serve me today, he says.

– It was so busy this lunchtime, Patricia replies.

– I got the sourpuss.

– Kathy isn't that bad.

– She always gets my order wrong.

– Hasn't been so busy for ages.

– You always remember.

– Tomato soup and an egg salad roll.

– Served with a smile.

– We try, she grins.

– Except the sourpuss.

They both share bright eyes, bury hands into coat pockets.

– I'm freezing, she says.

– Look, take this scarf, he says, unwrapping the tartan.

She shakes her head. – No, no, you'll only get cold then.

He throws the scarf around her as they walk, trying to tie it up as they move along side by side.

– Better? he smiles.

– It's all warm.

The man looks distinguished with his bald head and long face. She likes his smile and the crow's feet around his eyes. Her fresh skin glows as the sky darkens.

– I live up by the park, he says.

– Lucky you.

– Oh, I don't know. Fairfield Road is nice.

– Not as nice as the park.

The man blows on his hands. – Who do you live with?

– Family.

– Good?

Patricia shrugs.

– Come on, I'm sure it's not that bad, the man grins.

– I prefer being out of the house.

– Doing what?

– I like going to work.

– I can see that.

– It's nice to be busy.

– Boyfriend?

– No.

– I can't believe that. A girl like you.

Patricia looks at the man and his eager expression. She grins, slightly shy.

They reach the corner of the road. The man stops. – This is where I leave you, he says.

– Take your scarf.

– You keep it for now. Can't have you being sick and missing work.

– I'll be all right.

– Who will I look forward to seeing?

Patricia laughs.

– Maybe I'll collect it tomorrow.

– Tomorrow?

– Why not?

– OK.

– I'm Edward.

– I'm . . .

– Don't say, I know. I hear sourpuss say your name. Patricia, he says, making the name last a whole exhale of breath.

Conventional courting is impossible due to the age gap; the neighbourhood is small, word gets round. Even going further afield wouldn't avoid the comments and unwanted attention. And so Edward and Patricia meet in the park after work as he walks his dog.

Once a week, all through spring and summer, they wander along thin pathways and rose gardens, and over grassy banks and past the lake. Edward is educated in botany and introduces Patricia to the various species of plant and flower. Together with their formal names. They laugh at the strange words and her attempts at pronunciation. The joke soon progresses into changing the proper names into ludicrous phrases. *Euonymus japonicus* becomes 'humorous Jap on the bus'. *Potentilla fruticosa* becomes 'potentially fruity'.

They never touch. Their arms don't even brush as they squeeze together on the narrow tracks and under overhanging weeping willows (*Salix pendula* – 'Sally is a pendulum').

One evening Edward announces his fortieth birthday. He wants to celebrate, wants to take her to the coast for a weekend.

Such an idea is out of the question. Patricia is forced to tell him about Mother.

– You're eighteen next month, he says. – Surely she will allow you a night or two away.

– I'm sorry, Edward. It's not like that.

– Never mind. How about supper in town instead? Edward's gentle smile and suggestion offering consolation.

– She won't allow it, Patricia replies, rubbing hands nervously.

– Ask her. For me. I'd like us to have some proper time together.

– It won't happen.

Edward looks stumped. – If you don't want to come, I wish you would just say so.

– It's not like that.

– Do you really want to spend time with me?

– Yes. Yes.

The second yes trails off into reverie. She does have feelings for Edward. She does have desires.

Edward moves near. Near enough for breath to blend. They stand facing each other. His dark mouth doesn't move and the stiff, tweed jacket sets him in concrete. Set in the stench of dog and disappearing years and useless knowledge of plants and flowers that now mean nothing.

Patricia cannot look into his eyes. She stares at his chest; at the strands of hair poking through the shirt. Seventeen-year-old flawless face reddens with Edward's proximity and the heat of the descending sun. Her arms hang limply by her side in a state of resignation.

Edward and Patricia jolt as the dog barks angrily.

He turns to call the animal back as it chases a squirrel.

The following week Edward is quiet, paying more attention to the dog than Patricia.

– What's the matter? she asks.

Edward offers a shrug.

– Tell me?

They stop walking. Stand together on the path.

– I can't keep going on like this, he says.

– Like what?

– Like this.

– Like what?

Edward takes a deep breath, closes his eyes for an extended blink.

– I can't bear just seeing you in this way.

– But I explained to you . . .

– I know, I know, that doesn't make it acceptable.

Patricia strains with concentration as she stares at him. She looks older. – What's wrong?

– I want more than what we've got. Can you understand that?

Patricia offers empathizing eyes. – Of course I do, but it's just the way it has to be. For now.

– When will things change? I need to know, Patricia. When will things change?

– I don't know.

– Will you ever be able to marry me?

She throws her gaze to one side. – I don't know.

Edward did not return to the bakery for his egg salad roll and tomato soup.

3

On Patricia's twenty-first birthday Mother was angry.
   – You've let everyone down.
   – It's not my fault!
   – You're going to be an old spinster, an old unwanted spinster.
   – There's still time.
   – I wanted grandchildren.
   – You are joking? The way you treat kids?
   – You're the only one, you know. All the other girls round here managed to marry.
   – I didn't do it on purpose.
   – What could I expect from a daughter with an eye like that?
   – I wish you wouldn't.
   – Wouldn't what?
   – Keep going on about my eye.
   – This is my house, I'll go on about what I like.
   Patricia sighed sulkily.
   Mother interpreted the impertinence. – Now go, she said, waving her hand as if to a servant.

4

Mother has always been harsh. Dominating the family with her sneers, shouts, swipes, tears and excruciating silences. Her hair pushed behind, enhancing hawkish features. Her scowl that condemned. That the family at 26 Fairfield Road knew well. And how she punished Patricia in those early years. For spilling a drink, for not eating her dinner, for talking too much. For nothing.
   Mother had three punishments for disobedience: making

Patricia sit in a cold bath, stand in the living room under a blanket, or curl up into a wooden box used for dirty washing.

Mother didn't need to spell out the punishment: a one-word order was enough to get Patricia undressed, under cover or inside.

– Bath!

(Patricia shivers and coughs uncontrollably while the water eats into her white, feeble body.)

– Blanket!

(The blanket fibres tickle her nose and allow through the faintest of light that Patricia transforms into patterns. Her legs hurt from standing. They feel exposed and vulnerable outside of the blanket's covering.)

– Box!

(Crammed in among the damp, dirty underwear she tries her best to get comfortable, turning herself onto one side and pushing her back against the wood. She tries to sleep by thinking of the park and ignoring the noises Mother makes with pots and pans and curses in the other part of the kitchen. Waits to hear Dad's deep voice roll into the room that signals release.)

Good Times

1

Stanley Coppin, in his bedroom. Hiding away from the mornings that he finds so empty and vast. Lying in bed, the floor scattered with clothes and dirty mugs. A stark room: wooden chair, single wardrobe with door open and contents spilling, under a bare bulb. Painted walls blemished by fading colour and scars from Sellotape and Blue-tac. On third floor of Dewsbury House off Eversholt Road, NW1. Lives with mother, Sylvia, a well-known psychic.

Stanley's father died four years ago from lung cancer. Stanley's younger brother, Sausage, died twenty years ago. Hit by a car. The council later introduced speed bumps along Robert Street. Sylvia cannot walk past the ramps without imagining them as coffins pushing up through the tarmac.

It was Sausage's death that introduced Sylvia to the spirit world.

One week after the accident and the family of three is sitting around the flat in various states of bereavement.

In the kitchen, Sylvia hears a voice. 'Mum?' it says. 'Mum?' Sylvia thinks that it is Stanley. She goes into the lounge. Stanley hasn't spoken.

Back in the kitchen the voice calls out again.

– Mum! The cry is more distressed. – Mum, I'm scared!

– Is that you, Sausage? Sylvia responds.

– Mum, I don't want to be here.

Sylvia sits down at the table and closes her eyes so that she can concentrate on the voice.

– Speak to me, son.

– Mum, I miss you, it's all dark, I'm scared.

– Don't be scared. Mum's here now.

– I'm up here, above you. Can you see me?

Sylvia opens her eyes and bends her neck backward to look up at the ceiling.

– I can't see you, she says. – Whereabouts are you?

– Up here, Mum. Up here, look, I can see you.

– I can't see you, says Sylvia, beginning to cry.

– I'm waving, Mum.

– Where?

– I'm waving.

– I can't see you.

– I've got to hide, someone's coming, I can hear them coming. Help me, Mum, don't let them keep me.

– I won't, son. I won't let them keep you.

There is no more sound from Sausage. The room falls still.

– Are you still there, son?

Nothing.

– Are they keeping you?

Silence.

– Bring him back to me! Sylvia snaps, jumping to her feet.

No reply.

– Bring him back! You hear me, bring him back! she screams.

Stanley and Harry run to the kitchen and take her into a scrum of arms and affection.

– Calm down, honey, says Harry, stroking her hair and enveloping her in embrace, rocking in rhythm with the throbs of her fear.

Sylvia's spiritualist awakening opened up a route to the deceased. She found herself communicating with Grandad Coppin, Aunty Mo, Nanna Wilkes. Her skills attracted attention. Soon she was hosting gatherings and taking clients. Began to make a bit of money. Not a lot, but enough to make a difference to the household budget. Particularly with Stanley and Harry working only intermittently.

*

Sylvia knocks on Stanley's door.

– You ready? He's going to be here in a minute, she says.

Stanley comes out of the room dressed in his black suit with black shirt and black shoes. His hair is slicked back.

– I'm ready. Don't rush me.

Stanley acts as the sidesman during Sylvia's seances. He answers the door and leads the client through to the lounge, where Sylvia sits at the table. Stanley offers a drink: tea, coffee, vodka, gin. He moves about the flat slowly, attempting to add gravitas to the occasion. During the meditation he stands by the door with his hands pressed behind his back like a waiter, ready to assist. Ready for all kinds of scenarios. In the past clients have fainted, screamed at spectres, suffered blindness, had out-of-body experiences, fallen off chairs, jumped under the table, tried to attack Sylvia. During these episodes Sylvia maintains a detached otherworldliness while Stanley is left to manage things.

Mr Furtle arrives exactly on time and Stanley escorts him to the living room.

Mr Furtle is a regular; he likes to keep in touch with his wife, who died last year. Stanley pours the usual Scotch. Retreats to the doorway. Stands smartly.

– Is she there? Mr Furtle asks, noticing Sylvia twitch her head, with eyes still closed.

Sylvia does not reply. She moves around in her seat.

– Tell her it's me, Mr Furtle whispers.

– I've got her, I've got her, Sylvia smiles.

– How is she? Mr Furtle asks.

Sylvia chuckles to herself. – I knew it was you, Peggy.

– What did she say? he asks.

Sylvia moves her head towards Mr Furtle, as if she can't hear him properly through the noise of his wife's voice.

– What did she say? he asks again.

– She sounds so distant today.

Sylvia squeezes her eyes to hear better.

– Tell her how much I miss her.

– He misses you, Peggy.

– Tell her I love her.

– He loves you, Peggy.

Stanley watches Mr Furtle's face fill with pleasure. His red nose shines. He swallows the last of the whisky with a jolt.

Stanley is sweating under the suit and tie. Being enclosed in a room with spirits invariably makes the temperature rise. Even in midwinter they have had to open the windows to allow the air to cool.

With Mr Furtle gone, Sylvia recuperating in bed, and the spirits returned to the other side, Stanley sinks into armchair with beer and hops channels. Through the sports, the news, the selling shops, the US dramas, the nature documentaries, and on to the talk shows.

A tall black woman stands in front of the audience with microphone. On stage sit two middle-aged women, one rather drab-looking, the second with huge cleavage. The show's title scrolls across the screen: I PAID A MAN FOR SEX. Stanley places the beer on the coffee table, leans towards the television and squirts the volume.

They are in mid-conversation.

– Why don't you try and find a man to have a regular relationship with? the host asks the woman with the cleavage.

– I'm looking, don't get me wrong, but I just haven't been lucky, she replies.

– Does that make it all right to buy sex?

– But it's different. When you hire a man there is no emotional or psychological games. You get what you want without all the other stuff, you know, the unwanted phone calls and possessiveness. The girls in the audience will know what I'm saying.

There is a high-pitched murmur of agreement.

– But isn't it all a bit shallow and superficial? the hosts asks, folding her arms and leaning back.

– I know it's not ideal and when I find the right man I won't use the service. But, for now, while I'm in this situation I don't see anything wrong with it.

– But surely the man is only there for the money. He's not interested in you as a person.

– I totally disagree, the guest argues. – I've had some great relationships with my males.

Stanley reaches for the phone without taking his gaze off the screen. He calls Clive, orders him to get onto channel 36, clicks off the phone without saying goodbye.

The host turns to the other guest. – Aren't you really a victim in all of this?

– No, not at all. I'm not forced into anything. It's my money, I work hard for it, I should be allowed to spend it on what I want.

The audience breaks into a muted applause.

The host turns the microphone on a person standing up out of her seat.

– I think the two people we see up on the stage are just two very lonely individuals. I think they lack self-esteem, the person says.

Before the guests can reply, another audience member is on the mike. – I think it's absolutely disgusting and you two should be ashamed of yourselves. You give us women a bad name.

– Sit down, the guests shout.

– No, you sit down, you dirty old whore, the girl cries back.

Stanley grabs the beer and empties the can in one. His body is pumping. The seat is damp from his sweat.

2

Stanley and Clive pool cash (another small loan from Sylvia) and the first advert is placed in London's free newspaper, *Metro*.

GOOD TIMES
London's number one male escort agency
Dinner – Dates – Dancing
All occasions catered for
All men available
'Go on, treat yourself'
CALL 07575 776 90235

Fish Net

1

Pimp Papa and the Daddies run all the local scenes: the drugs, the insurance, the thieving, the brawls, the hits. And the ladies – Papa's speciality.

The young girls dumped from school – some still attending – or unable to get work find Papa able to offer an alternative career. Papa runs three houses that provide around twenty girls, age from fourteen to thirty, with food, shelter, security, regular income. They live well, with Jacuzzis and satellite television and mobile phones.

Papa is strict but fair. He has his regulations. All girls must:

1. Call him Papa at all times.
2. Not talk while he is talking.
3. Answer with just a yes or no.
4. Never lie.
5. Declare all money earned.
6. Do what Papa says do.

Papa grew up in the neighbourhood, when things were a bit different and no one knew whether it was New York or New Year and the police gave no space. Papa and his contemporaries grew the Afros large and then trimmed them down before wearing shorn heads. Grew up with school uniform; the ties with huge knots and the saggy blazer that fell to the knee. Grew up alongside the working-class whites who shouted abuse. Remembers seeing bananas being thrown at Garth Crooks on *Match of the Day*. And everything seemed so grey back then. So cloudy.

There were no opportunities. No consideration. Papa and his boys had to find their own way. Fight their own way. Looked for markets, established business, gave it their best shot. And, on their terms, made a success of it.

The sleek Mercedes glides about the community. The black metallic finish scattering reflections from the white sky. Silently drifting past the boys on bikes who stop to stare, the girls at the bus stop who wave, the kids outside the grocery store who sip bottled juice, the woman with the shopping trolley, a bus full of heads, a troop of gangsters in track suits sitting on a rusty car.

2

Brenda busies about the living room, trying to make order. A hard task with five children in the house. And only herself to hold things together now that her latest boyfriend has left.

Tyrone (16), Naomi (15), Emmanuel (13), Troy (10) and Sasheeka (5) do little to help. Pile their washing on the bathroom floor, run to the store when coerced, occasionally wash dishes. Things are really left to Mom.

Brenda's mother was an Irish-born bar-woman who pulled pints on the Kilburn High Road. Father was a West African who tried to make the relationship work but could not temper his wife's drinking, infidelity, volatility. Brenda grew up with her father in Harlesden and gave birth to Pow-Wow when she was sixteen.

Loved her children more than herself. Though she felt inadequate without a qualification, or a job, or a chance to give the kids what she wanted to give. Made up for it with time and affection. But determined that they would do better than she did.

Pow-Wow became the problem.

Things began to slip at school. Pow-Wow's teachers phoning, writing, visiting home. Giving the same message: so much potential but won't cooperate.

First school suspension came in Year 9 when he took a swing at the history teacher. Caught the man on the temple and got himself hauled in front of headmaster and sent packing for a week. A holiday for Pow-Wow, who spent the days practising his rapping and hanging with boys already out on the street.

– When you get back to school you're going to keep out of trouble. You're going to avoid the bad boys. You're going to change your ways, Brenda told her son the day he returned to school.

Pow-Wow sucked in one side of his mouth and shrugged.

– You need to rehabilitate yourself, she said.

Pow-Wow sniffed and stared at her knees.

– You're not going to end up wasting yourself.

– Man, he replied. – You gotta open your eyes and get with the real.

Within a month he was back at home for throwing a classmate through a window.

By the Easter term Pow-Wow was permanently excluded with a record covering five pages of A4. Referred to the Pupil Referral Unit in Kingsbury. Rejected. Given a course of home tuition that he didn't undertake – refusing to open the door to the woman holding a briefcase who arrived when Brenda was out.

And then Emmanuel began arriving home with black eyes and broken teeth. Around the same time as Naomi's first abortion. And Brenda could not understand what she had done wrong.

3

Tuesday morning – the same as any other day. Breakfast for Pow-Wow is a bowl of Cheerios. Eating on the lap, on the sofa, in front of the TV.

– What are you doing today? Brenda asks Pow-Wow, as she runs a cloth along the mantelpiece.

– Out, he replies with milk dripping from lips.

– Work?

– Come on, Mom, I'm too young for that.

Brenda shakes her head and starts picking plates off the carpet.

– One day you'll realize that life is not all about sitting in front of the television.

– Might be.

– You've got to have a future.

– I dunno.

– What are you going to do?

Pow-Wow juts out his lower lip. – Do something.

– Yeah? Brenda says, looking at her son from unblinking eyes.

– Work around here somewhere.

– Not with your little bunch of crooks.

– There's older ones.

Brenda huffs. – We read all about the older ones. You're not going there.

– Ease off, Mom. I'm only sixteen. I got lots of time.

– Yeah, my big baby.

Loud music blasts upstairs.

Brenda puts the plates on the kitchen table and goes to the foot of the stairs.

– Not so loud! she calls up.

The music stays at the same volume.

Emmanuel comes running down the stairs and almost collides with Mum.

– Not so fast! Brenda shouts.

– I've gotta get going, Emmanuel replies, pushing her to one side to get through.

The floor of the hall is a mess of shoes and bicycles and jackets.

Brenda picks up a token coat and hangs it over the banister.

The music continues thumping through the ceiling.

– Mom? Sasheeka cries from the top of the stairs. – Mom?

Emmanuel pushes past to go back up the stairs.

– What? Brenda shouts back.

– Mom? Sasheeka repeats.

Brenda looks down for a split second and then looks back up. – Tell Naomi to turn it down, she says to Emmanuel, who is a blur flying up the stairs.

– Turn it down! Emmanuel shouts.

– Mom? cries Sasheeka.

A rumble of door-thumping from Emmanuel rocks the house. The music stops.

The silence buzzes.

– Mom? Sasheeka bawls.

Brenda wipes her face.

Pow-Wow barges into the kitchen and throws the bowl into the sink. The spoon seems to break the china.

– What is it, babe? Brenda calls up to her daughter.

Pow-Wow grabs the coat off the banister and rolls his eyes.

– I'm out, Mom. Catch you, he mutters, flicking open the front door.

Brenda just gets the chance to say 'Wh . . .', before the door slams. And the walls shake.

4

Pow-Wow sits in the front of the Merc. Mister B spreads in the back. A rare treat to ride the Papa wagon. A chance for the All-Star duo to hear things from the top.

They drive out of Willesden towards Wembley. Papa has no worries about territory; he is too big to touch.

There is no sun but the windows are down and wind whips through the car and blows the heads. Papa nods and hums as Pow-Wow talks. All the while he watches the road, lightly holding the wheel, casually panning the pavement for girls. Papa is always on the lookout for girls; for himself, for the Daddies. Mainly for business.

– If it fucks it make bucks, he drawls.

The two passengers laugh.

– If she's cute, with a chute, she can make loot.

Two girls stand outside a chicken shop. Skirts slit to the hips, two-inch fingernails, braided hair wrapped into pineapple shapes. Papa recognizes the type, sees it in the way they sway from side to side as if listening to music, the way they blow kisses at the passing cars.

– Who wants to get some fried? Papa asks with a wide grin.

– Mmm, mmm, finger-licking, Pow-Wow smiles.

– Leg or breast in coated crumb, Mister B says.

– Now sit back and watch the P in action, says Pimp Papa.

The Mercedes rolls to a stop and Papa throws an arm behind Pow-Wow's seat to lean forward and greet the girls.

– Wha's down? he winks.

The girls move closer together, link arms and look more nervous than when they were left to flirt from a distance.

– Hi, says the bigger one of the two.

– Having a good day?

– We're doing fine.

– Where you sisters from?

– N-dubya.

The girls lower their heads and turn their shoulders to face Papa sidelong. The smaller one licks her lips.

– You want to eat something? Papa asks.

– Just filled up, the bigger one shrugs.

– Save us any? he jokes.

– I save chicken for no man, she replies.

– Oh, I hear you. I hear you, Papa says, taking a packet of cigarettes. – Wanna smokey?

– We're giving up.

– What about weed?

– You got?

Papa turns away in fake disgust. – Have I got? He turns back with a more serious face. – You riding?

The girls look at each other. They make coded eyes.

– We can't go far, the bigger girl says.

– You show me where you want to go and we'll be cool.

Pow-Wow, following a wink from Papa, hops into the back with Mister B and the smaller girl. The bigger girl bends forward to squeeze into the front, flashing big brown breasts in the process.

They stop behind a shopping arcade. Next to lock-up garages and discarded oil drums. Papa sparks a stick and passes it on.

– That is high quality, he nods. – I hope you sisters can take the force.

– I can take whatever, the bigger girl says, dragging on the reefer.

– Feels good, huh, baby? Papa smiles.

The girl nods and her eyes drift out of focus. The stick goes to the back seat.

– When you make money you get the best, you know what I'm saying?

– So you're a rich man, yeah?

– You see this watch, baby. Oyster Perpetual, five thousand bucks.

– For a watch?

– Check this, home-girl, Papa says, twisting and shaking his wrist so that the chain rolls over the hand. – Twenty-four C with diamond studs. How much?

– A thousand?

– Treble it, sister. Treble it.

– Where'd you make the paper?

– I do what's got to be done.

The girl fiddles with the glove compartment.

– What's your line, sister? Papa asks.

– I'm finding my feet, you know. I'm young, looking about for the right thing.

– You a pretty girl. You'll get stuff.

The stick returns to the front, to the girl.

– You like making out?

The girl exhales the smoke. – That's private business.

– You got men?

– I get what I want, she says, pushing the joint back between her lips.

– And what do you get?

– Satisfaction, she smiles.

– I hear that, girlfriend, her friend behind laughs.

Papa lets the fun fade. He takes his mobile and presses a couple of buttons before replacing it in the recharging cradle.

– So you let men go with you and all you want is satisfaction in return?

– They take me out first.

– You gotta understand your power potential, sister.

– It doesn't bother me.

Pimp Papa sniffs condescendingly. Gives the rear mirror a wipe. – Where they take you then? he asks.

– Wherever.

– Like where? Papa says, acting puzzled.

– Burgers or chicken. Maybe pizza.

Papa shakes his head. – You give it to men for a Coke and mother-fucking fries?

– You make it sound bad.

– Do you know how much some men would pay you?

– I ain't like that.

– You could be driving a Benzo within a year, you got me?

The girl moves her mouth about and sucks in her lips.

– Coke and goddam fries, Papa sighs.

– What you saying, I should be a fuzz?

– Listen, sister, if you're having it anyway you might as well make some dollars from it. Right or wrong?

– All those dirty men?

– If you work for a proper stud then that ain't gonna happen.

– Is that what you do, pimping?

– You're sitting in the proceeds of sex, baby. Feels good, huh?

The girl shrugs.

– Hey, sweet thing in the back. You get the fix?

– I've never thought about it, she replies.

– Well you think. This is the easiest way you'll ever get to own a drop-top, a penthouse, wear D&G and Versace, you name the cloth.

Papa starts the car and drives. Returns to the chicken shop.

– Here's what we do. I give you my number, you call me when you decided things.

Papa passes a card into the bigger girl's hand.

– Now show me a bit of appreciation, he says.

The bigger girl bends over the door and kisses Papa. The kiss develops and there is noisy nasal breathing and the lapping of tongues.

– I'll speak to you, Papa says, throwing the car into the road and back towards Willesden.

– Way to go, Papa, Mister B laughs.

Contact

1

Wednesday is shopping day. Patricia struggles along the high street, apologizing as she takes knocks from passers-by even though the collisions are not her fault. She is careful not to slip on the crushed bananas and apples that have fallen from the market stalls. Cautious of the sly stares from a gang of youths circling on the corner. Ignores the bad language and the spitting as she walks past. Balancing the bags of fruit, the bread from the bakery, the groceries from the supermarket. And the chips. Always chips on a Wednesday after the shopping.

The dense weight of the wrapped packets still the same as when Dad brought home chips after working late at Millwall. So Mother would acknowledge him, at least look at him, even if it involved merely brushing stares as she took the plate. Painful for Patricia to watch at the time and still hurts to recall.

But the chips weren't only an offering to Mother; Dad didn't forget Patricia. Bringing the portions home so she could breathe in the greasy steam that left a film on the face, and watch Dad at the hob cracking eggs into fat. Father and daughter would eat in the kitchen, safe in the knowledge that Mother doesn't shout while chips appeased.

Dad had worked at the docks before and after the war. During it he served in North Africa with the 7th Armoured Brigade.

While he was away, Mother joined a long list of other ladies in Bow vying for the attentions of a local ARP warden.

The warden cycles about Bow and herds the population towards the shelters in the parks. He walks tall among the East End while the younger men are absent. Inviting himself in for tea with the women of the parish. Spends the time boasting, winking and talking innuendo. Such a fit, strong man arouses the suspicion of the men who don't know of his reasons for active-service exemption. Unsure of his background, for he talks with a Welsh lilt though he calls Wapping home.

He is always immaculate in his black garb, polished helmet and eye-catching red and white stripes. Immaculate with manners and responsibility in front of the older men – behind whose backs he lathers the ladies.

Mother, despite her severity and coldness, doesn't discourage him. Mother, at twenty-six years of age, relishes the flattery and takes hours spreading precious make-up bought on the black market before the front door clatters with his officious call on Wednesday mornings.

The warden breathes condensation waiting on the doorstep. The air is still and quiet; frozen. When it is daylight, the war is forgotten. Even the fighter aircraft fly noiselessly above.

– How are you? he smiles.

– Still here, Mother replies, her face bleached with powder.

Inside, in the kitchen, the tea is made and poured.

– Any news of your husband?

– Nothing new, she replies, her teeth contrasting yellow next to the garish red lipstick.

The warden is not afraid to talk of spouses; to remind the women of their soldiers. It doesn't seem to deter.

– You're looking as gorgeous as ever, he winks.

Mother stiffly turns her attention to the teapot, giving it a shake to assess whether there is enough for a refill.

– Ah, all embarrassed? he says.

– Your tea'll go cold, she replies.

– Plenty of time for tea. What about that broken tap? You want me to have a look?

– Would you?

– Any excuse to get you upstairs.

Mother coughs to cover her unease.

44

– I won't tell if you don't, he jokes, offering a hand to lift her off the seat.

She takes his hand, briefly. The shared grip is sticky.

In the bathroom, she leans over the bath to show how the water dribbles out instead of gushes.

The warden, standing behind, edges close to her and presses into her bottom with his crotch.

– Yeah, I can see what you mean, he says breathlessly.

Mother doesn't move, feeling him against her.

They both stay locked in position, watching the trickle of water falling from the tap.

He places a hand on her shoulder, spreads the fingers wide and slowly squeezes.

She remains bent over, supporting herself on the fittings.

His hand slides down her back and stops just below the buckle of her belt. He runs his fingers along the rim of the plastic. Nudges forwards with his hips.

– I should be able to sort it out.

Mother gently straightens herself up so that the back of her head rests against his mouth.

– I should be able to sort it out, he repeats into her hair.

– We'd better finish our tea.

The following Wednesday he returns. The same confident knock on the door.

He swallows the last of his tea and asks her to sit on his knee.

She sits there awkwardly, face turned away, not noticing his smug expression.

– Don't look so angry, he says.

– I'm not angry, she replies, keeping her back stiff and her eyes averted.

– You sound angry, he grins.

She feels his hand as it clasps her shin and begins crawling up her stockinged leg, as it pushes aside cotton skirt, as it fumbles.

By the time they reach the bedroom he is half inside her.

The marital room becomes a foreign place as she watches his face sweat two inches from hers. The house smells differently as she lies on her back. The ceiling doesn't look like her ceiling as he presses his face into her neck and finishes.

2

Patricia dumps the shopping on the table. Puts the chips into the oven to keep them warm. Stands by the kettle as it boils for her lunchtime coffee. Looks out of the window at the houses opposite and their double-glazing and satellite dish and children's slide and basketball hoop and barbecue.

Patricia's fiftieth birthday is approaching. She wants to make it an occasion. 'Go for it', Lorraine told her. Maybe she should.

Fifty! Where do the years go? she thinks, pressing a spoon into the coffee jar, tipping the granules into the cup, melting them in boiling water. Where do they go?

Bow has changed; the customers at the chemist's are not what they used to be. Now there are the druggies who stagger through the door to sniff aerosols. There are the addicts who harass the pharmacists for a prescription. There are the shoplifters who carry guns; the headcases who find solace among the white coats; the pensioners who come to sit on the chairs and talk among themselves to escape the loneliness and vulnerability of home; the shoppers who shout at the staff; the people who spit on the floor; the drunks who piss over packets of Pampers; the street-fighters fresh from battle who want to be patched up, thereby avoiding the official channels of GPs and surgeries.

And the staff are different: the security guards who steal from the storeroom; the employees who gorge on the chemicals kept in the secure cabinet; the sales assistants who consider customers the enemy.

Tap-tap-tap. The sound of glass on bedside table. Time for Patricia to make lunch.

Patricia takes Mother her dinner on a tray. A few chips, a tomato, a cup of tea.

Mother, sitting skeletal on her armchair in the lounge. She prods at the food with a fork. With disdain.

– This is off, she says, sniffing the tomato.

– I got them from the market this morning, Patricia replies, from the sofa, with her dinner on her lap.

– Rotten.

– No it's not.

Mother throws the tomato at Patricia. It lands on her plate, sending chips flying to the floor.

– Mother! Patricia says, leaning over to pick up the pieces of food. Mother turns her attention back to picking at her chips.

– That's gratitude for you, Patricia complains, settling herself back on the sofa. – Shop all day, get your dinner ready. That's a lovely way to say thanks.

– Pah.

3

Later that day, Patricia takes Mother to the bathroom. She picks off the clothes and avoids scraping the skin with her nails. Winces to herself at Mother's atrophy. The skin barely papers over the jagged bones.

She collects the discarded clothes from the floor and goes to the corner of the bedroom where the box now lives. The box from the kitchen, the box from her childhood. She lifts the lid and drops the dirty washing in. The box closes with the same clunk it always has.

In the gloom of Mother's room the white box stands out. So much smaller than the mountain it once was. So much safer.

Fiftieth birthday approaching and, back in the bathroom, Patricia catches sight of herself in the mirror. Her own face is sinking into itself, the bags under her own eyes spilling over onto the cheeks.

Patricia soaps the sponge and rubs it over Mother, who sits uneasily in the bath. The white froth rolls down her back and collects in the water. Joan arrives tomorrow; Patricia will go to work. She adds hot water, pushing it onto Mother's legs and past her bony bottom.

Mother's nose is rutted with deep pores and red pimples. It is still pointed like a beak but lacks the definition of her youth.

Thread veins decorate the cheeks, forming a scarlet cobweb over the face. It carries all the history. And even in its old age the face still makes Patricia panic.

Patricia dries, grooms and places Mother onto the bed and turns on the side-lamp.

Mother lies still, not blinking. Intransigent.

– That OK for you, Mother?

A grunt of assent.

Patricia walks to the curtains to ensure that there are no gaps that will wake Mother before six. – Everything OK?

– Leave me alone, Mother says.

– I'm only trying to get you settled.

– I can look after myself.

– You don't realize how much you need me, says Patricia, turning to stare at Mother.

– You're no good. Never were any good, never will be.

– Thanks, Mother.

– You're a reject.

– That's not fair.

– Waste.

– Mother, stop it!

– Useless.

Patricia pushes Mother into the sheets, turns out the light and rushes upstairs to her own bedroom. Once inside she strikes at invisible tormentors. Lashing out with her fists, scratching at air. – I hate her! I hate her!

Cool Waiting

1

Clive lives on his own. Has done for a few years. On Housing Benefit and Job-seeker's Allowance. Above a drug addict who plays music all night long but whom Clive is too scared to confront – preferring to keep things amicable. At least it is better than staying at home – the house in Camden where he grew up as an only child. That is now a small outpost of poverty in a street filled with modern couples working in good jobs. Mum and Dad alongside a soap actor, a guitarist from some pop band and a blonde girl who presents television programmes.

Clive doesn't have a problem with his home or his parents, but for some reason, since the area changed, he no longer feels welcome along the street. It somehow shrinks him and makes his stutter worse. And the celebrity of the neighbours makes him feel less appealing in the presence of his parents. As if he is a failure. And so he prefers to live among his own in the flats, with the loud music. And visit, on most days, the house in Camden with the shabby front lawn.

Wednesday afternoon and the warm wind brushes Clive as he walks to his parents.

Mum is pleased to see him when he arrives, plopping a smacker on his cheek. Taking his arm, she leads him along the narrow hall to the kitchen, where she sits him down to feed him plates of buttered potato bread. Dad wanders in from the garden, where he keeps a big rabbit in tunnels of wire.

– That animal is getting too fat, Mum says to Dad.

– It's only potato bread, Dad jokes at Clive.

– Not Clive, I'm talking about Flump, out there in that run of yours, she says, stifling laughter.

– How's things? Dad asks Clive quietly.

– Mmm mmm, Clive replies, chewing a mouthful.

– Any luck on the work front? His voice as soft as the melted butter.

Clive shakes his head.

– It's just too hard to find work, Mum adds. – It's daft.

– You'll be all right. Dad gives a short nod.

Clive rips at another slab of potato bread, trying to forget that he is in his thirties. And that Mum and Dad have been saying the same things for fifteen years. They have such faith.

– And Stanley? Mum asks.

– He's f-f-fine.

– Any luck on the work front? Dad asks.

Clive shakes his head.

Clive's dad works for the Post Office as a sorter. The unsociable hours suit him. Often travelling against the commuter tide. Takes pride in his job, seeing letters and parcels organized and dispatched. It somehow connects him to the world.

And the house is full of postal memorabilia: Post Office posters, prints of the various Post Office uniforms used in service, framed stamps, and the odd trophy for the Post Office Best Kept Rabbit Competition.

When Clive sees a postage stamp he thinks of Dad.

– Been out recently? Mum asks.

Clive knows the code; the girlfriend question.

– No, Clive replies.

To Mum's disappointment. A silent, private disappointment because Clive has yet to meet somebody special. Mum is sad at the passing of time and the failure of her son to mention the names of girls.

Her only child and no hope of grandchildren.

Dad never talks of women – too shy. Wouldn't dream of treading on his son's toes. He knows how Clive feels. He knows how long it took himself to ask Mum for that first night out.

But Clive relishes Dad's nervousness. It almost redeems and legitimizes his own timidity. Like last week, when the three of them went to a small barbecue thrown by the actor next door. He was kind enough to ask them and they showed up in their best shoes.

A group stood around Dad, stood over him. They were all artists and actors and people who had flocked to London from the provinces to find success. Dad was asked questions and they demanded answers too quickly. Mum urged him to relax with her subtle, stinging stares, but Dad was tongue-tied and crushed the paper cup in his hand. And the group turned to Mum. She tried to smile and chat but they stared back at her without expression as if they didn't understand. They all looked at Clive to see if he could tell them what she was talking about, but Clive spilt his Fanta and drenched his arm. He looked down, saying, I-I-I-I-I'd b-b-b-etter clean up.' Leaving Mum and Dad to stand alone and fend off the group. He went into the kitchen to use quilted towel to absorb the mess and smile at a big man by the sink. To return to the garden, where the group around his parents had dispersed, abandoning Mum and Dad to their own talk. The three of them left to offer snippets of empty conversation to fill the gaping silence. And left to fill their own empty cups.

Clive certainly won't mention the Escort Agency advert placed in the paper. It would not be in tune with his parents' way of thinking. It's not really in tune with his. But Stanley is persuasive. And Clive regrets allowing Stanley to leave the phone with him.

– No one will ring for a couple of days, Stanley assured.

– You t-t-take it then, Clive argued.

– I'm busy with Sylvia. I can't have it going off during a meeting.

– I don't know what t-t-to say.

– Take the details, arrange a time. Piece of piss.

– You've got the g-g-gift of the gab, not me.

– You'll be fine.

– Well, don't c-c-complain if I don't do it r-right.

– Bring it over later.

– Don't w-w-worry, I w-will.

*

Mum pours him another cup of tea and he takes it upstairs to his old bedroom. Still with the Shalamar posters and photographs of Marvin Hagler. He places the phone on the bed and stares at it while sipping the drink. 'Don't ring,' he thinks. 'Please don't ring.'

2

Clive climbs the concrete steps. Knocks on the green door of Stanley's flat. Early in the afternoon and the day is taking a nap; no movement in the air, no effort from the stagnant cloud cover.

Stanley flings the door open. – Any calls?

– N-n-nothing.

– Bollocks.

Clive edges past a hangdog Stanley into the smell of stale incense.

– You sure about this m-m-male escort thing?

– It'll take time for the advert to be spotted.

Stanley leads Clive through to the lounge.

Clive slumps into a seat, Stanley kneels by the stereo system. He pulls out a vinyl LP. Harvey Mason. Puts the record on.

– This'll cheer us up.

The mobile phone lies on the dining table in the corner; the seance table.

They both pretend to ignore it and roll with the music until Stanley nods towards the phone and asks, – You sure it's working?

– I d-don't know.

– Let me try from the landline.

Stanley stretches over on the floor and grabs the normal telephone. Dials the number. The mobile rings.

– G-g-g-g-g-g-good Times, Clive says.

Stanley slams down the phone. – It's working. Shit. I don't know whether that's good or bad.

The second track on the album plays out into a fade.

– A drink? Stanley suggests.

– If you w-w-want.

– The Brewers.
– Always the B-b-brewers, Clive sighs.
– The Sons, man.

Love Life

1

Joan arrives at eight on the Thursday morning as Mother rocks at the breakfast table with egg spilling from mouth.

Patricia and Joan exchange knowing glances as they pass each other in opposite directions through the back door.

– All yours, Joan. Have a good day.

– Yes, you too, Joan smiles.

– Bye, Mother. Be good.

No reply.

Patricia walks the short distance to the shop.

Last week a man called Patricia a bitch, a young guy rubbed himself against her as she bent over, a women threatened to slit her throat because the receipt wasn't put into the bag with the purchase. Yet work is still Patricia's release: a chance to be herself, to feel appreciated, to laugh.

She arrives at eight fifteen a.m. with fifteen minutes to spare before stacking morning delivery and filling tills with the float.

Patricia tidies the shelves with Lorraine, straightening rows of shampoo, bringing forward toothpaste nearing sell-by date, returning misplaced lipstick to plinth.

– Soon be the big day, Lorraine grins.

– Oh, don't, Patricia laughs, waving her hand at her friend. – You'll make me feel old.

– Well, you are, Lorraine laughs. – Half a century.

– I'm bound to end up like Mother, Patricia says.

– Now that wouldn't be funny.

Patricia takes a cloth from pocket of overall and wipes dust off tubes of hair gel.

– Any plans yet?

– Oh, I don't know. It just seems so much trouble.

– You've got to treat yourself.

– I suppose.

A man knocks on the door, pushing his contorted face against the glass above the CLOSED sign. – Get this fucking shop open!

Patricia returns home for lunch. Through the door and into Mother's obstinacy.

– She won't eat, says Joan, standing over Mother, who huddles on the chair at the table.

– What, nothing?

Joan pulls in lips and shakes her head.

Patricia places her bag on the worktop and kneels beside Mother. – What is it?

There is no response, except for angry breathing.

– Joan's made you dinner, why don't you eat it?

– Leave me alone, you stupid girl, she growls.

– What is it? Patricia asks.

– Toilet.

– I know you don't want the toilet, Mother. Why don't you eat?

Joan offers a supporting sigh and digs fork into potato. – She only just went ten minutes ago.

– It's difficult when she's in one of these moods, Patricia says, rising to her feet and wiping her hair back.

Mother folds her arms and retreats into despondency.

– Let it go cold, I've had enough of her, says Patricia, moving to sink to clean hands and prepare for her dinner, left steaming over boiling pan.

Mother just stares loathing at Patricia. She is too old to control her daughter the way she used to.

Walking back to work the air is warm despite the rug of cloud filling the sky, in shades varying from strawberry to bleached blonde. The pedestrians, dressed for heat, strut lightly to and from the Roman Road, to and from the parks, to and from the gardens and front steps of friends. The girls, a flash of summer in bright dresses. The women, in shorts eating into buttocks and revealing cushioned thighs. And men whom Patricia studiously ignores as they pass. One with stripped torso and a silver chain that beats against his heart as he walks. Skin browned and layered in the lightest of sweat. Another wears shorts and vest showing off lean legs and sculpted arms. He offers Patricia a shifty smile as he sneaks a look up and down her body. The sun may be missing but summer still pushes men and women close.

Patricia shrugs off desire. Tired from a sleepless night in which her mind throbbed; visions of change. In which her body pulsed, needing relief. Tired of waiting for a man. The thought of embrace. That rusty smell behind male ears.

And she thinks of the muscular lines of the passing man. How she missed the company of men. Her last encounter was arranged through a dating club. She made the decision to join the agency on her forty-sixth birthday and met Melvin.

Melvin picks her up in his Ford Fiesta and drives her out to the Thames Barrier, where they sit in the car and contemplate the possible devastation caused by rising sea-levels. They drive back to the East End, to a pub that perches alongside the canal, sitting on a picnic bench that tips when they both go to sit on the same side. And so, facing one another, they clink a glass of white wine and bemoan the dark sky drifting above. But it does not rain and Melvin tells her all his best jokes and the story of his divorce and money-grabbing wife and how he relishes the chance to start afresh. He even manages to mention how they still keep in touch – for the sake of the kids – before he stops talking and turns away with sodden eyes. A minor setback, but they are soon on the road and arrive at the Indian restaurant twenty minutes earlier than booked. The place is empty and so getting the table is not a problem. Order a bottle of wine to sip with the menu despite Patricia's mild protestations about drink-driving. Which are soon forgotten by the second and third bottle and post-prandial port and brandies, all of which Patricia politely declines. Drinks that seem to fill Melvin's head with confusion as he staggers and sways outside the car, digging into pockets for the keys. Finally found in shirt pocket with the exclamation of 'Jome, Hames, and don't hare the sporses'. Pulls up outside 26 Fairfield Road at ten thirty p.m. and waits under dim bulb of car for next move. She is not sure about him at all, he is breathing through blocked nose and looking out of half-shut eyes. She thanks him for a lovely day and decides it is only fair to proffer a polite kiss before sleeping on things and making a decision the following day about the possibility of any future liaison. He seizes the opportunity and pulls her face onto his. She tries to move out of the clutch. He goes for the skirt and manages to get a finger against her pants. She flings her hand onto his wrist and stops the advance. He grabs her kneecap on the way out. She grunts with exertion as she pushes him away and grabs for the door. He groans with disbelief as she brushes herself down outside, slamming the door on his begging eyes. Closes the front door and hears the tap-tap-tap of Mother's glass coming from the bedroom.

2

How she made a fool of herself with her desire when the first home help arrived from Tower Hamlets. It was so unlike her. She still can't believe it happened and that she behaved in such a way.

Soon after Mother's first stroke, the council representative called to assess the extent of Mother's need, the extent of the state's responsibility. Forms were signed, promises made.

On the Wednesday Ian arrives on the doorstep.

Ian: employed to do the cleaning and give Patricia time to undertake the more personal aspects of Mother's care. It is the first time in an age that a male has been in the house.

For Mother it is a chance to shout and bully and make Patricia look scared in front of the skinny boy with the vacuum cleaner.

For Patricia it is a welcome change.

Ian is so near as he wipes the tables and sweeps the kitchen floor. As they share a packet of biscuits over mid-morning coffee away from Mother, who stays in bed till lunch.

He is so affable and quietly spoken that Patricia finds herself dominant. He is almost like a son who needs to be fed confidence and encouragement. And she enjoys watching him clean the house so timidly yet with such attention to detail.

It takes a few months of initiation and familiarity before Patricia finds herself waking in the night and thinking that the other pillow is Ian, caressing and whispering lust to it. Finds herself nervous before his arrival at nine. Finds herself applying a bit of lipstick.

This is how it begins, with the lipstick.

Opening the door casually and hiding her nervousness. Ian tiptoes in, as usual, as if a secret visitor. Stinking of leather and peanuts. His hair tied in a bunch and falling down his back to the belt of his tight, faded jeans.

He hoovers in the lounge while Patricia hovers about the room pretending to sort magazines and rearrange books on the shelves. They perform a little dance as he vacuums about her feet and she tries to move out of his way. Two bright laughs, the lipstick glowing.

When the make-up fails to have the desired effect, Patricia decides to reveal a little flesh. Maybe rouse Ian to realize that she is a woman and not just the lady at number 26 with an angry mother.

The tights come off, replaced by bare legs under the knee-length skirt. Wafting about the house and around Ian as he mops the bathroom. She continually fiddles with her shoes to draw attention to the skirt and legs, but Ian doesn't seem to notice. Sitting at the table, during the drinks break, the skirt tactic proves pointless.

And so, the next week, Patricia chooses to leave off her bra and wear just a T-shirt as her battle to make Ian interested intensifies. It has become a test of her femininity and attractiveness now that she is in her late forties. Just to make him look would be enough.

During the darkness of night, and while waiting for Mother on the toilet, losing the bra seemed such a good idea. But by morning her head is full of doubts and her body full of clumsiness. She cannot focus on herself as she assesses her appearance in the mirror, her ample bosom pressed cleanly against the shirt. She feels so stupid, so reckless, but in her own home, overtaken by urges and febrile determination, she finds strength knowing that Ian is so unthreatening.

She feels her smile break into panic as he walks into the hall and she is suddenly exposed. She does not lead Ian into the house but waits against the wall of the hall, thereby letting him brush past her, face to face. Her breasts seem huge under the flimsy top and her mouth, dry from anxiety, is unable to produce words.

She recharges herself in the loo and makes for the lounge, where Ian is dusting. She joins him, making special effort to reach up to the ceiling and lights, allowing the T-shirt to strain. In the kitchen she pushes against him as she pours the coffee. Sitting opposite, she leans back and forces herself to uncross her arms.

The week goes so slowly between Ian's visits, allowing Patricia too much time to think. It becomes obsessive, and nursing Mother and working at the chemist's become irritating distractions. Life centres on Ian's arrival.

Patricia knows that words would fail her if she tried to articulate desires or attract Ian through loaded conversations or subtle hints. And so she is left with the cruder and less personal method of allowing actions to speak for her: the lipstick, the unfettered breasts. And then deciding to walk about her bedroom in her underwear with the door left ajar so that willing eyes from the landing will be free to view.

Patricia doesn't know what to do as she hears Ian carrying the hoover up the stairs. She pretends to move purposefully about the room, checking the drawers, adjusting the duvet. She feels naked in her knickers and bra, waiting to turn and catch Ian peering through the door at her. She hears him make a slight cough as he fiddles with the plug. Was the cough a cue? She returns the sound with a clearing of the throat. She is shaking with expectation. Then the vacuum hums.

She watches his back as it lunges to and fro, refusing to face the bedroom door. Patricia coughs louder, over the noise of the cleaning. She moves nearer to the door, pretending to pick something off the carpet in case he turns. But he doesn't turn and she stands admiring the slim back and long hair, feeling absurd. She coughs again, and again, but Ian does not attempt to turn.

The following week her patience is paper thin.

Once again she hears him carrying the vacuum up the stairs.

She listens to his breath as he nears the top. She stands behind the door with her ear to the wood. Ian arrives on the landing, preparing to uncoil the lead. Patricia's head pulses as she discards the last of her clothes and, carrying a towel in one hand, emerges from the bathroom.

– Oh! Patricia says, with pretend surprise, standing in front of him naked.

– I'm sorry, Ian replies, turning away and putting a hand in front of his eyes.

– I thought you were downstairs.

– No, it's OK, mumbles Ian.

For a moment, Patricia does not move, she allows the initial terror to ease. Then she makes for her room, with half-hearted attempts to cover herself.

Inside the bedroom she remonstrates with herself, annoyed that Ian didn't see enough, that she didn't stay on the landing longer, forcing his gaze towards her.

But she can still hear him there. Can hear the shallow breathing and scratching of the plug on the wall.

She cannot contain herself, she is delirious from the encounter and the culmination of weeks of desire. She throws the towel on the bed and opens the door.

Ian looks up from the plug socket at her nudity.

– Look, don't you get it? I'm just not interested! Ian shouts, throwing the hoover to floor and rushing back down the stairs.

Daddy's Boy

1

Thursday afternoon in Willesden, Pow-Wow lies on the bed next to Ileasha.

Pow-Wow and Ileasha have been together since Christmas when she began floating around the circle of players. Pow-Wow took notice and acted the part of major gangster – that impressed her. They joined forces and gradually she moved her way into the heart of things. Moved onto the back seat of Pow-Wow's scooter.

Her soft chocolate breasts rest on Pow-Wow's chest as she leans across him to stroke his head. Mellow R&B plays on CD, the sweet scent of weed wafts about the room and through the gap in the open window. Every two minutes a train chatters over the music.

– Baby? Ileasha asks.

– Wha's?

– Am I your girl?

– Damn, what type of question is that?

Ileasha is not fazed and continues to stroke him slowly. – I just want to know.

– You're my woman, you know that.

Pow-Wow keeps his face aimed at the ceiling.

– You did say you were going to buy me a gold tooth.

– Yeah, baby, I did.

A pause sits between them.

Ileasha moves her stroking hand down to the stomach. – Well, where is it then?

– I'll get it. Hold tight. I'm just waiting for things to change.

– Like what?

– Like making it to All-Star Number One.

Ileasha smiles to herself. – When's that going to happen?

– Soon, baby. Things are moving.

Pow-Wow climbs out of her hold and sits on the edge of the bed. He reaches for a pair of shorts and rolls onto his back to slip them on. He stands up and goes to his exercise bench. Begins to curl two dumb-bells from his thigh to his chest. The veins push through the skin and the immature biceps slide up and down the arm. He snorts and blows as the weight begins to pull, finishing up by lowering the dumb-bells gently to the floor.

Ileasha smokes the half-finished stick and spreads herself out on the bed, pushing aside the duvet with her feet.

– You're not Mister Universe just yet, Ileasha smiles.

– Got to start young. Got to make an effort.

– You could make an effort getting some dollars.

– I'm working on it. Give me time.

– I could get me some money if you let me work for Pimp Papa.

Pow-Wow scans her nude brown body. – You ain't working like no brass.

She turns onto her back and pulls pillows beneath her head so as to watch Pow-Wow while recumbent – I sure could use the money. Mom's struggling.

– Your mom don't want no dish for a daughter. She don't want no mother-fucking ho.

– I wouldn't tell her, Ileasha says, blowing out a lungful of smoke.

– I'll get you your gold teeth. You stop thinking crazy.

2

The sea of cloud has made the early evening hazy. The sounds from the train track and road are dampened.

Pow-Wow and Ileasha walk the pavement to the walled playground on the way to Willesden. A handful of under-15s and All-

Stars stand alongside the brick sheets spraying tags. Some working on bigger murals with skyscrapers, stars, and oversized hands gesturing defiance.

– Yo, yo, a guy says to Pow-Wow.

– Wha's? Pow-Wow replies, standing behind the guy, admiring the picture in progress.

Pow-Wow takes Ileasha's hand and walks over to a bench. They sit and watch the walls changing colour. Listen to the hiss of the nozzle and the clack-clack of the shaken can.

Ringing mobile. Pow-Wow answers.

– Bro, it's Mister B, we need to talk. Urgent, yeah. Where are you at?

– Chapter Road play park.

– Don't move, I'm coming there.

Ten minutes later Mister B arrives. His skin is glowing, but his expression is dull. He ignores greetings from the artists and stamps over to Pow-Wow and shares a handshake.

– Good news, bad news.

– Good news first, says Pow-Wow.

Mister B shakes his head in shock, as if to say, 'You ain't gonna believe this.' – I get a phone call this afternoon. Pimp Papa. Tells me waltz down to the Daddies' crib on Carlton. I get there, get in, facing Spoonie, Race, Licence and Papa. I get nerves but I stay still and look smooth at the Daddies.

– What the fuck?

– Hold tight. It's coming. They sit me down, they stand up, look over me. I think I'm for a shot. Papa smiles and I know it's not bad. Race offers a hand. I shake. 'Welcome to the Daddies,' he says. I say, 'What?' He says, 'You're in.' I say, 'You're fucking me?' Licence gives me a swat across the head saying, 'You're a mother-fucking Daddy.'

– Get the fuck . . .

– Level, bro. I'm fucking down. I'm out of the All-Star, I'm a mother-fucking Daddy.

– Shit, Ileasha whispers.

– I'm going to be making bucks, having fucks. Making loot, man. You hear me?

– I hear you, Pow-Wow says, still rocked.

– No more peds. I'm in the saloon. No more crumbs from the table, I'm at the fucking feast.

Pow-Wow swivels on the gravel and faces the railway fence. He knew this was coming. It was always going to be a matter of time. But it shocks. Mister B is moving on. He'll be in a different world. End of an era. – This is the good news? he sighs.

– Don't fade on me, Pow-Wow, Mister B says. – You know how much this means.

– What's the bad news? Ileasha asks.

– Now don't tell me. Don't fucking tell me, Pow-Wow snarls.

– Step back, bro, Mister B says, holding out a hand to contain Pow-Wow's aggression.

– Man! Pow-Wow shouts at his feet. – I know it.

– What do you know? Mister B asks.

– All-Star Number One, that's what I know. I'm not getting it. Right?

Mister B puts his arms up into surrender. – That's not the deal. That may not happen. You're in the race.

– In the race? I've always been Deputy. I've always ran that job. It should be me without any fucking race.

– It's you and Ego.

– Mother-fucker.

– One on one. Sort of eliminator.

Ileasha grimaces, gags herself with her hand to prevent protest.

– When is this shit meant to happen? Pow-Wow asks.

– Tonight.

Pow-Wow blows out his disgust. – He'll fucking eat me up.

– You can take him. Believe.

– Daddies, man. They shit on your head and expect you to say thanks for the hat, says Pow-Wow.

Ileasha stands up and walks away.

– Where are you going? Pow-Wow yells to her back.

She spins round, tears of rage in her eyes. – You are full of shit! she shouts, pointing to her teeth where gold should be.

3

A dozen motors wait in the corner of the Sports Centre car park. Fifty faces avoid each other and scour the surroundings for the arrival of Pow-Wow.

Ileasha stands next to Pimp Papa, who drops his arm over her shoulder and whispers words that make her laugh and make her easy. And Papa is tempted to skim his hand down her curves but he will wait. No one looks at the two of them as they tease but focus on the weed sticks being passed about.

Track suits, baggy jeans, topless torsos, basketball tops and shorts, high socks with sneakers. Individuals strutting around in circles. Some shadow-boxing and kick-boxing moves going on in jest. The anticipation of violence pushing aggression into the veins of the spectators.

The young All-Stars show off in front of the adults, who sit on BMW bonnets and nod heads to the beats pumping from drop-top sound systems.

Ego staring at the concrete. Swinging his arms in circles to keep muscles warm. Flopping his head from side to side to encourage flexibility. Popping his eyes up occasionally to catch the glimpse of a friend with a wink and then slipping back into his trance.

Pow-Wow limps slowly across the open space from the road. Arriving alone now that Ileasha is angry and Mister B is neutral.

Pow-Wow strips off his top as he gets near. Throws it to an All-Star.

Ego, already topless, steps into the middle and pulls his head back so far onto his neck that he is peering down the nose.

A few seconds of staring, standing within inches of each other, copied from the pro fighters. Pow-Wow a small boy compared to the bulk and maturity of Ego. Two-stone difference in weight, with half a foot discrepancy in height.

They both throw their arms up into right angles.

Ego edges forward, Pow-Wow edges back.

Pow-Wow moves in, Ego moves out.

And then they both attack at the same time and meet in a flash of fists.

Pow-Wow throws punch after punch, trying to break through the size of his opponent.

Ego offers less in the way of quantity but aims a single big shot for every two of Pow-Wow's.

Pow-Wow's shots make the sound of a slap. Ego's thud.

They back off, take stock of the situation, then charge back into the slugging.

The crowd loses its passion. Fisticuffs are not as much fun as they remember.

Ego lands a heavy one and Pow-Wow folds. He bends over and tries to catch hold to recover, but Ego is slick and stands back and throws uppercuts to the head and rabbit punches to the kidneys.

Pow-Wow falls and Ego jumps on top, pressing his knees onto his opponent's arms. With Pow-Wow's head exposed, Ego starts dropping bombs.

Moving his face from side to side, Pow-Wow tries to escape the torrent of blows.

Pimp Papa steps in and hurls the new All-Star Number One off the battered Pow-Wow.

4

The crowd disperse quickly. The Daddies have business and pleasure to attend to. The All-Stars have new hierarchies to plot.

From the floor, Pow-Wow notices Ileasha drop a kiss on the cheek of Pimp Papa. Pow-Wow knows Papa's game. And he watches Pimp turn to Ileasha and give her elbow the slightest stroke before he sinks into a car.

Mister B tries to offer consolation but Pow-Wow can read the lack of interest in his eyes. Mister B is already gone; he's with the future. While Pow-Wow is left pummelled on a car park facing a reduced role in the Pack. Facing a lengthy wait before he can consider reaching Mister B's position. Facing humiliation in front of friends and Ileasha.

Ileasha waits near to where Pimp Papa departed. She looks over

at the bruised Pow-Wow. She looks so much older for her age –
much older than Pow-Wow. And her girlfriends call her over.
And she goes. Without a word.

Drip, Drip, Drip

1

Friday morning and a dull sky drapes over Fairfield Road.

Patricia sits reading *Metro* in the kitchen, reading about the Underground extension overspend, the rat infestations of a council block in Hackney, the rise in pickpocket crimes, a medal at the Karate World Championships for a Lambeth lad. Radio 2 adds music to the bubble of potatoes boiling on the cooker.

Joan has gone and the house smells of disinfectant. A little present and card perch on the edge of the table; Joan remembered Patricia's birthday. She will open them on the day. Along with a gift from Lorraine that is meant to be a bit risqué. There will be nothing from Mother – a lack of gratitude is one of the last weapons Mother has at her disposal.

Tap-tap-tap. Mother's glass knocks against the table. Patricia gets to her feet.

Mother is not feeling well. She is laid up in bed with three pillows behind her head.

– Do you want a drink? Patricia asks.

– Pillows.

– OK, let's be having you.

Patricia goes to the bed and leans over Mother, whose body is lying on top of the sheets, whose white nightie is scrunched about her midriff, exposing sallow legs.

– Lean forward, Mother.

Patricia grabs an armful of pillow. Accidentally pinches a section of Mother's arm.

Like a cat, Mother strikes. A flimsy claw rips against Patricia's face.

– What are you doing? Patricia shrieks, pulling away from the bed.

– You caught me, Mother growls.

– I didn't mean to.

– Pah.

– This can't go on, Patricia shouts, running towards the bathroom.

Mother stays motionless, staring through the gloom at her daughter throwing water over face.

The water is sharp and cold and it stings against the scratched skin. It washes away the beginning of tears. Which is good, because Mother likes to see upset, she likes to see the damage. Patricia pushes her head into a towel to feel comforted. A facial hug. Which makes things seem better. Gives her the strength to leave the bathroom and face Mother.

Patricia walks past her without a glance.

Mother stares from the corner of her eye.

– Drink, Mother says, as she notices Patricia leaving the room.

Patricia blocks out Mother's voice. Slams the door as she departs.

2

Patricia knows she shouldn't shut the door on Mother. It's like blocking one's ears to the cries of an infant. But this time Patricia is dogged in her determination to exclude Mother. Maybe give Mother time to regret her actions – which is unlikely. At least give her a chance to feel isolated. The way Patricia increasingly feels as each day and week turn to nothing.

Whenever Patricia closes the door on Mother and ignores the taps, and whenever Mother is too weak to climb out of bed, she knows that Mother's mind will return to the war. The claustrophobia of the bedroom invariably transports her back to Bethnal Green Underground station.

3 March 1943. Eight o'clock p.m. the sirens begin and Mother

walks along Roman Road towards Bow. She has been to see her friend Betty Ribbon and ended up staying late with chit-chat of the war, of houses ruined by bombs, of people killed. But also talk of cooking, clothing and recollections.

Mother weighs up the prospect of rushing the twenty-minute walk home or dashing back to the nearest shelter at Bethnal Green Underground station on the corner of Cambridge Heath Road. She decides to head for Bow and has to push her way through oncoming groups who shout, swear, laugh, all making their way towards the Bethnal Green bunker.

– Where you off to? a warden asks, appearing out of darkness, grabbing her arm.

– I'm getting home.

– Where's that?

– Fairfield Road.

– You'd better head back the way you came.

– I've an Anderson in the garden, Mother replies sharply.

– You ain't going to make it back there in time.

– I'll do it, don't you mind.

The warden, his face lit only by streaks of sweat over the nose and cheeks, shakes his head. – You just get yourself back to the station. They are going to start dropping any minute.

– Pah! Mother sneers and turns round to join the scattered crowds now running to the faintly lit stairwell.

The anti-aircraft battery in Victoria Park begins to unleash volleys of fire. The sky dances with searchlight and crashes with shells.

The steps into the station are packed with people panicked by the chaos above. The crowd pushes and heaves its way into the small entrance. Mother is pushed along with the momentum and finds herself halfway into the tunnel moving towards the ticket hall. Heads begin to disappear from view under the murky light from a single twenty-five-watt bulb. They are falling to the floor in front of her and yet the crush from behind increases. There is a shriek, a shout, and the good-natured cursing and complaining stop as the atmosphere turns fearsome.

– Stop pushing, someone yells from where bodies are sinking into blackness.

– Go back, go back! screams a man.

The sound of the battle outside escalates and the anxious hollering inside is drowned out under the ack-ack roar. The pressure from the top of the stairwell increases, forcing more and more people into the human waterfall. Mother sees legs around heads. There are hands emerging out of the scrum, seeking a grip; arms waving in distress; hoping that someone will see and come to rescue. But no one can offer assistance, everyone is trapped. And the heat becomes burning. And Mother struggles to breathe as she folds up between the merging, melting bodies.

It took rescue workers over three hours to untangle the 173 dead; mostly women and children. It has taken Mother over fifty years to try and forget that evening; mostly unsuccessfully.

Every time she returned to Bethnal Green she heard screams and saw shadows floating about the station. So she stopped going back and left the ghosts to their torment.

3

Patricia puts her feet up in the lounge and lays her head back on the cushions. Turns her mind off to the tap-tap-tap from across the hallway. Reassured by the knocking glass that Mother is OK. Safe for her to stretch on the sofa and relax on a Friday afternoon. After another weekly routine creaks to a halt, like Mother walking from bathroom to bed. Equally strained and ultimately meaningless. And Patricia is fifty tomorrow. So determined to do something special and show Mother that she is not beaten and that there is life in her yet.

She thinks it would be nice to go out. But there is no one to go out with. Joan is too much of a help to be a friend. Lorraine too young to want to spend her evenings away from her boyfriend and social group. Patricia is not the type to ask to tag along as they drive into London or watch the latest horror flick. What would they think of her? What would they say to her?

But where could she go alone? Certainly not into town. Or into any of the trendy bars that have sprung up nearby. Or into the grubby local pubs that have not changed in fifty years and are dying on their feet, like their clientele.

Recalls seeing an advert for a new Mile End Indian restaurant in *Metro*. Takes the paper from the coffee table and shakes through the pages to the adverts. Patricia likes a curry. The only colour classified in the section. Enjoys a spicy one. The Bengal Tiger. Sounds vicious.

Checks that Mother's door is closed. Presses her ear against it to hear Mother coughing lightly. She's OK.

Dials the number of the restaurant.

– Hello, Bengal Tiger.

– Hello, I'd like to book a table for tomorrow night.

– Let me look, the South Asian accent replies.

A muffled rustle of paper. – I'm sorry, we're fully booked tomorrow.

Patricia thinks quickly. – Tonight?

– Yes, we've got a few spaces.

– Yes, tonight then. Can I book a table?

– How many?

– One.

– One?

– Yes, it's my birthday.

– What time?

– Seven?

– Name?

– Patricia.

Patricia is empowered and pushes into Mother's room.

– I'm going out tonight, she says.

Mother stares ahead and says nothing.

– Too late to get Joan. You'll have to be on your own for an hour or two.

Mother begins to cough violently. Trying to push her lungs through her chest.

– Don't act, Mother, Patricia says.

Mother continues to cough, bringing herself close to retching.

– Stop it! Patricia snaps.

And Mother begins to wheeze like she is suffocating. But she isn't. She is just desperate.

4

Patricia is in her special blue dress. Her hair is washed and blown into a wavy block. But the perfume is stale. The make-up is crude. The wonky eye is accentuated by the eyeshadow.

She is nervous, leaving the house alone in the evening. It is not a time she is used to outside. Her hands shudder with the keys and she can barely lock the door.

Her shoes are too tight and too tall in the heel. She feels like somebody else. Scared to see anyone she knows as she closes the garden gate and goes onto the pavement.

It is her birthday tomorrow, why shouldn't she go out and enjoy a meal? she thinks. Conjures up images of the curry and naan bread. Hobbles along the street. Conjures up images of Mother lying in bed alone. Two boys ride past on bikes and shout out, 'Cor, you look sexy,' in sarcastic tones. They laugh out loud. She recalls the questioning voice of the man at the restaurant as he confirmed the table. 'One?' The waiters will no doubt be waiting. To laugh at the sad woman who wants a table for one on a Friday night. For her birthday. Why did she tell them that? They will be making bets about what she looks like. She looks at herself in a house window. The garish face and unfashionable frock. And what will all the other customers think as she shrinks into a corner by the toilets and sips tepid wine? As she tries to avoid eyes out of an unnecessary sense of guilt. Will they laugh, too? Will they feel sorry for her? What will her Chicken Madras taste like surrounded by all this sympathy and sniggering? And she realizes that she is not hungry. Her stomach is as tight as a noose. Strangling her from the inside. Mother wants her back home, she knows it. And Patricia can't face the restaurant. Cannot face sitting down and wanting to cry because she knows she shouldn't be there. That she should be with company or at home, but not sitting alone pretending to enjoy the evening without a friend. Why did she have such a stupid idea? Why didn't she think about it properly? Why is loneliness so hard?

She turns around and walks back towards Fairfield Road. With much quicker steps. Almost running. Passing the cinema tagged onto the end of the shopping parade.

A gaggle of youths and families shuffle about the entrance and look at watches. Standing below the huge colourful canopy with the film titles written in black. Patricia notices *The Lady in Waiting*. Has seen the trailers on TV. She stops awkwardly outside the cinema and peers in through the posters. The blue décor and pictures of food. A small queue for tickets. How she loves a film. Has been a long time since she went to the movies. Nothing like the big screen and the surround sound. And the murky darkness that shuts out the world.

Inside, the children are laughing and running around with lollipops the size of their heads. The youths in baseball caps carry armfuls of food and mingle easily with the mums and dads in the gentle light of the foyer.

Patricia initially pretends to look around for an imaginary friend. Acts as if she is a little late. Walks determinedly towards a woman only to pull back at the last minute to feign mistaken identity.

She then realizes that no one is looking at her. Even the serving staff waiting behind the food counters are refilling frankfurters and adding candy chews to giant glass tubs.

Stands behind a couple holding hands in the ticket line. Clutches her handbag for company.

– One for *The Lady in Waiting*, Patricia says to the girl behind the screen.

– Standard or luxury? the girl asks.

– What's luxury?

– Bigger seat, more leg room, central view, the girl reels off quickly.

– Luxury, please, Patricia grins. – Why not?

As the girl fiddles with the computer booking system, Patricia is conscious of the queue forming behind her. She once again looks over her shoulder to fake a search for the non-existent friend.

74

– I hope my friend makes it in time, she says to the girl.

– Do you want me to reserve the seat next to you? the girl asks.

Patricia pauses and turns around once more to give herself a chance to think.

– I'll leave it for now, she says, pulling open her handbag, unwilling to touch eyes with the girl.

They exchange ticket for cash.

– Hope your friend makes it, the girl says.

The thick carpeting makes Patricia feel important as she walks along the lane for Screen 3. The other people around her walk slowly and calmly, all mollified by the civilized ambience and the smell of caramel popcorn.

The luxury seat is not a lot bigger than the standard seat but it is more like a compartment with red velvet wings that act as walls. Patricia smiles to herself as she sinks into its arms. Content at having made it through the public process to end up alone with the screen.

The auditorium is relatively empty considering it is Friday night. Patricia assumes that it is the film. *The Lady in Waiting* is a quiet, thoughtful movie. Little in the way of Hollywood. And the locals who have gathered to watch are an ageing bunch. In couples. Only Patricia sits alone, at the back, in her booth. Hoping that Mother is all right. Glad that she did not go to the restaurant. Here among the faint lights, her solitude is invisible.

5

When Patricia returns home, Mother is in the lounge. Staring at a blaring television. Furious that her daughter went out and left her alone.

Patricia notices the frail wrists shaking with rage.

– Sorry I'm late, Mother, she says, standing in the doorway.

Mother is unsure how to play the situation. Chooses to ignore.

– I'm in now and so there's no point being angry, she says, going over to the TV and turning down the sound.

– Where've you been? Mother growls.

– I went to the cinema. Had a lovely time, thank you.

– Pah.

– Just a little birthday treat for myself, Patricia says slyly, reminding Mother of the date.

Mother does not bite the bait. – Who would take you?

– I went on my own.

– Who would want you?

Patricia thinks of the film and its sad ending, which made her cry on her own in the booth. The film made life become easy, become beautiful. Away from the ugly smells of Mother.

– A woman with a face like yours, Mother continues.

The film made Patricia hopeful and filled her with energy and optimism.

– Spinster, Mother hisses.

It left her cocooned in a make-believe world where everything is possible. And so Patricia looks at Mother coolly, almost with sympathy. Unperturbed by the usual ire-inducing insults.

She feels apart from her Mother, looking down on the tiny body as if the size is not because of shrinking bones but because of perspective. Mother is far away.

– Going out alone, you're pathetic, Mother says, trying to tighten the argument.

– I had a great time, Patricia smiles, bathing in the detachment, the lack of care.

– A grown woman, going out alone, Mother tries to continue, but her tiredness drains the power of her attack.

As Mother wilts, Patricia grows. Her head seems to be against the ceiling. Mother is a virtual speck on the chair. And Patricia feels the urge to brush the speck off the seat and into nothing. She searches the mind for the blow.

– Yes, I went out on my own tonight because I've got a date tomorrow, Patricia says, surprising herself.

– Date? You? Mother's voice is all that is left and it is incandescent as it flashes across the room to Patricia.

Patricia sees the minute figure swaying on the chair, ready to fall.

– Yes, a handsome man who comes into the shop, she says.

– Lie, Mother squeals.

– Quite wealthy, I hear.

The speck of Mother is fading. – You are ugly. No man wants you.

Patricia is invincible tonight. The words of Mother are harmless.

– Well, my date for tomorrow obviously doesn't think so.

Mother falls off the chair to the floor.

Patricia runs over and reaches down to lift the old lady back to her feet.

– I'm hurt, Mother shouts.

– You're tired, Patricia reassures, supporting Mother as they limp to the bedroom. – You should have been asleep hours ago.

Mother begins to cry. It is an uneven, self-indulgent cry that is meant to affect Patricia.

Which it does. But not enough to knock Patricia off her perch.

With Mother in bed, Patricia has to consider the date she promised in front of Mother. The date that leapt on her from the thought of an advert in the paper. An advert near the Bengal Tiger.

The film's effect is fading but she is still resolute. Still determined to show Mother that she will not be beaten.

Patricia has heard of male escorts but not for one minute has she considered them to be of any relevance to her. Who would pay a man for a date? But how it will show Mother. A few pounds for such a performance. Mother will ignite. And it will be over in a couple of hours. And she is fifty tomorrow. What the hell. The thought makes Patricia want to laugh. It is nearly ridiculous. Then she thinks of Mother's face when she told her about the man. It was a picture. She goes to the kitchen to find *Metro* while enthusiasm still burns.

6

Clive's flat throbs to the sound of music from the flat below. Clive and Stanley sit in half-darkness watching the film credits roll past. Empty drink cans and biscuit wrappers lie around their feet. The movie was a let-down – it just wasn't funny. But it killed a Friday night. And kept their minds off the mobile phone sitting on the table behind. That has not rung since the advert appeared. A lack of response that generates relief and disappointment in equal measure. That has begun to make the friends think there is no future in the escort game.

And then it rings.

Clive looks to Stanley. Stanley looks alarmed. Its shrill tone causes panic.

– Shit, says Stanley.

– I'm n-n-n-n-not answering it, Clive mumbles.

They both sit stuck in their seats. Listening to the sharp trill. Hoping for something to happen.

Then the ringing stops.

Stanley blows out and shakes his head.

Clive keep his stare on Stanley. – We should h-h-have answered it.

Stanley nods quickly to himself. – I know.

And the phone begins to ring again.

Stanley jumps up and rolls his shoulders to shake out the tension. Picks up the phone and taps the green button.

– Good Times. How can I help? he says, as Clive curls into a ball on the armchair and covers his head with a cushion.

– I'm sorry to phone so late, Patricia says.

– Not a problem, Stanley replies, rushing out the words just before he has to have a nervous swallow.

– I saw your advert in the newspaper, Patricia says, equally anxious. – I was hoping you might be able to give me some more information.

– What do you want to know? says Stanley, grimacing.

– It is just dating, isn't it? Not anything . . . more.

– Just dating, Stanley says firmly, angling his pitch.

– And you have proper, respectable-type men?

– Oh yes, nods Stanley, then wincing as he sees Clive poking his head out from beneath the cushion.

– I was hoping to . . . hire . . . a man for tomorrow night. It's my birthday. Maybe go for a meal, says Patricia, embarrassed.

– Not a problem.

– How much would it be? For the evening?

Stanley has thought about price but he found it difficult to strike a balance between offering good value and sounding desperate. – Call it one hundred, he says, confidently.

– Yes, I thought it would be expensive, Patricia replies. – Is that the cheapest price?

– Eighty?

– It seems funny to haggle.

– We can give you a lovely guy for eighty. Tall, dark, handsome, Stanley squirms, studying Clive's frightened face.

Patricia is hesitant. She is on the verge of agreeing to a date with a stranger. Closes her eyes and thinks of Mother. Recalls the little speck on the armchair. – OK, OK. That'll be fine.

– For tomorrow, you said?

– Can I call back and give you a time and place?

– Course you can. When you like.

Stanley hangs up and drops himself to the floor. – Oh my God!

Patricia gently replaces the phone in its cradle and tries to stop herself from shaking. She now has to think about a restaurant. Attempt to get that booked by tomorrow. Will be difficult. Will start tonight. Go somewhere special. Once-in-a-lifetime treat. What will the date look like? What will he think of her? Maybe go up the West End. Yes, why not? Live a little. Fifty years old. Time to go for it.

Riding

1

Pow-Wow has kept his head down since yesterday evening. Turned the mobile off, turned away callers at the door, laid on the bed dreaming of a way out. Without the energy to lift any weights, or stand by the window watching trains, or getting out into the air and hoping the dead sun will find a way back to life.

Ileasha hasn't made an effort to get in touch. Not an offer of sympathy or encouragement. It seems an age since she was last lying on the bed, draped over the sheets like a long brown pillow.

Blows out smoke rings to the beat of the music.

Extinguishes the roach in time to a knock on the door downstairs.

A rumble of feet up the stairs.

– It's Mister B, Emmanuel whispers through Pow-Wow's bedroom door.

– Let him in, Pow-Wow says, willing to see the only person he could face.

He struggles from the bed and throws on a vest and unlocks the door.

Mister B taps twice and then pokes his head into the smoky room.

– Yeah, yeah, he says.

– Come in, Pow-Wow replies.

Mister B steps in trying to hold a gait of despair but he is too excited to repress a swagger. Dressed in a crisp suit, now out of the All-Star sports gear. Dressed like a Daddy.

– Fucking pimp, Pow-Wow sneers, half jokingly.

– Friday night, Pow. I just wanted to touch base before I headed out.

– Look nice, Pow-Wow nods. – With the Daddies?

– You know it.

Pow-Wow offers a painful smile.

– It ain't all over for you, Mister B says urgently.

– Maybe not, replies Pow-Wow, flopping onto the bed.

– You gotta play the time game. The Daddies know what you can do.

Pow-Wow shakes his head. – Man, did you see Ego eat me? How does anyone come back from that?

– It's forgotten. Done. You're still a player.

Pow-Wow shrugs.

– I'm speaking for you. I'm looking out.

Pow-Wow shrugs again. – I understand that. But, whatever.

– Believe it, Mister B says, trying to look deep into Pow-Wow.

– You have a good night, yeah.

2

Ileasha sits in the passenger seat of Pimp Papa's Mercedes. Her long legs push against the glove compartment.

Papa scans the naked thighs. Papa in his velvet suit, eau-de-toilette, and smoothly shaven face. Driving slow through Harlesden with cars straining at the leash behind. Papa whispering deep into mobile before turning the phone off and giving attention to the seventeen-year-old girl next to him.

– Tonight, baby, I'm going to show you the world, Papa smiles.

Ileasha returns the smile.

– Tonight, sweet thing, I'm going to make you see things the way I see them.

As he speaks, a group of guys standing outside a store wave to the car. Papa downs the window and returns a slow salute.

– Go, Papa, go, one of the guys shouts.

Papa snorts a laugh and hits the button to redraw the darkened glass.

The late-summer evening melts the shadows. A murky sky

drifts over the Brent side of the city. Bringing with it tension. The gait of the pedestrians becomes more hunched and intense.

Papa hits the headlights and the dashboard erupts.

Ileasha likes the lights as they appear around her: the greens, the blues and the yellows. The heat from the fan trickles up her skirt. The scent of Papa envelops. The CD throbs jazz.

Papa does not speak, allowing the ride to speak for him. The cool, clicking fingers of indicators. The muscular moan of engine. The heating whispers. And he sparks a number and draws long and slow, exhaling in gushes. Losing Ileasha in smoke. Letting out a little moan of pleasure as he pushes back into the headrest. Guiding the steering wheel with thumb and forefinger. Past dissolving streets.

Mister B waits at the end of Pow-Wow's road.

The Mercedes glides to the kerb.

– Wha's happening, Daddy? Pimp Papa says.

– Hey, Papa, Mister B replies, climbing into the back, surprised to see Ileasha sitting in the front.

– You OK, Ileasha? asks Mister B.

– I'm fine. How are you? she sings.

They drive for ten minutes before coming to a halt outside a club called Tino's. To a welcome of security staff in black bomber jackets.

Papa collects a cane from the back seat.

Mister B jumps out and tries to look cool, fighting his nerves in front of the bouncers.

Pimp Papa slides his hand around Ileasha's waist to saunter under the flickering sign, through a dark double doorway, into a hallway of black and chrome, along a corridor to the main room. Quarter-filled with groups drinking in cubicles. Girls in transparent catsuits carrying drink trays. A DJ stuck in a booth above the main floor. A handful of guys in tight-fitting threads mingle in front of the bar.

Mister B living real in the Daddies. Hair sliced short, and trimmed into smart lines over jaw and chin.

– Champagne on ice is my advice, Papa chuckles.

– The wine is fine and always on time, Mister B laughs back.

– But first I gotta dine on a line.

– I hear that, agrees Mister B, reaching into his jacket for his tin of cocaine.

Tino's fills up with the faces of NWL. Papa circulates and arranges and compromises and offers and slaps hands. Never sweating or hasty. Always ready with the right quip or calming word. Strutting from friend to friend with the cane tapping. The turquoise suit buttoned. The neckerchief knotted loosely.

Mister B sits with Ileasha, on opposite sides of a table. On a raised platform. They sip drinks and follow Papa with their stares. Sitting together as if they are strangers. Pow-Wow is not mentioned. Those days are gone. Mister B pretends he's Al Capone. Ileasha acts the film star. Both trying out new roles and happy to accommodate the other. But so little to say. It is all said and done in the way Mister B snorts on the powder, the way Ileasha coquettishly shakes the hands of introduced guys.

Papa escorts a famous boxer, Trey Benson, over to the table to introduce.

Trey strokes Ileasha's hand as he shakes. His knuckles like rocks. A hot stare. A cursory press of flesh for Mister B as Trey hones in on Ileasha.

– Your first time? he asks.

Ileasha comes over shy, responds with a blush.

– How about I come and make myself easy next to you?

– Yeah, sure, Ileasha mumbles.

Papa and Trey exchange the subtlest of glances. Both pairs of eyes slightly close.

Trey drops onto the leather seat that runs alongside the wall. Pushes himself close to Ileasha. Close enough for knees to touch and her bare arms to rest against his suit.

– You are pretty, Trey says.

A waitress places an ice bucket with Moët on the table. The table watches silently as she pours two flutes.

Mister B takes the hint and grabs his drink to move to the bar.

Trey drops a hand onto Ileasha's leg and rolls his fingers about the kneecap.

– You're going to like it here, Trey says. – We all look out for each other, cookie.

– I'm not really used to this type of place, Ileasha replies quietly.

– You soon will be.

– It's the first time I've had real champagne.

– You won't taste nothing sweeter.

– Papa says it's good for me.

– He likes you a lot. You're a lucky girl.

– I feel safe here.

– Baby, you ain't got nothing to fear in this world. I can see that you've got what it takes to roll with the kings.

– It's like a different world, she says with a disbelieving shake of the head.

– What do you want out of life?

– I got some plans. I don't know.

– Hit me.

– Singing, acting, dancing.

– You make friends in the right places and then there'll be no limits.

– A model?

– With a face and body like yours, that should be a tease.

– I'd like to be able to help out my mom.

– See, you've even got a conscience. You got it all, cookie. We come from nothing and take it all. Like me. Local boy, yeah? I ran with the rats before I let my knuckles break out. You want to go to the States?

– I guess.

– You'll not see anything else like it, Trey says, tipping another glass of the fizz. – It's new, you see. Modern.

Trey stops playing with her knee. Reaches for a packet of cigars on the table.

Papa returns and reaches over to talk to Trey's ear.

Trey slides away from Ileasha, pulls himself up from the table. Swaps a hug with Papa. Swaps another whisper. Turns back to Ileasha. – Next time, cookie. Me and you, yeah? he says, pointing with the cigar.

Ileasha smiles over the taste of champagne.

Papa moves along the seat to sit on the warmth of Trey's imprint. He pours himself a glass and refills Ileasha. Puts his arm around her and tugs her in tight.

3

Papa and Mister B sit in the front of the car, Ileasha and a girl called Serena sit in the back. Cruising home in the early hours of Saturday morning. Rain dribbles down the screen.

– This is the life! shouts Mister B over the sound of music, puffing on smoke, rocking excitedly in his seat.

– Wooo! encourages Serena.

– I am the man! Mister B cries out.

– You are the man, Serena replies.

– You hear about Serena, Papa? Mister B asks.

Papa flicks his head up for an answer.

– She's going to double the hours, man. Double bubble!

– That's steadfast, Papa nods.

– Me and you, girl, Mister B says, turning to Serena. – You's the first lady and I's the President. We're going to go all the way.

Ileasha smiles as she watches Mister B swell. – I think you've had a good evening, she says.

– What an evening. I'm down with the town.

– Thanks to Papa, Ileasha says.

– Damn right, Mister B replies. – He's a king and I'm going to be the prince.

Papa shrugs off the admiration. – But how do you feel? he asks Ileasha.

– Good, Ileasha grins, catching Papa's eye in the rear-view mirror.

– We're all happy! yells Mister B. – We're all kings!

Papa takes the weed off Mister B and slots it between his lips. Sucking the stick dry. Changing through the gears as he slows for traffic lights on Willesden High Road. – Mother-fucking red, he curses.

– Mother-fucking red, Mister B repeats. – Break the fucks.

– Mother-fucking cameras, bro.

– Fuck them.

– Easy, man. We're easy.

– They ain't got no fucking film.

– Take a chill-pill. You're blowing up.

They wait without talking. The music left to thump melodies. The girls in the back begin to sleep.

Mister B sinks lower into his seat and rubs his hands over his head. Pimp Papa drops a long sigh that marks the end of the evening.

Date

1

The Tactics

Stanley spent the night thinking about the first phone call. The initial panic gradually subsided and he settled into dreams of success. Imagined making loot from the business, imagined walking into the Brewers with a wallet full of dough and women on the end of the mobile. The Sons can keep their bonuses and family firms if I can live like that, Stanley thought. The Sons will soon be asking me for work.

Clive had a more difficult night, after being coerced by Stanley into taking the date. Always the fall guy. Therefore spent the night working himself into a terror. 'Need to overcome your shyness,' Stanley argued as usual when he volunteered Clive for the job. 'See it as a treatment.' Clive was not convinced and frowned.

'This is our big chance,' Stanley said with huge eyes. 'And you get to shag,' was his final thought.

It was hard for Clive to say no to Stanley. The way he pleaded and pressurized. The way he played the emotional strings and made things sound easy.

Now five thirty on the Saturday afternoon.

Patricia rang earlier that morning with the details. She has booked a table in a restaurant near Covent Garden. Could only get the first sitting at seven thirty.

Tall, dark and handsome, Stanley said on the phone when Patricia called. Now, looking at Clive, he is not so sure that he said the right thing.

Clive looks shattered, with puffy eyes. He looks terrified as he winds up the tie and slips on his mauve jacket. As he pushes a comb through his hair and wipes gel off the plastic teeth. At least he's dark.

They set off for the station. Humid evening, white-mist clouds, daytime heat trapped in the air and inside clothes.

– Is that the best clobber you've got? Stanley says, staring the question at Clive.

– You know I d-d-don't have much in the way of c-c-clothes.

– But still, what made you buy a mauve jacket?

– Mum and Dad b-b-bought it for me.

– You should have worn your old dancing gear.

– My s-s-s-satin pegs don't fit me any more.

Stanley pulls his mouth to one side. – At least you could wear pegs. I always wanted a pair of pegs.

– Why d-didn't you get some?

– You must remember. I saved up my pocket cash for a whole winter. For my pegs. Big day came and the bloke in the shop told me I could never wear pegs.

– Why?

– Legs too short.

– Bit of a b-b-blow.

– I can still hear the bloke's voice. Still see him. There's some things you never forget.

They carry on walking to the station. The evening light exposing the faded streaks on Clive's jacket. Exposing the cracks in his demeanour.

– What am I going t-t-to talk about? Clive asks.

– Whatever, Stanley replies.

– Well, what?

– Yourself, for starters. Women aren't interested in talking about themselves, you've got to get the conversation onto you. Impress her.

– Impress her?

– Make it up, you schmuck.

The Piccadilly line is full of going-outers, windows steamed up by failing ventilation and cramped bodies. Clive and Stanley nestle by a single door in the corner and stand with faces pressed close, merged heat causing Stanley to melt and Clive to panic.

– I d-d-don't know if I can do this.

Stanley breathes out with disgust. – Get a grip, you're going to have the night of your life.

– What is she expecting?

– Just stick by the rules.

– Who m-m-mentioned rules?

– Ladies' rules, you know?

Clive pushes his bottom lip out.

– Forget it, Stanley says, harassed by a moving body behind.

They both walk from Covent Garden station towards the restaurant, Ad Nauseam, looking drained.

Clive is immersed in himself, attempting calm but achieving little.

– T-t-t-tell me about the rules, he asks, once the main tourist traffic has began to ease.

– I should have gone over this at home.

– What is she g-going to expect?

– Listen, keep it simple.

– What if she doesn't l-like me?

– Drink what she drinks, yeah? Match her glass for glass. Women hate drinking alone.

– But I d-don't like drink.

– Keep smiling.

– What if she tells me something s-s-s-s-sad?

– Complain about the food. It's a must. Shows confidence, shows a bit of class. You're used to certain standards.

– What if she likes the f-f-food?

– When it comes to the bill make it clear that she's paying. That'll make her feel special. Remember, it's her evening.

– What if she's f-f-forgotten her purse?

The restaurant pushes out of the surrounding buildings, edging onto the pavement. Flower pots and hanging baskets decorate the façade. The menu framed in metal sticks to the wall.

Stanley pulls Clive into a doorway as if attempting to avoid someone. He smoothes the creases in Clive's shirt caused by the manhandling.

– Now, I want you to go in there and do the business. Feeling good?

– No.

– That woman in there wants you!

– She h-h-hasn't even m-met me yet.

– You've got to be confident. Wiggle the hips and push that door aside gunslinger-style.

Clive's mouth turns down at the edges.

– Don't forget the most important rule of all, Stanley adds. – If in doubt, lie, just fucking lie.

2

The Tizer

Patricia is at the bar, sipping a gin and tonic, trying to avoid the glances from barman, diners, and the standing groups who mingle as they wait for their tables. She is wearing the bright blue dress she specified on the phone to aid identification.

She is trying to forget about Mother, who shouted and swore when Joan arrived to take over for the evening. When she saw daughter in make-up and dress and gold chain bought for her by Dad on eighteenth. Who tried to make herself vomit as Patricia turned handle on back door. And whose howls faded as Patricia made her way along Fairfield Road.

The chatter of the restaurant and the metallic clink of formal dining waft past Patricia and into Clive as he slips through the entrance door.

A tall, elegant waiter holding a clipboard sidles alongside Clive.

– Yes, sir?

Clive squeezes out a smile. Without words he points towards the blue dress at the bar and implies his purpose with eager eyes and a pointing nod. Without returning a look to the waiter he treads carefully towards Patricia seated at the bar.

Behind her back he composes himself for the introduction, mouthing the name Patricia so as to avoid a lengthy stammer. She turns to check the door just as Clive closes his eyes to concentrate. When he opens them she is staring straight at him.

– P-p-p-p-patricia? he mumbles.

– Clive? she replies.

A clumsy handshake commences the transaction.

– H-h-happy birthday.

– Thanks.

Sudden silence. Two strangers stare at one another.

– Would you like a drink? Patricia asks.

– Yes, s-s-sure.

Patricia turns back to the bar and attempts to catch the barman.

Clive scans the optics, the pumps and the fridges.

– What would you like?

He is scared to take an alcoholic drink so early. There is bound to be wine with the meal and he doesn't want to humiliate himself. His thoughts cause him confusion. – D-d-d-do they have Tizer? he blurts out.

She beckons the barman with a timid smile.

– Do you sell Tizer?

– No, I'm afraid not.

Patricia shrugs helplessness at Clive, who bites his lip.

– Coke? he suggests, remembering what he usually drinks in pubs.

The barman looks to Patricia attentively, awaiting her acceptance of his choice.

– Don't you want something alcoholic? I'm having one.

Clive recalls 'Drink what she drinks.' – Oh, r-r-r-right, he says, wide-eyed with fake realization. – I'll have what you're having.

Patricia grins and nods uneasily at the barman, who prepares another gin and tonic.

– Ice and lemon?

Clive bends around Patricia to study her glass. Sees the shrunken cubes and yellow hue. Nods.

Clive notices that one of Patricia's eyes stares at her nose. He thinks of Stanley's advice ('Keep smiling') and stares unblinking at her with a tortured grin.

– I guess you don't like to drink too much, being out so often. You could turn into an alcoholic, she laughs.

He continues to smile, standing erect with his arms down the side of his white trousers. Patricia reaches for her drink and sips.

Clive knows that he should start talking about himself but Patricia sits there, too real.

– Where are you from? she asks.

– London.

– Whereabouts?

– Finchley, he says quickly. Too quickly.

Patricia nods lightly. – I'm from Bow. Do you know it?

– Yes, he says seriously, as if he is going to add something else. Nothing comes and he reaches for the drink.

A group encroaches alongside at the bar, bantering loudly. Clive is pushed closer so that he presses against her stool. The strained smile betrays his embarrassment.

3

The Table

Clive finds the situation impenetrable as they take their seats on a table for two tucked discreetly beside a square pillar. Social interaction swells and subsides around them while waiters rush about carrying huge white plates full of colour and sauce.

Clive and Patricia sit silently at the table admiring the cutlery and decorations. Patricia bows in her seat, repelling the invasion of others. She peeks at Clive and notices him wearing the same grin as if he has got something stuck in his throat.

Clive is aware that his shyness is making Patricia retreat. His awkwardness is rubbing off and causing her to regret making the date. He wants to start talking, to smile cleanly, but the more he observes her deflation the harder it becomes to act.

They order the house white and stare about the restaurant. Other couples draw a blind around themselves as a stare from Clive or Patricia seeks release.

Patricia, once again, thinks of Mother, probably sitting in front of the mirror having her hair dried by Joan. Home seems distant. Patricia feels isolated. As if cooped up inside a larger box.

Clive looks at Patricia, dressed like a flower. Looks at her wilt.

And, regardless of the date, the money, the escort agency, he wants to rescue her. To make her happy. Her sadness is his motivation and he decides to attack.

– A toast, he declares, swiping his glass off the table.

Patricia slowly takes her glass and gives Clive a surprised grin.

– To Patricia, on her b-b-b-b-birthday.

They clink drinks. The silence becomes warmer. The smiles, more honest.

The waiter lights a candle.

– This is a l-l-lovely place, isn't it? Clive says.

– I read about it in a magazine. It was an article on the chef. I've never had a meal by a famous chef. I bet you're used to it?

– Well, you know, I-I-I-I've been around.

Clive is sweet, totally unlike what Patricia expected for a male escort. She assumed it would be all chin and chest. How wrong she was. But she is not disappointed. There is something decent about him.

The waiter delivers the starters and they begin to eat; Patricia with careful movements, Clive with a clumsy, slippery manner – the knife and fork jutting from his grip like broken fingers.

– Mmmm, superb, Patricia moans with full mouth.

Clive is ready to join her in the appreciation until he remembers the rules ('Complain about the food'). He throws up an arm.

– What's the matter? Patricia asks anxiously.

– It's the f-f-fish, it's cold.

– Isn't it meant to be cold?

The waiter arrives.

– This fish is c-cold.

– Yes, the fish is served cold. Would you prefer it to be warm?

– Yes, please. I d-don't think it should be this cold, he suggests.

– I mean, this really is c-c-cold.

The waiter dips in to remove the unsatisfactory starter. – How warm would you like it: hot, warm, tepid?

The waiter does not intend to sound patronizing but Patricia squirms and lowers her head into the salad.

– Just warm, please, Clive says, trying to salvage credibility with certainty in his decision.

The waiter floats away and two confused expressions meet over the candle. Other diners turn away with raised eyebrows and climb back into their privacy, pulling down the blinds.

Patricia and Clive are left marooned in the middle of the restaurant. Patricia's cheeks flush a little and she gulps on a slice of mozzarella that is not chewed to a convenient pulp. It sticks in her throat and needs to be coaxed down with a glass of water.

Clive looks at the pillar to avoid her struggle with the cheese. To await the return of his fish. Warm. The slight boozy film that had entered his vision fades and returned sobriety makes him shuffle in his seat.

– Do you w-w-work? he asks.

– Chemist's. Not very interesting.

– I'm sure it is.

– I used to enjoy it but I'm not so sure nowadays. Things have changed so much.

The waiter slips the returned plate back onto the table. Clive sheepishly nods a thanks.

The couple eat. Sip wine. Make appreciative noises. Wait for that moment when conversation must recommence.

– Some of the older customers are nice, Patricia continues.

– I bet they're all after y-y-you.

– I don't know about that.

– You're still v-v-very attractive.

– Still? Patricia raises an eyebrow.

Clive recognizes his slip and chews faster, unable to find mitigating words.

Patricia chuckles. – I'm only teasing. It's nice of you to say so.

– Th-th-thanks, Clive says, reprieved.

– Even though I bet you say to that to all the ladies.

She throws Clive a questioning stare. The word 'ladies' fires across the table. Clive looks back blankly and then suddenly ducks back into the food before the word hits.

– Do you see many ladies? Patricia persists.

– No, I'm new to all of this.

– Good answer, she smiles.

The starter plates are stacked. The wine bottle removed. The drinks have flowed but neither Clive nor Patricia is affected, the initial dose merely equalizing the adrenalin. Another bottle arrives. Opened and poured just as the main course appears; two heaped plates, steaming with flavour.

The lights of the restaurant have dimmed and the sway of the candlelight evokes intimacy and belonging.

He may stutter, wear a mauve jacket, occasionally act a little strangely, but for Patricia it is sheer relief that Clive is the way he is. With hindsight, staring at a hunk all evening would have been too corny. She would have felt too desperate. Whereas, in Clive's company, she is almost on an equal footing and they are able to share the date together rather than one of them going through the motions.

They eat slowly, offering comments on each mouthful, on each part of the meal. They even swap forkfuls and laugh as errant pieces of food tumble from the mouth to the table during the exchange.

The other people in the restaurant no longer exist.

The marooned table for two is now an island paradise.

4

The Tab

Their serenity is disturbed by the waiter drifting alongside the table.

– Would you care for the dessert menu?

– Not for me, Patricia replies.

The waiter turns to Clive.

– No, no, I'm f-f-fine.

– Could we just get the bill, please? Patricia says.

The bill? The bill? Clive rummages about his inebriated mind. ('Make it clear that she's paying'). – I'm not p-p-paying for this, he blurts out to the retiring waiter.

– I beg your pardon, sir? the waiter says, stepping back to the table.

– I'm n-n-n-not paying for this meal, he repeats.

– What's wrong? Patricia intervenes.

– She's paying for this m-m-m-meal, aren't you, P-patricia? You're p-p-paying?

– Yes, that's right.

Clive calms himself down. He knows that it all came out wrong.

The waiter shares an understanding glance with Patricia and leaves for the till by the door.

– What was all that about? she asks.

– I j-j-just wanted to let him know that you're p-paying.

– I think you just about managed that, she smiles, patiently.

Clive goes to speak but the words stay in his neck.

Then Patricia begins to laugh. – Are you teasing me with all this cold fish and bill paying?

– No, of c-c-course not, Clive says as earnestly as he can.

The voice and strained stare makes Patricia laugh all the more.

– I'm serious, Clive insists.

Patricia falls forward with the giggles. – You are so funny, she laughs.

– I'm not t-t-trying to be, he says.

Patricia thanks the waiters and the tall man with the clipboard who opens the door for them to depart.

It dawns on Clive that he didn't talk about himself enough. He didn't complain enough. And so, halfway out, he collars the elegant holder of the door.

– I've had a l-l-lot better, you know.

– I'm sure you have, sir. Good night.

Outside, the chilled air slips into their clothes and they both fold their arms.

– What would you like to do? Patricia asks.

– I don't m-m-mind, Clive shrugs.

– We could get a nightcap around here?

– Yeah, Clive says with a succession of small nods.

– But . . . Mother . . . she mumbles to herself.

– Pardon?

The street outside the restaurant is quiet. A couple meander past as if window-shopping.

– We could have coffee somewhere, she says, lost in options. The dark sky and late-night city and second bottle of wine add confusion.

– I've had such a good time, Clive. Thanks so much.

– It's b-been great.

– Maybe I should just get back.

Clive tries to smile.

– You've been such wonderful company. I shouldn't really say that.

– Why n-not?

– This is just your job.

– I d-don't think I'm cut out for this type of work.

– This is just another evening for you. You don't want to know the last time I went out for a meal.

– But as I said, I'm n-n-n-new to all of this.

– Maybe we'll go out again.

Clive and Patricia reach for each other's hands and stand there rubbing thumbs against fingers.

Make Things Better

1

Pow-Wow wakes up feeling a little better on Sunday. A couple of days alone has eased some of the grief. Determined not to hold grudges against Ego and Ileasha. They're just trying to make their own way. Doing what they see fit.

But the isolation has sown a seed of determination – time to wake up and make moves. Pow-Wow can see that the only way to make things happen is to do them himself. Time to get outside and breathe the world.

Skips down the stairs wearing a long T-shirt and baggy shorts. High-fives Troy and pops head into kitchen to say bye to Brenda before crashing out the front door.

Keeps his face low as he saunters to the station. Wants to jump a train, get out of the community and see somewhere else. Unlike most of the others in the All-Stars, who prefer to stay on home turf and panic the moment they see a street sign without an NW postcode.

The Pack regularly rob commuters, jack cars, dip on the Underground, bust houses and flats. But today, none of it appeals. Neither does the patrolling, the gang-banging, the dealing. It all seems so negative. And temporary. OK for a youth but not for a life. He's already sixteen and days aren't as long as they used to be.

The Jubilee line runs elevated through Kilburn and West Hampstead, where north-west London spreads out like rubble.

Pow-Wow gets off the train at Bond Street and hits Oxford Street by midday. Under dented clouds that threaten rain. Into the pedestrian crawl. Through a cloud of dust thrown up by a

Routemaster. Over to the north side as the traffic lights show red. Inside a burger bar for a cheese and bacon double and king-size Pepsi. Then browses a music store to hear the latest garage from headphones. To sports emporium to pluck expensive sneaks off the walls and admire the latest basketball shirts from the States. Plays video games in an entertainment centre buried beneath a department store.

He is reminded of the Daddies by the layers of postcards covering the windows of telephone kiosks: *Oriental Beauty, Swedish Au Pair, Black is Beautiful, Massage, Domination, O and A levels, Watersports, TV Times, VIP Service.* Reminded of how badly Pimp Papa wants Ileasha.

Spots a small park to the south of Oxford Street and decides to take a seat and take things easy. The fevered air is making him tire. Happy to sit on a bench and watch the working girls eating sandwiches on the grass. A check of his text messages does not take long. Unwilling to read some and certainly not going to reply. Quite enjoying the isolation from his friends. Though he feels odd sitting alone. So he leans on the armrest and pretends to sleep, though his ears are attuned to every passing step and distant voice.

Pow-Wow follows a trail of high-heel taps as they approach. He marginally opens an eye to glimpse the legs: a woman wearing loose black trousers and leather boots. She walks with a swing, with a handbag flowing alongside, and he peers up to the head. Italian-looking lady with sunglasses resting on fox-coloured hair. Pow-Wow quickly shuts his eyes again as she nears.

Her footsteps slow, to a hesitant halt. Then Pow-Wow feels her presence lower onto his bench; the wooden slats descend with the extra weight.

– Isn't it warm? she says.

At first Pow-Wow stays in sleep mode, hoping that she is talking to herself. He can sense her looking at him.

– I wish I had a pair of shorts like yours, she says, clearly directing her speech at him.

Pow-Wow finds it difficult to ignore her so blatantly. She knows he's not asleep. He opens his eyes and shakes his head a little to feign interrupted nap. – Say what?

She smiles patiently. – I wish I had a pair of shorts to wear. Like yours.

– I'm not sure they're quite your style, Pow-Wow grins, brushing down the material.

– And what do you think is my style? she asks, with a glint.

Pow-Wow stops grinning and looks threatened. – I dunno.

The woman reaches into her bag and takes out a packet of cigarettes. – Do you smoke?

– Sure I smoke, Pow-Wow replies, still on the defensive.

She offers and he takes. She ignites an elegantly thin lighter and he dips the fag in the flame.

– Bad for you, you know, she says, lighting a cigarette herself.

Pow-Wow shrugs. – Only live once.

– My type of attitude, she says, blowing smoke from the side of her mouth.

She keeps her stare on Pow-Wow. Casually sliding her gaze onto his legs and arms.

Pow-Wow is uncomfortable with her attention, but he does not know how to escape. He has taken a cigarette; it would be rude to leave. She is attractive but he is tense.

– How old are you? she asks.

He tries to turn his head to look her in the eye but he is too awkward and his gaze meets her halfway. – Sixteen, he says.

– Are you really? she says thoughtfully.

– I ain't no child, Pow-Wow snaps, attempting to reclaim some of the initiative.

The woman tilts her head right back and sucks on the cigarette. Keeps her soft glare on Pow-Wow. – I can see that, she says slowly.

Pow-Wow finds the nerve to face her. He follows the pristine white shirt up to her neck and then scans the delicately decorated face. She must be in her early forties, he thinks, quickly turning away to fiddle with his sneakers.

Inside there is an element of uncertainty. Pow-Wow is still too young to have beaten the sense of vulnerability around an older woman. He has the sudden, bizarre thought that the woman is a Mafia wife.

– Have you a girlfriend?

– Sure, man.

– Is she pretty?

– Yeah, man.

The woman nods to herself as if she can see the girlfriend right in front of her.

– Don't you ever get bored? she asks.

– What with?

– Your girlfriend.

– Not really.

She edges a little closer up the bench towards Pow-Wow. As if she is about to tell him a secret.

Although the bench is in the cool cover of overhanging trees, Pow-Wow boils.

– I've been married for twenty years. I can tell you, I get bored. Yawn, yawn, yawn, she laughs.

The Mafia scenario rears up again.

– Oh, to do something different, try something different. Wonderful, she says, turning the last word into a picture.

Pow-Wow notices her stare on him. It's watching the beads of sweat drip down his cheek.

A wave of quiet sweeps over them. Her breathing is loud.

– What do you say? she says calmly.

– I guess doing different things is good, he agrees.

The woman chuckles away his comment. – Come on, you know what I mean. What do you say?

This is not a situation Pow-Wow can deal with. It's happening without a plan, without a chance to step back. He can't get the Mafia thing out of his head.

– Look, lady, he says, looking her in the eye.

– Shit! the woman says, staring over Pow-Wow's shoulder. She grabs her bag and stands up, brushing down her trousers and stamping on the cigarette. – Wait here, she hisses with her head down. – I'll be back.

Pow-Wow watches her walk to the park entrance and step into the kiss from a man wearing a suit. The couple turn back from the park and saunter, arm in arm, into the pedestrian traffic. Not even a quick glance back from the woman.

He waits on the bench and reruns the encounter in his mind.

Acknowledges that she wanted him. Acknowledges his own timidity. Annoyed, he throws the cigarette butt onto the path. Decides to sit tight and hope for a rematch. He will not be intimidated when she returns.

The woman wanted him. That was the deal. She wanted him. The sophisticated, attractive lady wanted him as he sat snoozing on a bench in his shorts and sneakers.

He sits patiently for an hour before deciding that she is not coming back.

2

Back on the train, Pow-Wow sits confidently with his legs stretched across the aisle. Hurls a couple of glances in the direction of a lady in the corner – his appetite whetted by the woman in the park. But this lady won't connect. In fact, she seems nervous and his stares merely make her blush. The skin around her neck erupts like a rash.

Pow-Wow leaves her alone. Different rules apply now the train heads away from Finchley Road. He picks up the newspaper lying on the seat next to him. Flashes through the paper, offering disdainful sniffs at the stories. Until towards the back, in the classifieds, he sees the advert.

Does it happen? Do women really pay men? he thinks, reconstructing the face of the woman in the park. Recalling her asking, 'What do you say?'

The opportunity gives him ideas. Offers a route away from the All-Stars and into his own success. Makes him optimistic when he thinks of the possibilities. Building his own business, getting paid. Getting laid. Without treading on the toes of the Daddies. He will need to see how things work. Good Times will be the starting point. He'll ring them.

Speak About It

1

Stanley stands by the front door of the flat in his black suit. Sylvia sits in the living room at the table, prepared for Mr and Mrs Pickle. They come every month, on a Sunday, to talk to the daughter they lost ten years ago in a bus crash in France.

Sarah Pickle smashed skulls with a boy sitting in front of her. There was not too much for Mr and Mrs Pickle to recognize on the school-hall floor in Grenoble. Except for the devastation of the gathered families. The Gendarmerie stood about the bright space like museum guards. Keeping a watchful eye on the corpses laid out on blankets behind movable screens.

Stanley greets and leads them through to Sylvia. Hands are shaken, pleasantries exchanged, and Stanley brings in the tray of tea and lightly buttered crumpets that the Pickles enjoy. And then the curtains are drawn and heads lowered as Sylvia reaches into the ether.

Just as Stanley gets to the telephone to take it off the hook it rings. The room startles and Sylvia's eyes flash open.

– That is meant to be off, Sylvia says.

– I thought it was, Stanley replies before speaking into the mouthpiece.

– She w-w-wants to see me again, Clive says.

– What?

– Patricia. She's just called up, she w-w-wants to see me again.

– Great.

– What shall I d-do?

– Just go.

– She wants me to g-go this afternoon.

– So? You're hardly a busy man.

Sylvia gives a sharp hush.

– I got to go, Clive.

– What am I g-going to do?

– Charge the same price.

2

The house is a terrace, with concrete slabs for a front garden. White pilasters adorn the entrance. A lone milk bottle hides in the shadows of the porch.

Patricia opens the door and looks unsure.

Clive smiles and allows Patricia to settle. Maybe he knocked at a bad moment; though he is bang on time. He hears an old woman shouting. Another woman's voice tries to call for calm over the top of the shouting.

Patricia attempts to hold the door, welcome Clive and listen to the noise all at the same time.

– It's Mother. I'm sorry.

– No p-p-problem, Clive smiles.

– She can be quite demanding at times.

– Don't w-w-worry.

She teeters on the doorway, turns to the voices, holds her hand out to prevent Clive from entering. – Maybe it's best if you don't come in. I hope you don't mind?

– I'll d-d-do whatever you want.

– Wait there, Patricia orders, rushing into the house.

The shouting stops. Then there is a yelp, like a dog. The shouting recommences.

Patricia returns to the door with her left cheek reddened. – I think it's best if we go, she says.

– Are you OK? Clive asks.

– Yes, I'm fine.

– Did she h-h-hit you? Clive asks, looking shocked.

Patricia does not reply. They go through the gate and onto the street.

– Joan will be OK with her, is all she says.

Despite the lack of sunshine, the day is dry and the park busy. Bikes and dogs, benches full of silent people.

– She doesn't like to see me going out like this, Patricia says.

– L-like what?

– I don't normally wear make-up.

– Did she h-h-hit you for wearing make-up?

– She's very lonely.

– S-s-still, it's a bit tough on you.

– There's a lot of history there, Patricia says quietly.

A jogger lugs his huge weight past them. His breathing indicates that he is near the end of his exhaustion.

– But she m-m-must expect things to change, says Clive.

– She's still living in the war. Nothing changes for her.

– I guess her L-l-london is different to ours.

– She's only just started hitting me again.

– I b-b-b-bet she's seen some changes.

– She never hurts me, hasn't got the strength.

– I've seen some changes m-m-myself.

– She thinks I've gone and got myself this man.

– What man?

– You! You silly thing.

Clive feels quite proud at being considered the man. – I s-s-see.

Patricia sniffs out a laugh with little shake of the head. Then a sympathetic smile at Clive. – I thought I'd show you off. It didn't quite work out.

Clive looks to the sky, at the dense bushes of white.

They stroll along some of the paths that she and Edward used to walk. They have changed. As has the rest of the park: gone through cycles of tending, despair, renovation, neglect. And now the flowers are trampled into mud and at night it is no-go.

They stop under a tree and sit on a bench. They hold hands.

– I had it all wrong about you, didn't I? Patricia says.

– I d-d-did try to explain, Clive says.

– I should have realized when I first met you.

– I h-h-hope you weren't too disappointed.

– Not at all.

– I'm n-n-no stud.

Patricia grins. – I'm glad it's not like that.

Clive wants to escape the subject, but feels obliged to set the record straight.

– I've got a friend, Stanley, who sort of g-g-got me into it.

– Recently, I think? Patricia asks knowingly.

– Am I that b-bad?

Patricia chuckles and then begins to burst into loud laughter. – Oh, Clive, I'm so glad we met, she says.

Clive joins her laughter as a cheerful gust of wind brings with it the scent from the grass.

– I guess I just wanted to talk to you, Patricia says.

– I was g-g-glad you called.

– We had such a good time at the restaurant, didn't we? Even if you have had better, she smiles slyly.

Clive blushes. It seems a long time ago. He doesn't recognize himself in the memory.

– With Mother, I haven't been able to keep in touch with my old friends.

– I'm no good at staying in t-touch either.

– I've got Joan at home and a friend at work, but they're not what I'd call close friends.

– I've g-g-got Stanley.

– If I tell them too much about Mother they might feel I'm looking for help or sympathy. But I'm not.

Clive nods cautiously, not wanting to pretend that he knows how things are.

She rubs his hand harder.

– And the way things are going with her. Well, I don't know. It's no good.

– Is she ill? asks Clive.

Patricia raises her eyes and then closes them. – She's just lonely.

– Don't b-b-be so down on her.

– And she's so angry.

– Angry?

– It's inside of her.

– What would she do w-w-w-without you?

The bench becomes uncomfortable, they both move their bottoms. The shared hands slip apart. Patricia uses the free hand to push her hair back. Clive leaves his stranded between them.

– I've lived too much of my life for other people, she says.

– You're a c-c-c-caring person. That's n-n-nothing to be ashamed of.

– But what if those other people don't appreciate what you do for them? What have you got left of your life then?

Clive thinks for a while. – The s-s-s-satisfaction that you did what you thought was right?

– Is that really enough?

Clive strokes the question in his mind. Answers don't come naturally to him.

3

The Pickles leave in tears. Happy. With messages from Sarah. Messages of comfort, of how things will get better. Ten years down the line and nothing has changed for Mr and Mrs Pickle. The wound won't close.

And how Sylvia tries to contact Sausage to ease her own pain. But, unlike Sarah, he won't speak. He might cough or whistle, or even hum, but he won't speak.

But there are many things that Stanley won't say either. Things about Sylvia's work, his brother's death, his short stature, failed relationships, lost fights, etched insults, the fears that occasionally keep him up all night and drown out the sound of trains running into King's Cross. That smother the noise of the taxis turning in the street below and the local street gangs brawling over terrain.

He recalls so many people saying things to him over the years. Things that have stuck inside. Things that he would like to forget. Like the bloke in the shop condemning his too-short legs. Doesn't remember the positive words, only the negative.

The coach of the Somers Town Boys' Club dismissing his desire to play in the five-a-side team with the phrase, 'We're not that desperate.'

The family friend being told that he got only one O level and saying, 'We never realized you were that thick.'

The foreign girl in Regent's Park Stanley was trying to hit on saying, 'Don't English boys wash their hair?'

Stanley misses Sausage. Misses having a brother, or someone else around to be on his side. There are things he could say to Sausage that he couldn't say to anybody else. Not even to Clive, who is a loyal friend.

Clive has never doubted him, always allowed him to spin his yarns and lay down the law. Clive listened and considered the things he had to say. The older he gets, the more Stanley finds people not listening.

Stanley's recent anxiety is of a tidal wave. He is running from a tidal wave. It's coming for him. Time is not on his side. Ideas are being taken, jobs are going, money is harder to find, if you're not inside you're outside. If you're not on you're off. If you're not up you're down. Somers Town is now full of people he doesn't know. He used to know everyone. And the wave is going to hit him in his own neighbourhood. He is running from this wave. He is shouting at Clive to run faster but he's so slow and too busy trying to ask the question, 'W-w-w-w-w-why?' His own legs are tight and stiff. He can hear a roar. He doesn't want to go under. He doesn't want to be washed up.

It is late and dark and Stanley listens to Atmosfear records in his room. Sylvia sleeps and Stanley thinks of Dad; how he used to laugh at anything. 'Keeps me sane,' he said. Laugh until he winced and folded in pain. Until he fell to his knees in agony. And suddenly there became a thin line between laughter and distress. Stanley got scared at the sight of Dad rolling tortured on the floor.

4

After the date with Patricia, Clive goes straight to his parents in Camden. Unless Stanley tries to drag him down the pub to be near the Sons, Clive will invariably spend Sunday evenings with his parents. It is something of a ritual, using each other to ease the heavy weight of the approaching Monday. In younger years, they watched television as a family: *Last of the Summer Wine, Dad's Army, Songs of Praise*. How those programmes filled him with sadness as the week reared its head after two days of freedom. And Sunday evening still creates a bitter taste in the mouth that is not cleansed by cups of tea, ham sandwiches and Cadbury's chocolate fingers. Clive will stay the night and use the toothbrush that he has kept there, unchanged, for ten years. Will use the own-brand toothpaste that Mum buys. Wash with Imperial Leather.

Instead of Sunday evening television, Dad now prefers to polish some of his Post Office paraphernalia. Mum reads a musty novel. Clive sits at the table with a deck of cards, playing solitaire.

Tempted to tell Mum and Dad about Patricia, Clive finds it hard to concentrate on the cards. He knows how good it will make them feel if he told them about her. Yet it is early days. And she is still paying him, which seems to detract from the intimacy built up between them. Maybe he should ask Stanley to let him see her as a proper date. The response would be obvious.

His parents wouldn't worry about the age gap. In fact, they would probably see it as an advantage. They've always said how he needs someone with a more mature outlook. Someone who will take charge. How they disliked some of his earlier conquests that came round the house in track suits and smoked the house into a fog. That was a long time ago, though. Five or six years since the last girl.

Clive is exhausted and retires upstairs before Mum and Dad. To the toothpaste and soap. And blankets and sheets that Mum still insists are best. Though, for Clive, they are always starchy and impossible to free from their fold under the mattress.

Relaxed and ready for bed, he is not prepared for the mobile phone to ring. The phone that Stanley had persuaded Clive to take with him as the only calls coming in were from Patricia.

Tempted to leave it ring, though part of him hopes for Patricia.

He does not recognize the number on the screen, but Patricia could be calling from a friend's or a call box. Mother might have got too much.

– G-g-g-good Times? Clive says.

– Male escorts? asks a man.

– Yes? replies a nervous Clive.

– What type of men do you have? says the confident voice.

– All t-t-t-types, Clive stutters, wishing Stanley was there to lie.

– Sun-tanned and hairless?

– That c-c-can be arranged.

– Muscular?

Clive feels his chest thump. – Y-y-y-yes.

– W.E.?

– W.E.?

– Come on.

– I'm n-n-not sure, strains Clive.

– Big, you know. Big.

– Oh, s-s-sorry. Yes, big. Y-y-y-yes.

– What will he do?

– It's up t-t-t-to you really.

– Up to me? the man guffaws.

– Like w-w-what?

– Unprotected.

– I d-d-don't know about that.

– What do you know?

Clive audibly swallows. He is breathless. – You could call b-b-b-ack tomorrow.

– I want someone tonight, not tomorrow.

Things begin to clear in Clive's mind.

– You want a m-m-man?

– At least you've got that right.

– Not for a w-w-woman.

– No, I want a man.

– We d-d-d-d-don't do that stuff, Clive struggles to say.

– Male escorts?

110

– For w-w-women.

– Oh, for God's sake, don't restrict your market.

Clive doesn't respond, he just switches off the phone and tucks it into a cupboard with the spare blankets and pillows. How did he get into this?

Knock, Knock

1

On Monday morning Mister B arrives on the step of Pow-Wow's house. Still buzzing from another night out on the town, on the coke. The sharp look has blunted throughout the twelve hours and now his suit is hanging slack and the orange shirt is askew. Wants to see Pow-Wow, misses his partner. Especially last night, when he stood about sipping cocktails at Tino's and watching fifty-year-old men taking sixteen-year-old girls away on their arms. It didn't feel right. Neither did the suit that restrained him and made him too hot. Until the snuff kicked in and everything began to roll.

– He's not in, says Brenda.

– He is, argues Mister B.

– You look terrible.

– Let me up and see the man.

Brenda keeps hold of the door. – Come back another time.

Mister B sucks in his lips. – I'm a Daddy.

– Well, I hope you enjoy prison.

– Don't switch on me.

Brenda gently closes the door, minding Mister B's foot resting on the ledge. – You come back another time.

Pow-Wow is upstairs. Back on the weights. Back with inspiration on his side. Last night as he lay back and listened to the mopeds screaming up and down his road he felt happy to be away from them. Maybe he'll sell his scooter to some up-and-coming gangster. If he's going to be a ladies' man he'll need some real wheels. By the time he's seventeen he intends to have enough cash for something fast. In the meantime he'll take the train.

Looks at himself in the mirror and likes what reflects. A cute babyface that the girls die for. A lean torso that needs a little fill-out. A cropped head that could do with a little trim.

Still anxious about making that phone call. Though it's got to be done if he wants to move forward. Will probably have to lie about his age. What about being black? What about being from Willesden? Maybe they want posh people? And the nerves calm and the confidence rises when he thinks of the woman on the bench. He's willing to do whatever – that must be in his favour. Don't mind dogging it for dough, he thinks. Got to learn the ropes, he keeps reminding himself. Got to learn the ropes.

2

Monday is always a difficult day in Fairfield Road. It is the one day Patricia keeps clear, knowing how bad it can get. There is an ambience of endlessness and emptiness when she goes to Mother in the bedroom. They both feel it and both hate it. And keep their feelings locked inside themselves so they can gnaw. Released only in the mutual hostility.

Patricia pulls the curtains to a damp day. Condensation drips onto the window sill. She notices the black mould running along the frame. Ignores it; it's Monday.

The pillows raise Mother's head high above the mattress. She lies there, watching Patricia with squinted eyes.

Leaden light creeps through the room and neither of them speaks.

In the kitchen Patricia makes tea and toast and soft-boils an egg for Mother. She reaches into a cupboard and takes out an eggcup, scratching solidified yolk off the side. The tray is kept by the sink. She loathes the routine. She is suffocated by the routine. The start of the week is bad.

Yesterday, in the park with Clive, the world brightened. But the colours do not last. Today, things are the same and dull and Clive doesn't exist as she walks the food through to the bedroom. He is a happy memory, no longer part of life. Reality is the heavy door and cold room and the lifting of a withered body into clothes.

Mother dribbles when Patricia puts the tray in front of her. She inspects the spread with critical eyes and waits for Patricia to pour the tea. Mother uses a scrawny hand to wipe away the spit on her chin and winces as the steam from the tipped teapot envelops her face.

– Shall I break the egg for you? Patricia asks.

– I can do it, I can do it, says Mother, grabbing the spoon.

Debris from the smashed shell scatters over the tray and bedclothes. Patricia dips in to clear it up.

– It's not done, Mother says, spooning out the uncooked egg white and throwing it onto the plate.

– Go into the yolk. That'll be fine, Patricia suggests.

– Pah!

Tea spills over the tray as Mother's legs twitch and kick under the sheets.

– Watch it, Mother, says Patricia, seeing the drink splash onto the toast.

– It's not cooked, Mother continues.

– It's OK.

– I want it cooked.

– Go for the yolk.

– My toast is all wet.

– You spilt your tea.

– Look at this mess!

– I'll get a cloth, says Patricia, moving for the door.

– Take this egg back, Mother shouts.

– Take it back yourself.

Before Patricia can get through the door, the egg crashes into the side of her face.

Mother looks away sharply to stare at the window.

The shattered egg drops from Patricia's cheek onto the floor.

– You bitch! Patricia says.

And Mother turns. – How dare you, she hisses, attempting to climb out of the bed to attack Patricia.

– You can't keep doing this to me! You can't keep doing

this! Patricia screams, and leaves the room with a thunderclap door.

The aftermath drifts about the house. A cold silence. That reaches into Patricia's room, where she sits on the edge of the bed crying. Wiping away tears with shivering hands, and mopping nose with wrist. Being pushed to the brink of her tolerance. Despite doing her duty as best she can. But things are not getting better. And she will end up old and alone without a daughter of her own to bring her breakfast. Without a friend, who have all been sacrificed by the domestic demands. So tired of Mondays. So tired of it all.

The thought of Clive offers a little warmth in the frigid atmosphere of home. How nice it would be to hold his hand again and let him listen to the pain inside of her. To watch his innocent face and allow the stutter to serenade her. But she is not made of money. He is not cheap.

Patricia won't go into Mother. Mother won't tap or call for Patricia. And the day limps towards evening without a word being spoken. Patricia will hide in the lounge. Mother will drift back to Bethnal Green. The static in the air pricks at both of them. But they stay locked behind doors and hope for the darkness to come and cloak their misery.

3

Clive and Stanley sit in the lounge at Clive's flat. Sipping 7-Up, bouncing feet to the sound of Maze. Reminding themselves how much has happened in the past week. From signing on last Monday, without much on the horizon, to running their own cross-London escort business.

Stanley drinks his can with a regal air. Though he is fully aware of the business's limitations. He is not deluding himself; it hasn't been a blockbuster week despite almost 200 quid in the kitty.

Clive frowns into the tin. Hasn't yet found the courage to tell Stanley about last night's call. Doesn't want to interrupt his friend's satisfying smirk. He was reluctant to bring the phone into the living room. Showed willing.

As Clive looks at the phone with fear, its electronic notes play.

– Answer it, Clivey-boy, says Stanley.

– Oh no, Clive moans.

– Could be money, Stanley says with a grin.

– Can you answer it, please? I'm too t-t-tired.

– For fuck's sake, Stanley growls, reaching over to take the phone.

He looks at the number and spends seconds remembering the right button to press.

– Good Times.

– You an escort agency, yeah? asks a voice.

Stanley struggles to catch the words thrown out by the accent – a mix of West Indian and West Coast. He has heard the patois used by the current crew of schoolkids running out of the SCCS.

– We are *the* escort agency, Stanley says.

– Got a big operation, huh? the voice continues.

– They don't come any bigger, says Stanley, trying to impress the prospective customer.

– How many guys you got working?

– Oh, loads.

– Nice.

– We can always find someone to suit the women's needs, Stanley continues.

– All ages?

– Certainly have. Eighteen to . . . eighty? Stanley grimaces.

– Eighty?

– You'd be surprised at the amount of older clients we have.

– You have black boys? Pow-Wow asks.

– No problem. We've got all colours.

– And you send men out anywhere in London?

– All over. All over.

– How much do the men charge?

Stanley thinks for a bit. – Depends.

– Average?

– Thirty pounds an hour.

– Not bad, Pow-Wow says quietly. – And you're always busy?

– It can sometimes be too hectic.

– Peach, Pow-Wow says.

Stanley is now eager to make a sale and pushes the conversation towards a deal. – Who's the escort for? A friend, a relative?

– Actually, man, I was hoping there might be some work for me.

– What are you saying?

– I'm a good-looking guy. Know how to deal with ladies.

This confuses Stanley. He didn't see the angle coming. – Er, yeah, right, he stumbles.

– You can trust me, bro. I'm real.

Stanley thinks quickly. He doesn't need another man because there is no work coming in. But if there did happen to be a surge in demand, the new guy could take the extra work and save him from getting involved; Stanley, despite the talk, is not confident about doing a date.

– Give us your phone number and some details and we'll contact you in the next day or two to discuss things.

– OK, sounds good, Pow-Wow agrees.

Going Under

1

Roman Road shops on a Tuesday afternoon. Pavements slanting towards the road. Market stalls tucked into gaps, squeezed between kerbs. Pigeons pecking at the red flagstones. Patricia looking out of the chemist's window onto the street. Thinking of Clive and how calm he makes her feel. How young. How there becomes more to Bow than the shop and Mother. How the world appears lighter, shapes sharper, other people less threatening.

They kissed that afternoon after their walk in the park. A brief, natural kiss outside the front door of Fairfield Road. Clive smelt of toffee. And he took the keys from her trembling hand and opened the door. And left, without seeking an invitation inside. Without counting the money that she passed to him in an envelope. Looking round only once to grin and look chuffed as he turned the corner by the estate agent's. By the property shop where they sell the locale for fortunes and recommend the natives move out for the money and value 26 Fairfield Road at a lot more than Mother and Dad ever dreamt of paying for it. But Patricia does not know, or look, for Mother is going nowhere.

Mother does not see the changes taking place. The huge black gates being erected around buildings. The uniformed guards sitting inside each renovated and resold council block. The constant crawl of police cars along Bow's streets. Streets that Mother had known so well but would now recognize only by the retained names. All Mother hears are the sirens, the shouts, and the weekly rain that beats at the window and splashes from the broken drainpipe.

Patricia has said little about her fiftieth to Lorraine. She thanked her for the present (a pack of male-model playing cards) but said nothing about Clive. The subject of birthday came and went like an awkward customer, forgotten until the next time. And the shop settled into survival as profits continued to dwindle and customers continued to complain and staff continued to search the newspapers for better work.

Patricia continues to stare out of the window and see Clive in the walk or figure of someone else. The unmistakable gait with hands flapping and back dead straight. The walk makes him appear taller.

Sunil, the shop manager, calls to Patricia from his backroom doorway. The other staff look over with concern. Patricia rolls her eyes back into reality and moves out from behind the counter.

Sunil asks her to sit down in his office. He takes off his spectacles and wiggles his eyes. He lets out a sigh. He does not beat about the bush. As soon as he begins to speak Patricia knows what is coming. She does not hear the platitudes, the gratitude, the words about long service, good relationships with colleague and customer, reliability, balancing work with a difficult domestic situation. She barely hears the words about falling revenue, overstaffing, part-time, changing hours, a new Boots the Chemist opening, uncertain future for all.

She takes off the white coat, unclips the name badge, collects her handbag from the staffroom that already appears like a memory. She falls into Lorraine's arms and they cry together while the other staff continue to slip lozenges into paper bags and stack the shelves with dental floss. Customers walk around the embracing couple as if they are a pillar, holding up the whole building.

2

Clive is up early and over to his parents before ten. Happy to have left the phone with Stanley and not having to dread the ringing tone. Free for the day. To join Mum and Dad as they take the car out to the country for coffee and cake in a tearoom. Maybe near a river or next to a village green. Not often they get a chance to go out as a family.

Clive in the back seat, his neck bent over to fit inside the small hatchback. Conscious of Dad's eyes flicking on and off the rearview mirror.

As soon as they are beyond the North Circular Road, Mum begins to smile at the other cars. Often the occupants of the other cars look back perplexed. Occasionally, a fellow traveller will return Mum's greetings and a short exchange of mouthed words follow: 'Nice day', 'Where you off to?'

There is silence in the vehicle. Dad likes to concentrate on driving. Mum likes to watch the different places pass. Clive twiddles his fingers and feels thirteen not thirty-six.

By one o'clock they arrive at the village.

3

Joan is in tears when Patricia returns home – it is Mother. She is lying in bed. She has been rude and vicious. Joan does not stop for a cup of tea, she is keen to get out of the house and away from Mother. A grab for the summer jacket, shopping bag, money left on the table underneath the sugar bowl. The back door slams.

Patricia lets her go; it is no time to discuss the redundancy and, therefore, Joan's future.

Patricia approaches the bedroom cautiously. Mother has been uncontrollable recently. Ever since that first date with Clive. She is deteriorating, working herself up into a fury. Like a camel she spits. Like a cat she scratches. And the words are always sharp.

– Mother? Patricia whispers through the open door.

There is no reply.

– Mother, it's me. Are you awake?

– Leave me alone.

Patricia creeps into the room. Mother is sitting up in bed on a mountain of pillows. The room is gloomy with the curtains drawn. Mother's white face shines and it moves to face Patricia.

– Why have you been upsetting Joan?

– Why are you back so early? Mother asks in return.

120

– Can't you treat anyone with the slightest ounce of respect?
The face is spectral. – Got rid of you, did they?

– Mother, I'm really not in the mood.

– Finally realized that you're no good, did they?

– Have you eaten?

– Couldn't put up with that silly eye any longer.

– I'm not in the mood for this, I've had a bad day. Please stop.

– All the customers laughing at the girl who swallowed the fly.

Patricia uses her sleeve to crush the tears.

– Toilet.

– Take yourself! Patricia hisses back.

– What a disappointment you were to me and your father.

– Don't you ever stop? Patricia cries. – I've told you, I've had a bad day, I don't want to listen to any more.

– How we used to laugh at you behind your back.

– Stop this!

– The way you used to stand under the blanket and curl up in the box. How we laughed.

– Dad never laughed at me!

– We all used to laugh at you.

Patricia draws a hand across her nose and mouth and walks to the bed. – Please, Mother, I'm begging you to leave me alone. Just for today.

– How I hate you, Mother says.

– You have treated me so wrong, Patricia suddenly says, quite calmly. – You just don't listen, do you?

– I have always hated you, Mother grins.

– That's it.

Patricia is engulfed. She is burning, feeling flames inside of her. Without control, she finds herself lunging for a pillow from behind Mother's back. The pillow is as pale as Mother's face and the two merge when compressed by Patricia's furious grip. Mother is too weak to fight back and Patricia pushes onto Mother's head with all her resentment and agony. A scrawny leg, riddled with veins and lumps, flicks over the side of the bed. Patricia is gripping the pillow so hard that her fingernails cut through the slip.

The flames subside, the heat cools, and left in the embers are a bone-white corpse and a woman holding a pillow.

4

The eyes are terrified, not looking into the distance but backwards into herself. Mother's body lies stretched out over the blankets.

Patricia stands over the bed, over a whole landscape of pain and past rather than the tiny, withered collection of bones and bleached skin. She is surprisingly composed. Absorbed instead of repelled by the scene below her. But the situation calls for action. The corpse must be disposed of – unless she wants to call the authorities. Which she doesn't.

Patricia scours the house for anything in which to hide the body. She returns to the bedroom, to the laundry box in the corner.

Taking the corpse in both arms, she carries it towards the wooden case. She lifts the lid with the tips of her fingers and gently folds the limbs as she places Mother into the box.

The house smells dry and stony like a church.

5

Whenever Clive is out with his parents he is reluctant to talk too much. He doesn't like to embarrass his parents in front of strangers with his stammer.

His parents, in fact, are not in the least concerned about his speech. They rarely hear the impediment, have grown immune to it.

When the young girl comes to the table to take the order he thinks of the easiest words to say on the menu. Chooses a tea and a scone. Said without a stutter, just an extended S at the start of scone.

Their table is set in the bay window and they can look out on the gentle sloping hill that leads to a pond.

– This is my t-t-treat, Clive says, having made a bit of money in the past week.

– No, no, Dad protests. – This is ours.

– Let him if he wants to, Mum says.

Clive looks at Dad, nodding to confirm that he does want to.

– You need your cash, Dad continues.

– Let him if he wants to, Mum insists.

The tray of food and drink arrives. Any further discussion is halted as plates and knives are distributed and minds focus on eating.

They eat quietly; just the sound of moist mouths and the gentle clink of spoon on saucer.

Suddenly a sense of uneasiness drops over Clive. He sits guilty in front of his parents, knowing how upset they would be if he told them what he had done for the money he now wants to use to treat them.

The tea tastes horrible when he thinks of the escort work. Especially when he looks at his happy parents.

– We used to come here when we first got a car, Dad says.

Clive doesn't want to hear it. It will only make him feel worse.

– All those years ago, says Mum.

Clive manages a moan of fake interest but is eager for a return to silence.

– Maybe one day you'll bring your wife up here? Mum continues.

A lump of scone hits the back of Clive's throat and causes a cough. He gets up to go to the toilet.

– You OK? Dad asks.

Clive nods as he walks away.

In front of the urinal he feels sad. He washes his hands at the sink and stares at a face that looks dead. In that instant, he decides that he will not work as an escort again. He will see Patricia properly, bring her to places like this, take her out for meals. Leave the seedy business for others. It was never him, even around the enthusiasm of Stanley. Around the goodness of his mum and dad, it just seems wrong.

Clive settles the bill at the till, while his parents shuffle their way out of the door.

He leaves a big tip, keen to off-load the tainted cash filling his pocket.

He wants to call Patricia and tell her that there is to be no more money. That he wants them to be a proper couple.

Boxing Day

1

Patricia crouches on the floor next to the box. She has to get rid of
Mother but doesn't have the strength or means to take her away
from the house. She cannot consider disposing of her at home;
the gruesome stories of butchery and burial repulse her. The
predicament exposes her isolation; no one to turn to who would
accept the situation. Lorraine would scream. Joan would faint.
The only possibility is Clive, whom she has thought of so much
since they kissed. He is her one chance. He might understand. He
might carry Mother away.

2

Mr Furtle has just left. Sylvia retires to her room. Stanley takes
the whisky glass and rinses it out in the kitchen sink, taking
care to wipe the rim of the tumbler where Mr Furtle's cracked
lips sipped. Stanley strips off his tie and stuffs it into his jacket
pocket. The weather is close and sweat collects around his
neck.

He takes care to hang the suit correctly, zipping it up inside a
bag to defend against the carbon that carries up from the road
and smothers the window sills, the shelves, the television, and
infiltrates the drawers and cupboards.

The mobile rings. Stanley steels himself – aware that Clive is
not around to do a job should one arise.

– Good Times.

– Is Clive there?

– Er, no. Not at the mo.

– This is Patricia. I'm a, er, friend of Clive's.

– Hello, Patricia, I put you and Clive together. How you doing?

– Yes, fine thanks. Is Clive going to be available for . . . work?

– When?

– The sooner the better, really.

– I don't know.

– When will you know?

Stanley doesn't want to lose the custom. – I'll get him there. Can I take your details?

– I think he's got them.

– I'd better take them again just in case.

She dictates her address and phone number.

– I really do want him as soon as possible.

Stanley raises an eyebrow, impressed at Clive's effect.

3

Escort required, but Clive away. Stanley considers the problem. He is certain that he isn't going to go on any date. But more determined not to lose the money. Remembers the guy who called looking for work. Checks the phone memory for Pow-Wow's number. Calls.

Pow-Wow screens the number, recognizes it as Good Times.

– Yo.

– It's Stanley from Good Times. We spoke yesterday.

– Wha's going on?

– We might have a job for you.

– Thrill, man. What, where?

– It's an older woman, I said we have a few.

– No challenge.

– Will you do it?

– Damn right. How much do I get?

– Just charge her thirty pounds an hour – you'll get half.

– What sort of thing will it be?

– It'll be just dating. Nothing heavy. Just a walk or something. Go with the flow. She's a regular.

– No slamming?

– No, that's not going to happen.

4

Pow-Wow is apprehensive as he approaches the house on Fairfield Road. The terraces may look the same as the rows in Willesden but they are different; they stand stiff rather than slouch. The streets in NW10 smell of Coca-Cola, in Bow they smell of chips. Pow-Wow couldn't eat before he left and felt sick when he watched a person on the Underground scoff a burger. Told Brenda he was off to see about a job. She was pleased and volunteered to pay the train fare. Pow-Wow found it hard to respond to the offer. Didn't know what to say. Didn't want to talk to Mister B when he called that morning, though listened to the mobile phone message in which Mister B shouted, 'I'm the nigger with the trigger.' The wildness in his friend's voice made Pow-Wow uncomfortable. Clearly been given his first gun. Pow-Wow could also hear the cocaine. The message made him more resolute to go to Bow and begin a new career. Even though he was filled with shivering nerves. Chewing lumps of gum all the way to east London. Hoping that the other passengers couldn't sense the fear in his gaze, and didn't notice the bouncing legs. Maybe he should have taken something to ease the stress, in the way the Daddies lick chuck to make things better. The way Mister B is now pigging performance-enhancers. The All-Stars used to smoke the weed and do a little of this and a bit of that when it appeared. But it was part of things rather than the crux. The Daddies seem to treat the deal differently. More personally. As part of personality.

The door knocks. Patricia opens. Pow-Wow stands on the step.

– Yes? Patricia asks.

– Good Times. I'm your man for the day, you know what I'm saying? Pow-Wow says quickly, in a release of anxiety.

– Where's Clive?

Pow-Wow frowns. – I guess he couldn't make it.

Patricia's immediate instinct is to close the door, cancel the deal. But she is desperate. Tragedy has heightened her awareness. She thinks like a criminal and assesses the situation for advantage.

Before her, dressed in designer jumper, sneakers and jeans, Patricia sees the next victim.

She takes him into the lounge and rushes to the kitchen to make him a drink. It seems the right thing to do, although her mind is screaming for a scheme.

His aftershave drifts about the house.

She can barely direct the spoonfuls of tea into the pot.

He stands in the room and casts a cursory eye at the pictures, at the television guide. She is not as old as he thought. Yet there is a sense of desperation. And the house feels unwelcoming.

She breaks out in sweat and guzzles a glass of tap water.

He slumps on the sofa and waits to evaluate the woman at close quarters. Wonders what she'll want to do.

She tries to clear her head from the chaos of killing and now the noise of plots and plans. She was alert and clear, holding it all together when the door knocked, but now things are clouding over. A summer drizzle dots the kitchen window. The aftershave is too sweet.

Patricia goes through with two cups of tea and sits on the armchair adjacent to Pow-Wow.

He notices her drained demeanour; a mustard complexion. Notices the funny eye. He doesn't know what to say. The tea is too hot to sip.

– Nice crib, he says.

– Pardon? Patricia says, distracted by her thoughts.

– Nice house.

– I've been here all my life, she says, to the cup, not wanting to catch his eye.

Slips back into silence, mollified by the steam rising from the cups.

Pow-Wow gives her a quizzical stare.

She pretends not to notice, and doesn't offer anything else to fill the puzzled gap between them.

Pow-Wow wants to chat to smooth things down, but he joins in the silence when he realizes that she is not keen to speak. He can tell by the shrunken eyes and tight lips. The lack of connection.

– How old are you? she suddenly asks.

– Eighteen.

Patricia accepts the age. Young people all look the same.

– And you? Pow-Wow asks, indiscriminately.

She doesn't answer at first, dipping her lips into the tea. Then she says, defensively, – Too old for you.

– Whatever, he shrugs, seeing the deal slipping away.

– I don't mean that in a bad way, she says, attempting to plaster the situation. She needs him there. She just needs time to think. Her mind is floating and the room is fuzzy.

– What do you want to do? Pow-Wow asks.

He is rushing her and this makes her resent him. She wants to scream and run away, but things have gone too far. He is so young but he is her only chance. And now he's hurrying her. Why is he hurrying her?

– I need to get ready, she says, standing to leave the room. – I look a mess, she continues, referring to her obvious dishevelment; the murder of Mother has soiled her and left her in disarray.

– No fret, Pow-Wow nods, happy for her to go and leave him alone. The situation is more difficult than he imagined. He is doubting his skills.

Patricia creeps through the doorway and into the hall, where she closes her eyes and prays for strength. How did she get into this?

Limps up the stairs with the youth's face imprinted on her mind. But she must disregard sympathy. There is no place for it any more. She must save herself, and the thought is strangely comforting.

In the bedroom she calls the police. Her words rush out, leaving her dazed and unable to remember the things she is saying.

Speaks of the boy in her house, who went into her mother's room, who killed her and bundled her into a box. Begins to break down and sobs desperation into the mouthpiece. Her voice seems to come from the inside of her head rather than the mouth.

Replacing the phone, composing herself, wiping the wet eyes with the back of a hand, she stands at the top of the stairs and calls out.

– Hello? she says. – Hello?

Pow-Wow sits up. – Yo, he shouts back.

– Can you come here a minute? Patricia asks.

Pow-Wow goes into the hallway and looks up to where the voice comes from but without seeing Patricia. – What's up?

– Would you mind going into the room by the front door on your left and bringing me my hair-dryer? I think it's under the pillows on the bed.

He enters the room, rummages through the bed and pillows and finds nothing.

Returns to the hallway. – Can't find it, he yells.

– Try underneath the bed, I think it's underneath the bed.

Patricia hears him walk back towards Mother's room. She slips down the stairs without a squeak and follows Pow-Wow into the room. She stands by the door, looking at the boy scrabbling about on the floor.

As he huffs resignation and pushes himself back out from the tight squeeze beneath the bed, Patricia raises the side-lamp above her head.

It breaks in two as the heavy stand crashes against Pow-Wow's skull. He falls flat like in the movies, exhales a grunt. She slams the remaining half onto his head once again. She is not thinking. She is not really conscious. It is as if she is watching herself from the ceiling. Looking at her madness, staring at the starfish in jeans and sweater.

Patricia drags the unconscious body nearer to the box. She is full of strength, a powerhouse of adrenalin. She even manages to press his dangling hands against the lid to imprint fingerprints. The story is already written in her mind.

It seems no longer than a second before the door is rattled and then flattened by three policemen.

– In the box! In the box! Patricia shouts hysterically at the officers. Releasing her pent-up horror, the screams are real.

One of the policemen pushes past Patricia and pulls up the lid of the box. A scraggy corpse is revealed.

Is That Everything?

1

More police arrive as the first three officers leave with the dazed Pow-Wow hanging from their arms. Forensic teams carry big black cases through to the bedroom, plain-clothes officers stand by the garden gate making mobile phone calls, a policewoman sits with Patricia in the lounge.

Patricia is ready for the questions, she's thought through the plan; it all came to her in a flash. Got the boy into the house, got his fingerprints all over the pillows and box. Understands, first hand, the extreme measures that individuals will take to save themselves. She is even happy to tell the policewoman about the escort date with Clive; shame is a small price to pay for innocence. Tells her about the arrival of Pow-Wow and how she found him throwing Mother into a box and how she went for the lamp. The tears break out again and the policewoman mistakes Patricia's sobs for shock and sadness rather than their true provenance, the realization of what she has done.

She is lying to the police officer, she is crying on her shoulder. There is no limit to her desperation as she throws all her accusations at the boy, at the black killer who came into her home and killed her beloved Mother. Patricia works herself into a fury and the officer suggests a Valium. It is all so unlike Patricia, all so unreal. But she must make them believe, she must convince. She has never been so close to the feeling of hell. Never has she been so deeply in the wrong.

2

Patricia has always tried to do the right thing. She loved her dad. She washed up and swept things and made her bed and kept her room clean. She did OK at school. Had lots of friends, who went on to marry, move away, have children, divorce, return and move away again. She tried to be polite, keep in with the neighbours, offer a helping hand. Church became boring but she maintained a faith, a kind of faith that didn't come from reciting the same old lines from a service book. People can easily forget her devotion to Mother, whom she has served for such a time. And whom she has obeyed to the limits of reasonable expectation. She has done her best to keep the garden trim. To smile at passers-by. To wear the correct clothes, keep her hair sober, steer clear of drugs and drink (except for the odd glass), visit the dentist once a year and not bother the doctor with flu or colds that everyone should know are untreatable and require only rest, fluids and time. Invariably found a haul of clothes and books to donate to the Scouts' Jumble Sale collection. Slipped coins into charity boxes outside Somerfield. Paid the television licence on time every year. Cooked the potatoes and greens and steak and kidney pies at the optimum temperature to the designated minute – when the pastry was tanned and the spuds sank under the masher with a slice of butter and dollop of cream. And showered with salt and/or pepper, and/or vinegar, and/or Worcestershire sauce, and/or horseradish. Kept the mustard in the fridge as stated on the label. Polished the table until it gleamed like a horse chestnut. Danced to Radio 2 on her own. Sang songs to Mother as she soaked in the bath: 'A Nightingale Sang in Berkeley Square' (the favourite). Giggled at Dad as he did his monkey impression, ran from Mother as she chased for a haircut. Has seen the sky white, blue, black, grey, red, purple, orange, yellow. Thrown snowballs at the post box. Jumped into the lido fully clothed. Eaten ice-cream cornets with Raymond Hunt. Walked to and from the chemist's for God knows how long. And told Lorraine all about certain things (Mother, Joan) and nothing about others (Ian). Never met a man to love properly and cherish and forsake all others for. To read next to in bed. Plenty of nice-looking chaps, just out of orbit, in other worlds. Noticed them from afar, or touched with her eyes and then watched them go. Got used to being alone, and/or independent, and/or lonely. Reached fifty. Met Clive. Lost job. Killed Mother. Framed boy.

3

The interview room is small and grey. The seats creak. A policeman and a policewoman sit opposite Pow-Wow. Smug as they watch him squirm. Knowing that the kid is guilty before they ask the questions. Basically caught red-handed. They've run up the record and seen the Willesden connections. Identified the circles the boy moves in. They all progress to murder at some point. Natural-born killer.

Though, procedures have to be satisfied. What they really need is the lad to loosen his tongue.

– I was working as an escort, Pow-Wow says.

– So how do you explain the body in the box? asks the police officer.

– I didn't know about that.

– Kill herself, did she?

– I don't know anything about an old lady.

– What did she say to you?

– Who?

– The old lady.

– Nu'ing.

– So you did see her?

– There was no old lady so nothing was said, you get?

– Did she insult you?

– I don't know what you're saying, man.

– You know how racist the old ones can be.

– You're not listening.

– Found her an easy target, eh?

– I didn't find anything.

– Oh, looking for things to nick, eh? Was that the ruse?

The policeman checks the tape is still running. Nods to his colleague sitting beside him.

Pow-Wow lights another cigarette.

– Why did you kill her, Tyrone?

– Shit, mother. I didn't kill no one.

– Did she say something that made you flip? Provocation is a defence to murder.

– Murder? No way. Don't drop this rock on me.

– Well, what would you call it?

– No, no, this shit ain't real.

– We have you with a dead body.

– I didn't kill no one. Come on, man, you're busting me up.

– Do you know how people like you are treated inside?

– Black?

– No, granny-killer.

4

Patricia declines the offer of counselling and victim support – she doesn't want other people involved. Well aware that no one at this stage doubts her innocence. Doesn't want to rock the boat.

The house is cordoned off as a crime scene but Patricia tells the police that she has nowhere else to go and so the chief officer promises prompt action. He will soon have his men out of the way so she can grieve in peace.

The body has been taken away and the house feels deserted despite the few remaining investigators drifting about the house, taking prints off cups and looking for clues.

Patricia is aware of the police's presence and she struggles to maintain misery. For when she thinks of Mother and her absence, there is too much relief and not enough guilt.

The house needs to be cleaned. Purged of the strangers' presence. The footprints of the police pattern the carpet. The boy's aftershave lingers in the lounge. The cups of tea left lying on the coffee table look like strategically placed props.

Going to Mother's room and peering over the black and yellow tape, Patricia stands in the doorway and smiles. She doesn't want to smile, it actually hurts her face and exposes her true emotions. But it flashes, just for a split second. Just before Patricia fights it back and chews it into a frown.

It is no longer the same room, despite the familiar items on the dressing table. And the box in the corner. Which seems content, standing squat against the wall.

Reaching

1

The Sons of Arsenal used to ruck. Look after their own and show no fear when travelling with the football or celebrating in town or inside the pubs planted along the Seven Sisters Road. The world may have been theirs but other people tried to snatch it away. Tried to slip in or muscle in or make more noise. The Sons put things right.

Stanley still has dreams of making it as a Son, even though the heyday is long gone.

He can't wait around for Clive to get back from the country. He's feeling too up-for-it. The day is bright, although the best of it has gone and the sun is a haze.

The claustrophobic streets of Somers Town, squashed between towers and tall brick town-houses, expand under the summer light.

He'll take a walk to the Brewers. Hopefully rub shoulders with a few of the lads, a few of the Sons. Attempt a little bit of ingratiation. The same ruse he's been up to for years. Not that the Sons are against him – they're not. They exchange banter, the odd beer. But they won't ask him to come to a game, or a party. Stanley would never ask himself: the height of failure. He prefers to get his face known, drink in the Brewers, clutch at conversational straws.

Having cash in pocket helps his cause. As does having a scam on the go. Chuffed to think that he has two escorts on the books, even if the client list is yet to explode. Working as a spiritualist sidesman can have its pluses but it doesn't quite have the kudos on Camden High Street as being a gigolo. Not that he undertakes the work himself – he's the governor. Leaves the hands-on aspects of the game to his trusted team. But for the Sons it's all about principle. And as far as principle goes, he's a gigolo.

Can hardly wait to see Dean or Kenny's face when he lets them know what's happening. Watch their expressions crash to the floor, just at the moment he reaches deep into pocket and pulls out a roll. Will talk them into spending an evening on the lash, regaling them with his stories of seduction and sexy ladies queuing for his time. Will make it sound nothing; business as usual. Make up a few bored housewives. A couple of rich bitches. Won't have to lie about the mature broad in Bow. Obviously a bit of a goer is Patricia.

Stanley jogs all the way from Eversholt Road to the Brewers. It is late afternoon and people will still be in for a drink and an evening schedule.

The car park and kerb outside are vacant. Stanley ignores the empty spaces and goes into the pub. To see no one.

Ron the landlord raises his head from the fridge.

– The Sons?

– Gone, says Ron.

– Where?

– Hertfordshire, I think.

– When they getting back?

– They ain't coming back.

– What do you mean? Stanley asks, holding the door, puffing from the run.

– They moved out.

– Dean? Craig?

– As far as I know.

– All of them?

– Yeah.

– Gone?

– Yeah.

Stanley heads to the house on Copenhagen Street. Past the row of shops, past a discarded sofa, under the arches. Climbs the steps to the large front door. No cars parked outside. No light through the thick, velvet curtains. Throws his fist against the door. Waits. No reply. Hammers the door again. Puts his ear against it to listen. Nothing.

He stretches across from the steps to rest a foot on the window ledge and taps heavily against the glass. Looks for a gap in the curtains. Hears a car horn from the road and turns to see an Audi estate. Barry Stainer, a Son, gets out.

– You won't find no one in, Stanley-boy, he cries up.

– What's going on?

The guy opens up the back of the car and pulls out a length of wood with a board attached. FOR SALE. – Moved out.

– What's this all about? I've just been to the Brewers.

– We're all finished here.

– Where you going?

– Out of town.

– Like where?

– A little place called Radlett. You won't know it.

– I don't get it.

– Leave London to the grannies, graduates and gangsters.

– But you can't just up and leave like that, argues Stanley.

– You get to a certain age when you want a bit of space, a change of lifestyle.

– Don't give me that, Barry.

– It's all done and dusted, he says, looking around for a suitable site in which to plant the sign.

– But this is our land.

– Stanley, Stanley, think. Who's left round here?

– My old dear's still here.

– Yeah, and she talks to the dead, Barry says, knocking the sign into a patch of mud at the bottom of the steps. – You want to think about it. You don't want to be the last of the Mohicans.

Stanley cannot think of anything to say.

Barry Stainer jumps back into the car and drives off.

Winded by the conversation, Stanley sinks onto the steps. He sits perched on dusty concrete staring at the road.

2

Clive was deep inside of himself all the way back from the countryside. His parents didn't take any notice; familiar with the quiet
emanating from the back seat. They couldn't hear his contempla-
tions on Stanley and Patricia. His resolve to tell Stanley that he
didn't want to be an escort any more. His passion for Patricia that he
is uncertain about. She phoned for an escort, not a relationship.
They get on well and clearly have feelings for each other – the kiss on
the doorstep showed that – but she is probably working from a
different agenda. He doesn't want to misread things.

Clive stands by the phone in his flat. He has Patricia's number
in his hand and he thinks about giving her a ring. He really missed
her today. It would have been great if she had been there. Mum
and Dad would like her enormously. They would see her kindness
and humour. They would ignore her age, and the eye.

Maybe Patricia's mother will answer the phone? That will cause
a rumpus. Perhaps he will phone at a bad time and Patricia will
resent him for it?

The thoughts scatter like startled birds when his telephone
pierces the room.

Stanley is on the other end. – Got a client for tomorrow in
Leytonstone.

Clive is anxious. Determined to tell Stanley how he feels about
the escort work, but wary of his friend's persuasiveness. Stanley
has a way of making Clive submit. – I'm n-n-not doing any more
escort stuff, he says.

– Get out of here, Stanley replies.

Clive grips the phone harder to hold his ground. – I'm s-s-
serious. I'm not doing any more. It ain't right. I feel bad around
Mum and Dad.

– Don't bail out on me, Clivey-boy. Things are picking up.

Clive shakes his head, sucks in his lips. – N-n-n-no. No m-
more.

– There's a job tomorrow. Think of the cash, Stanley argues.

To no avail. The telephone line has given Clive courage.
– You'll have to d-d-do it yourself.

– Up to you, Stanley says casually. – I'll just get the new bloke to do it.

– New bloke?

– That young guy that phoned yesterday. Sent him down to Patricia's earlier today. I'll send him to Leytonstone tomorrow, says Stanley, baiting Clive.

– P-p-p-patricia phoned?

– Yeah, geezer.

– She's m-m-my client.

– You were out of touch. What could I do?

– Waited.

– I thought you weren't interested in escort work any more?

The face drains as Clive struggles. – What happened w-w-when he went to Patricia's?

– Haven't heard back yet. I'll call him now. Tell him about tomorrow.

– I d-d-don't know why you did that.

– Business is business. I couldn't keep a client waiting.

Clive realizes that Patricia obviously didn't feel the same way he did about her. He was right, he was just an escort. Stanley's presence fades. Clive's hopes of a relationship with Patricia also dim. And the empty flat seems desolate as he stands in the middle of the room looking out at the dirty block opposite.

– Clive, Clive? calls Stanley down the wire.

Hearing his name, Clive breaks out of the trance. – L-l-leave me out of it. P-p-please.

– If that's what you want. Even though I think you're taking it all a bit seriously.

A grunt is Clive's reply. All he can think of is hiding or running away. Tries hard not to imagine Patricia with the new bloke. Everything seems lost. So glad he didn't mention Patricia to his parents.

3

Patricia wakes in the night with horror. Her stomach heaves. She jolts upright and vomits all over the duvet. She killed Mother. She retches again and the sick flows out of her mouth. The nightdress clings with sugary sweat. Her face is bright red and feverish. She throws aside the soiled quilt and is steadied by her feet touching carpet. She tears off the nightie and staggers from bed to bathroom. Hurling water over her head, she shivers with the realization of yesterday. With the terror of her half-dreams, half-hallucinations. Poor Mother, the poor boy. What is going to come of it all? The stairs creak as she descends.

Mother's bedroom light is on and the sombre glow crawls along the hallway to where Patricia walks with bare feet. Patricia feels she can't, but her body impels her to the doorway of the room. And there, standing in the corner of the room, is the box. As she edges forwards, the room shrinks and all attention focuses on the white, wooden trunk. The lid is down. The house has never been so quiet.

Over to You

1

Stanley is in a panic. Wednesday morning and he can't get in touch with Pow-Wow to delegate the date in Leytonstone. Now eleven a.m. and the date is on for one p.m. Things are looking bad. Stanley doesn't want to take it on. He has all the mouth and trousers but no confidence in his looks and his ability to charm the ladies. Clive is no Casanova but at least he is gullible enough to go along and let the lady take the lead. But Stanley perceives himself differently. He is too aware of his short-comings – short being the operative word. Let alone his ferret-face that has failed to impress a girl in years. What would he wear? Couldn't turn up in his Fred Perry and baggy jeans. Would have to wear his seance suit. Look like he's turning up for a funeral. That's if he goes. Tries Pow-Wow's number again. Time ticks on. A decision is imminent. His stomach is writhing with nerves – a gutful of snakes. Flicks the sweat off his palms and he reaches for the suit in its dry-cleaning bag. He could cancel the deal, but then he'd lose the money and feel even more of a flop. He's got to get to grips with the fact that he is going to have to do it himself. He resists the temptation to climb back into bed.

2

Leytonstone lies flat and Victorian. The layers of rusty terraces are set against summer trees. Stanley follows the directions from the station that the woman gave him.

A car pulls up alongside Stanley. A man in a suit leans out of the window.

– You on the way to the crematorium? he asks.

– No, mate, Stanley replies, nervous enough without having strangers harass him for information.

The man in the car apologizes and drives away.

It is only then that Stanley realizes the man's mistake and murmurs 'cheeky git' under his breath. The encounter makes him even more uncomfortable. And hot. He releases the black tie a little, crosses the road to walk in the shade.

Out in the open air, his nerves have subsided a little. Walking gives the adrenalin a chance to escape. If only the collar wasn't so stiff.

Finding the right house, he wrestles his way through the gate that grates against the path. He notices a twitch on the net curtains and the front door opens before he can ring the bell.

The woman gives a huge smile from her strawberry face. – Are you my man? she says.

– Stanley, he replies, offering a hand.

– Ooh, I could eat you whole, she laughs, her enormous body wobbling.

Towering above and around Stanley, she leads him, with a waddle, into the living room. The gas fire is on despite it being summer and the room swelters.

– Make yourself at home, she says.

Stanley is calmer than he expected. She is a lot bigger.

– Anne, wasn't it? he asks.

– That's right. Call me Crystal. Drink?

Stanley could kill a juice. He's sweated himself slim on the journey. – What have you got?

– Beer, whisky, rum?

He shrugs, and accepts that it will be something alcoholic. – Beer?

– I'll stick with my rum, if you don't mind, she says, heaving herself out of the room.

The leather cushions make Stanley stick. He shuffles free and sits upright, perched on the edge of the settee. Notices that the orange walls match the bars of the fire. Black curtains that match the series of dark pictures hanging bunched together on the opposite wall. The clock says one thirty – arrived a little late.

– You like art? Stanley calls out.

Crystal doesn't reply.

She returns with two drinks. Leaning back as she walks to compensate for the weight at the front of her body: the stomach, the breasts. Sits on the armchair adjacent to Stanley and, like him, perches on the edge. Her flowery dress hangs loose over the seat and brushes the carpet.

Sipping the beer, Stanley is aware of something stuck to the lip of glass: a crusty speck, picked up from the washing-up bowl and left to solidify in the cupboard. It makes him retch and he surreptitiously tries to scratch it off with his fingernail. He feels in a strange place, in an odd situation. His nerves reignite. He wants to be confident but he is vulnerable next to the huge woman. Drinks the beer quickly, from the opposite side to the speck.

– What did you want to do? he asks cautiously.

The dress is short-sleeved and the fat on her arms droops as she lifts the rum to her lips. She licks her lips as she looks back at him. – What's on offer? she asks with a raised eyebrow.

Stanley swallows the beer with a grimace. Can't stop himself looking at the size of her thighs beneath the clingy frock. He panics a little, unsure how to deal with things. – What did you have in mind?

She pushes her bottom lip under the top one as if she is toothless. The eyes close halfway. – Would you like to play strip poker?

Trying to appear calm makes Stanley appear more frightened. His legs bounce up and down on the toes as if tapping to a frantic beat. The heat of the room blocks his nose and he breathes through his mouth.

– I've got less clothes than you. You've got an advantage, she says, sweat rolling down her forehead.

– I'm a bit hot. Can we turn the heater off? asks Stanley.

– You'll soon be getting out of those clothes.

– I'm sweating.

– I'll go and get the cards, she says, pushing herself up from the sides of the chair with great effort.

The shirt collar is so stiff that Stanley can feel a red mark being ground into his neck. Normally he would only wear the shirt for a couple of hours at most. Maybe it will be a relief to get the shirt off. Then he worries about his body. He wondered whether the date might come to this. It would not have been so bad if the room had been half-lit with candles and closed curtains. However, the living room is as bright as day. And as warm. Which will make the spots on his back inflame.

While she is away for the playing cards, he stands up and shakes himself down to get rid of the awkwardness. He is Stanley, a male escort, a businessman, a friend of the Sons, a lad. He is not fazed by a date. He can talk the talk. Shoot the breeze. Lay down some lines that will make her pant. He's seen Dean in action; the way he wins the women over with a glint, a joke, and then a slight touch and the next drink. He can do the same. He can treat Crystal like a game. He may not be the best-looking bloke in the world, or the tallest, or the richest, or the most successful, or the most educated, or the funniest, or the coolest. But he isn't afraid to give things a go – that counts for something. How many other people can say that they've run their own hot-dog stand? He needs to get hold of that go-getting spirit before she comes back to the room and deals the pack. He needs to imagine himself in the Brewers telling the tale of today.

– Do you know how to play pontoon? she asks, coming through the door.

– Twenty-one, you mean?

– Ace is eleven or one, that game.

– I know it, Stanley sighs, the confidence found in that second of solitude immediately draining from him.

– The loser in each hand takes off one piece of clothing or a pair, Crystal says, clearly having played before.

If Stanley is going to change the course of this date, he has got to think smart. Unless he nips the poker in the bud, he and Crystal are soon going to be naked and ready for the next part of the game. That is, if he wants to stop any sexual encounter. It has been a long time since he went with a woman. Maybe Crystal will reacquaint him with the procedures. Her greedy eyes seem keen for the chance.

146

Two cards each. Dealt onto a pouffe.

For Stanley it is a Jack and an eight. He'll stick.

Crystal, as dealer, turns her cards over. A queen and a nine. Normally a stick but Crystal grins and twists. A ten. Bust.

Stanley realizes that this is not a game that Crystal intends to win.

She slips off her shoes – a pair.

He deals the four cards. His fear mutating into something nearer to panic.

She twists. Twists again. And again. Bust. She rolls down a pair of pop socks, holding the edge of the chair for balance.

Stanley can hardly look as he puts his two kings to the bottom of the pack and passes the cards to Crystal. At least he knows he is wearing his best underwear: a pair of pants he bought about a year ago and has saved for a special occasion. This is the first time he's worn them. – You should think about your hand more carefully, he says, trying to be helpful.

There is no reply, as Crystal folds her bottom lip under the top again. Gaze concentrated on the cards as she flips out another four.

Again, Crystal contrives to lose the hand. She moves away from the chair and more into the centre of the room. Fiddling unsteadily with the buttons of the dress, she pulls the frock apart. It flaps to the floor, she steps out of it, supporting herself with the mantelpiece.

A small string is wrapped around her crotch that allows the bulges and belly to overflow. The bra entraps white mountain breasts.

Stanley grabs the deck of cards and tries to stop his legs shuddering. He wants to go to the toilet. His bladder suddenly throbs.

– Well? she asks.

Stanley gulps and looks at her through squinting eyelids. He nods slowly.

When she edges towards Stanley, he smells her body. Bready. Her hands are sweaty and hot, stroking the side of his head. Pulling him slowly into her stomach, burying his head in flesh.

He can't take it. She is too much and the money no longer

important. Stanley pulls himself out of her clasp and makes for the exit.

Crystal stands there forlorn, unable to understand what's happening.

– I've got to go, I've got to go, Stanley blurts out as he pulls open the front door. – I'm really, really sorry, he shouts over his shoulder.

Out on the street, he runs from the house. Trying to put as much distance between him and Crystal as possible. Realizing and accepting that he is not a natural gigolo. The whole business is too scary.

As he passes over the Underground line, Stanley turns the phone off. Doesn't want any more calls that will lead to any more débâcles like today. Other male escorts can keep the work and the money, he'll think of something else. Nothing can be as bad as this.

Arrivals

1

Since the last policemen left, Patricia has been happy to hide out in the house. Things seem quite normal as she makes tea and cooks dinner and avoids the door to Mother's room. The television is a reliable companion. When the telly is off, the silence in the house is more bearable than she imagined. The only unnerving noises are the stairs that occasionally belch.

Joan has called, as has Lorraine. She told them the business with Mother. Didn't say too much about the boy being in the house – difficult to explain. They've offered this and that, but Patricia has gratefully declined their assistance. Let them both know that she needed some time alone to grieve.

'Lost her job then lost her mum' is the phrase circulating on the narrow pavements of home. The neighbours have knocked but Patricia hasn't opened the door. Being shut away inside has prevented her from facing any awkward moments. She is aware that with many of the concerned greetings cards slipped through the door there is a voyeuristic invite attached. How some of the locals want to know all about the murder, all about the black boy in the bedroom.

With the worry of neighbours, and the funeral arrangements, Patricia has had little time to reflect on the events of Tuesday. If she did, she feels her nonchalance would be unlikely to be replaced by anything more sinister, or emotional. Her mental state has calmed. She is erasing the guilt and forgetting about the boy. She is focusing on the life she had with Mother. This offers solace and a sense of release. How does anyone else know what it was like to live with Mother? How could anyone tolerate such tyranny? How many know the meaning of sacrifice? It was a mercy-killing. It was instinct.

The brief thoughts flash through her mind, like subliminal advertisements. At the end of each show, all she can think about Mother is 'good riddance'.

Patricia is eager to clean the house. She has collected a number of cardboard boxes and fills them with Mother's ornaments, clothes and various possessions. She wants to wipe out any trace of Mother and allow the home on Fairfield Road to recover.

She undertakes the clearing of Mother's bedroom in subdued silence. The gentle 'sh' of drawers at the dressing table. The rattle of bottle and container in the bathroom. The ruffle of bedsheets. Patricia quickly checks an urge to laugh. Packing away Mother's things is satisfying. Like wiping up a mess. How immaculate everything looks all of a sudden.

The one remaining stain is the memory of the innocent boy she has sent to prison. It won't seem to shift, regardless of how much effort she applies. Tries to forget, tries to reason and justify with the 'either him or me' approach. But she cannot forget his nervous smile as he sat in the lounge. Forces herself to think of something else, anything else. And Clive merges from the haze.

2

There is nothing like dunking a digestive into a cup of coffee. Apart from maybe a ginger nut, Patricia thinks, bent over the smallest table from the nest.

The TV rolls out the repeats of an American sitcom. She doesn't laugh as she watches but the action and non-stop gags are funny enough. And forgettable. Allowing Patricia to forget.

When the phone rings, she is loath to answer. But, in the hope of hearing positive news from the police, she answers.

– Hello? she says sadly.

– Patricia. It's C-c-c-c . . .

– Clive?

– Yes.

– Oh, Clive. Oh, Clive, is all she manages to say, genuinely delighted to hear his voice. She has missed him. When he didn't arrive on Tuesday, she assumed feelings weren't mutual.

– I just wanted to call and s-s-s-say hello. S-s-see if we could m-m-meet.

– What have you heard?

– That you had another e-e-escort c-c-come round?

– Have you heard anything else?

– Like what?

– Mother.

– No.

– It's terrible. So terrible.

– What's h-h-happened?

– Come and see me?

– I'll b-b-b-b-be there in about an hour.

There are bunches of flowers in the porch. Clive steps around them to knock.

Patricia is at the door almost instantly, pulling Clive into the house and then into an embrace that says more than any hello. She grabs handfuls of his jumper and pulls at it.

His arms feel too long and thin as he holds her and gently pats her back.

Clive has grown to huge proportions in Patricia's mind. On the first date he impressed her with his naïveté, his childlike honesty. He tried so hard. So different to her preconceptions. The second date was more settled, and they were able to talk. He actually listened to what she had to say. He never judged – she liked things like that. And in his way he was very attractive. His simplicity was seductive. Reassuring. She was too seasoned for muscles and egos.

Clive's friend Stanley obviously knew his onions when it came to allocating a man to a voice.

Seeing Clive so close again, she is overwhelmed. He is like a beautiful scent that takes her away from the stench of tragedy. The first time they met there was Mother, the chemist's, a routine. And now all things have changed, except Clive, in the same shirt and jeans he wore last Sunday. For a walk in the park, when she complained about home and they kissed at the door.

– Why didn't you come on Tuesday? she moans into his chest.

151

– I d-d-didn't know anything about it.

– Why weren't you around? she sniffs.

– What's h-happened?

She grips him tighter – The boy they sent. He killed Mother.

Clive stops patting her back. – He what?

– He killed her. The police have been.

After the shared tears and consoling hugs. After the desperate words of comfort that Clive managed to stutter his way through. After a cup of tea drunk next to each other on the settee, shoulder to shoulder, Clive tries to call Stanley to let him know what's happened. He calls the flat but Stanley is not there. He calls the mobile but there is only a worryingly continuous beep.

3

Clive travels on the train back to King's Cross. He tries Stanley's phone again but to no avail. Instead of hurrying home, he walks via the Two Brewers. If Stanley is anywhere he will be in the pub, sitting on the periphery of the Sons, hoping for a nod or a greeting from Dean. But why no mobile? Perhaps Stanley has heard about Patricia's mother and is lying low.

The pub is empty and its large open spaces surprise Clive; never realized it was so big. Not a single Son. Stanley is sipping a bottle at the back of the bar. Clive rushes over. – You ain't g-g-going to believe this, he says.

Stanley is drained. Drinking to recover from yesterday's fiasco. Bruised ego and broken business repaired by half a dozen bottles of Beck's. – No, you ain't going to believe this, Stanley says louder.

– It's that guy you s-s-sent to Patricia's.

– It's the woman I went to see at Leytonstone.

– Something terrible h-h-happened.

– You're right there, Stanley groans.

– He killed Patricia's mother.

– If I'd have let this broad get on top of me she would have killed me.

– It was m-m-murder! Clive says, trying to break down Stanley's self-absorption.

– You should have . . . Then Stanley stops speaking and stares at Clive properly for the first time since his arrival. – Say again?

Clive takes measured breaths, falls onto a stool. – That g-g-guy you sent to Patricia's on Tuesday k-killed Patricia's mother.

– How? says Stanley with open jaw, ready to swallow the answer.

– Suffocated her.

Stanley closes his eyes. – Oh, my fucking God!

– The police arrested the guy. He's b-b-banged up somewhere.

Putting his hands on his temples, Stanley moans to himself. – What the fuck have I done!

Not for one minute did Clive think that Stanley was incriminated. But now, seeing his friend wilt, thinking about the arrangements behind the scenes, he can see why Stanley is worried.

Clive is too loyal, too rational. He knows that Stanley would not have done anything intentionally or recklessly. He reaches out to rescue his mate. – It's not your fault. D-d-don't get on yourself about it. The g-g-guy was obviously a madman. You weren't to know that.

– The police, Clivey-boy, Stanley replies. – What about the police?

– Where's the phone?

– Turned off.

– P-p-permanently?

– Who knows?

– You c-c-could always go and tell them w-w-w-what you know?

Stanley tries to sip from the shaking bottle. His hands trembling. – No, no. That's not the way.

Clive bows his head as if thinking. But he isn't, he's just confused.

– First the Sons and then this. What have I done so wrong? he mumbles, pushing his fingers through his oily hair.

– W-w-what about the Sons? Clive asks. – Why's the p-p-place so empty?

– They've gone.

– W-w-where?

– Bloody gone and left us.

– Permanently?

– Course they have. Just when I'm moving things along.

– Why?

– I haven't got a clue.

The last dregs of the bottle are digested and Stanley winces with the bitter aftertaste. The shudder fills him with reality. – That's it, then. We've really ballsed things up this time, he says, with a clear voice. No longer muttering at the table.

Clive can only stay speechless and imagine the Sons' migration. He can only dream of getting away from Somers Town, the escort work, the relentless tragedy of Stanley.

Stir It Up

1

Thursday afternoon. Cheetham Young Offenders Institution, west London. Stripped of chains, coins, clothes and issued with sweatshirt and blue joggers. Standing in line with ten other guys transported from all over the South-East, processed by silent men with moustaches. Marched into the compound through gates and doors. Taken to stores and thrown bedding. No one speaks. No one looks at each other. Everyone beginning to consider the role they intend to play while inside. The head-down feel-sorry-for-me type. The head-up don't-fuck-with-me type. Pow-Wow keeps his chin pointed towards the ceiling. He ain't afraid of none of these bums. Even drops a stare on a couple of the others. They don't look back.

Shown into a cell on remand wing, where a skinny black guy in glasses sits at the table. Nothing is said as Pow-Wow puts his gear on the vacant bed on the right-hand side of the room.

The skinny guy closes his book, marking the page with a slip of paper.

– What's? he says.

– Yeah, yeah, what's? Pow-Wow replies aggressively, deeper-toned.

– I'm Lewis Robinson.

– Pow-Wow, he says, going to the table and offering a hand. They shake.

Pow-Wow returns to the bed and sits on the edge. – Let me get this straight with you, yeah? I'm an innocent man and I ain't done no shit, you get me? Pow-Wow says.

– I'm not so innocent. But don't tell them that, Lewis smiles.

Pow-Wow stares straight through the smile. – I'm a soldier. But they's nailing me up for some slant.

The cell is bigger than Pow-Wow expected. Two single beds on either side of the room. Table and chairs in the middle – occupied by Lewis and a pile of books. Sink and toilet in the corner by Pow-Wow's bed. A kettle and cups on a shelf in the corner by Lewis's. The bulb makes the room white.

– How about a tea? Lewis asks.

– Yeah, nice.

Lewis fills the kettle while Pow-Wow kicks off his sneakers and stretches out on the bed.

– You been in before? Lewis asks.

– No. Just visited.

– My first time too. It's rough.

– What's on?

– Look at me. I'm not cut out for this kind of setting.

Pow-Wow assesses the tiny arms and fragile build. – It ain't the size of the man in the fight but the size of the fight in the man, he says.

– I'm no fighter.

Lewis empties the kettle into the cups. Stirs the spoon quickly.

– I'm not going to take no shit, Pow-Wow says.

– It's all crews in here.

– I'm down with a show.

– Where you from?

– NWL.

Lewis passes Pow-Wow a mug. They drink in silence.

Lights out at ten. Pow-Wow closes his eyes after a long day. He listens to Lewis whispering to himself in the darkness.

2

Friday morning, after breakfast, the cell door is unlocked for prisoners' Free Association.

Pow-Wow stumbles off his bed with a stretch and groan and struts to the door.

– You on, Lewis?

– No, I'll do a bit of reading.

– You crazy? Stretch the legs, man. Catch some air.

– No, seriously, I'm OK, he says evasively.

– Everything cool?

– Cool.

The yard is bright and one hundred boys litter the space. Sitting on picnic benches, throwing basketballs, or wandering in groups. Pow-Wow stands with his arms folded. Walks the edges of the yard, ignoring the others. Enjoys the time alone. Under a chalk sky. Filling his head with thoughts about the escort date and the whole fiasco. Convinced that justice will out and that the bitch at the house in Bow will get her comeuppance.

Time runs quick and he begins a saunter back towards the entrance.

– Yo, Pow-Wow! comes a shout.

Pow-Wow looks over to a picnic bench, where he spots a Daddy called 'Coach'. Sitting with a number of unfamiliar faces.

Three-stage handshakes and a chest slam. Slides onto the tabletop next to Coach.

– What's this? Coach asks, looking pleased with himself.

– The bulls are making a big mistake.

– When'd you get in?

– Yest.

– Papa was in to see me. Says you took a beating.

– History.

– Been keeping your skull down, yeah?

– Making plans.

– Not too well, ending up in the can, Coach laughs. – What happened?

Pow-Wow dismisses the question with a snort; doesn't want to go down that road.

– I get, Coach grins.

Pow-Wow knows Coach. Knows Coach's reputation as a warrior. A member of the War Committee. His arms painted with tattoos. Razor cuts through cropped hair. A chain around his neck as thick as a dog's lead.

– We could do with another hand in here, Coach says, looking past Pow-Wow at a group sitting on an adjacent bench.

Coach introduces the other faces; none of them NWL but from associated firms in east London with whom the Daddies have pacts.

– We work B wing. Where you at? Coach asks.

– Remand.

– Easy shit.

– Seems sweet.

– We'll soon get you over to us.

A horn sounds for the end of Association. Shared shakes and back through wire to wing.

Since his arrest, the only person he's spoken to is Brenda. Told her as little as possible and said that he'd be home in a few days. She was not happy and demanded detail. Pow-Wow blocked her out. He is tempted to phone Ileasha but what good would that do? Would be better to give Mister B a bell and see if he can pull a few strings.

Pow-Wow won't mention the charge to anybody. It could cause problems inside and out. The police gave him warning and he knows the deal for himself having heard stories through Lewis about unacceptable crimes. Forget the nonces – they're protected. There's a big burden to carry if you're down for doing anyone weak. An old lady counts him in. No one's going to listen to his claims of innocence; he's on a murder tag.

Back in the cell, Pow-Wow watches Lewis at the table, feverishly flicking through textbooks and scribbling notes on paper. Pow-Wow sucks slowly on a cigarette and exhales in short, delicate bursts. Stretched out on the bed, his feet jut against the metal bar that runs along the bottom.

– What are you studying, man?

– Sociology, Lewis replies, looking up but keeping a finger pressed to the page.

– What's all that about?

Lewis is surprised at the interest. – Oh, society, culture, things like that.

– What do the pages say?

– Depends on the book.

– That big mother, Pow-Wow says, pointing with a smoking fag.

Lewis pulls the book out from underneath the others. *The Clamour for Glamour.* – Well, it says that people who crave fame lack self-esteem. They want to be actors or pop stars not because they love acting or music but because they want to be famous.

– What about that skinny fuck? Pow-Wow smiles, nodding to a thin book.

– *Watch This Space* by Penfold Little. He says that one day we will all end up the same skin colour. Probably a medium brown.

– How'd he float that?

– He uses this thing called the 'mixing-paint theory'.

– Am I that colour?

– More or less. I'm a bit too dark.

Pow-Wow laughs.

– Just trying to educate myself, Lewis adds.

Lewis gets up to fill the kettle. Rinses two cups and fumbles with the tea bags. – There's so much to learn. You should have a look.

– Easy, homey.

Lewis pours water into cups. Spoons out the tea bags. Adds powder. Hands a drink to Pow-Wow. – I'm going to get something out of the time I've got to spend in this place.

– How long do you think you're going to get?

– Ten. Though I'll probably only do four or five.

– How did a guy like you end up facing that?

– A mistake.

– No bail?

– No way.

Departures

1

Patricia climbs into the limousine. Patricia behind a veil.

A horse-drawn carriage waits at the funeral director's. Decorated with white flowers, chaperoned by undertakers in tall hats and black gloves. To take a slow trek to Bow Road Methodist church for the ceremony. Then on to Grange Road, West Ham, for the cemetery.

The end of a life displayed on the wooden cart on a Saturday morning. Being pulled through roads under a dusty sky that begins to leak. Umbrellas unfold along the route. Flower petals flicker as pearls of rain hit. They trickle off the waxy coffin.

Mother had not attended church for a number of years. Even when she used to go she would sit unhappily in the back row and mumble the hymns. The current vicar did not know her yet he conducts the short service with a respectful dignity. The congregation is small: Patricia, Joan and Lorraine; a few of Mother's contemporaries.

The old women sit with hunched backs and furrowed, bleached faces. Huddled together on pews inside the church dwarfed by surrounding apartment blocks. Wearing coats and brooches that they have worn for thirty years. Mourning a friend whom they remember as a young, headstrong woman. Someone who could be fierce yet fun.

Clive sits at the back. He wears a navy shirt with a black pullover – he doesn't own a suit and felt that the only jacket he owns, the mauve one, would be inappropriate.

He tries to catch Patricia's eye but she doesn't turn around. Since seeing Patricia on Thursday, Clive has only spoken to her once – she called for a quick chat and to tell him about the service.

On top of the coffin is a framed photograph of a youthful Mother. She is standing in the middle of a street, growling at the camera, wearing a fur around her neck. The severe face is instantly recognizable. The street is busy behind her, with men pushing bicycles and boys in oversized caps.

– Isn't that the Roman? one of the old ladies whispers to her neighbour.

– It looks like Bethnal Green Road to me, the neighbour replies.

– That's next to where they've built that new precinct, the first lady continues.

– No, it's where they put that estate.

– We should know, shouldn't we?

– It's hard to say, really. The picture's a bit faded.

– But still . . . the first lady sighs.

– I must find my photos.

– It makes me sad to look, it really does.

– Doesn't seem so long ago.

The first lady pulls a hankie from sleeve and dabs her eyes.
– This sort of thing ought'n happen.

– We mustn't dwell on it.

The first lady pulls in her lips and shakes her head. – Who would have thought it?

– Doesn't she look grand in her fur?

– Better off where she is.

– Our heyday.

– Of all the people . . .

– It's a shame that the picture is so faded.

– It's just age.

The journey from the church to the East London Cemetery is slow. It is also ugly, taking the short route along Cody Road past the industrial park and disused gasworks.

Clive kills time walking about Bow and Old Ford. He gives Patricia an hour before arriving at the house.

– Clive, she smiles from behind the veil.

– I h-h-h-had to come, he says softly.

Patricia reaches out and takes his hand. – It's so good of you.

– I felt I sh-sh-should. F-f-f-for you.

The shroud does not hide the tired face. – Come and get a drink. No Tizer, I'm afraid, she manages to joke.

Clive smiles. He relaxes a little.

The handful of mourners have returned to Fairfield Road. The original dining room was converted into Mother's annexe and so the food (quiche, sausage rolls, slices of ham, French bread, pickle, pizza, bread sticks and cheese) and drink (red and white wine, whisky, gin, tonic, beer and fruit juices) are laid out in the living room on an extendable table.

Clive picks at a plateful of bits and pieces, trying to hide his discomfort. Watches Patricia perform bravely in front of Mother's friends, filling glasses and offering seconds. As if Mother wasn't murdered. As if the pensioners aren't living in fear. He admires Patricia in black. Wishing he could hold her.

Clive waits alone and is one of the last to leave. He goes to the door, where Patricia stands nervously.

– Thanks so much for coming, she says.

– No p-problem, says Clive, taking Patricia's hands. – Do you need me to stay b-behind and help?

– No, no, I've got Joan.

There is a silent pause and they hold hands.

They both think about what happened to Mother. Clive does not answer with words, he merely shakes his head and frowns. His eyes are stretched wide with disbelief.

The hands squeeze more tightly.

– When w-w-will I see you?

– Call me later.

He reaches forwards and places a kiss on Patricia's cheek. He pulls away slowly.

– Thanks, she whispers, letting go of his hand and allowing him to leave.

– I'll call you l-l-later, Clive confirms.

Patricia nods as she pushes the door closed.

2

With the house empty of guests, Patricia is left to hoover the crumbs and wipe down the tables. Puts the uneaten sausage rolls into a tin and the ham back in the fridge wrapped in foil. She played the part of devastated daughter effectively. There were no suspicious glances or shady stares. And Clive being there offered encouragement.

The departure of Mother is still a relief. There are not even the hot flushes or unwanted outbreaks of shivering that accompanied the first couple of days following the death.

The only nagging thought is the boy. She may have got her freedom but he is not so free. The balance upsets Patricia the more she considers it. An uneven deal that uses the boy as a pawn in her game. But she will never tell the truth. It has to be this way. It has to be. What was a young boy like that doing anyway?

She mustn't have sympathy for the boy. She can't or the whole plan will collapse. She must put it all out of her mind. Out of her thoughts.

3

For tea, Patricia eats the leftovers from earlier. The sausage rolls are more soggy than she realized – no wonder there were so many left. She eats from a paper plate with the plastic cutlery to save on the washing up. Everything takes so much effort when weighted with guilt. And there is still so much of the house and Mother to purge.

The telephone rings and she knows it will be Clive. She leaves the plate on the table and goes into the hallway to take the call.

– I t-t-told you I'd phone, Clive says.

– I didn't doubt it.

– How are you f-f-feeling?

– Fine. You were a great support earlier.

– Is e-everything in order?

– Everything apart from the sausage rolls, she laughs.

Clive doesn't get the joke but gives a moan anyway. It sounded funny. – At l-l-least it's all over.

– I suppose so. Start trying to get back to normal.

– And w-w-what about work?

– I can't think about that yet. I'm kind of glad I don't have to go in. I couldn't face it.

– You m-must be shattered by everything.

– I can't tell you. I'm so run down.

– You need something to take your m-m-mind off it all.

Patricia sighs. – I just want to get a break. Clear my head.

– C-c-can I ask you something? Clive almost interrupts.

– Yes, of course.

A quick cough to clear the nerves. – Please d-d-don't think I'm being forward. But what would you think about g-going away for a few days?

– With you?

– If you l-l-like. I reckon you need a r-r-rest. A chance to r-r-recharge the batteries. Clive speaks nervously, scared of rejection but excited by the prospect of acceptance.

– Where would we go?

– I d-d-don't know. Where do you f-f-fancy? Clive tries to be as accommodating as he can.

– Are you sure about this?

– Yeah.

– It's a big step. Have you thought this through?

– We c-c-can stay in s-separate rooms and stuff.

– You are so sweet.

– Maybe go somewhere you've always wanted to g-g-g-go.

– Have you been to Constable country?

– Where's that?

– I'll take that as a no, then.

– W-w-we can go there, I don't m-mind.

– Or Brighton. How about Brighton? I haven't been there since I was a girl.

– Are you saying y-y-yes?

– Are you asking me as an escort or as a friend?

– You know I'm n-n-not an escort any more.

– So if we go out to eat, you're not going to tell the world that I'm paying? she jokes, recalling the first date.

– I'm trying to f-f-forget that!

In a Sense

1

Sunday morning. Pow-Wow sits on a chair staring at the television in the communal space. His feet rest on the seat in front. His arms dangle on neighbouring backrests. Waiting for eleven and the first chance to go outside in days.

Stuck inside for most of the day, the time is spent on the wing where there is a pool table, ping-pong and the TV.

The thirty guys on remand don't really talk and during a game of pool the only words exchanged are calls for the next player.

Whispers have got round about Pow-Wow's All-Star connections and he's getting space. Though at night things close in. The cell and the sound of someone else sleeping is claustrophobic. And the shouting from the other blocks goes on till the early hours.

Verbal bullying is rife and Pow-Wow closes his mind to the constant taunts thrown between windows, between Bigs and Birds.

The Bigs are the rulers of Cheetham – regardless of outside gang affinities. The Birds are the ruled.

On arrival at Cheetham, newcomers are assessed by the Bigs; assessed for servitude suitability as a Bird. This assessment is tested at night, when the doors are locked and windows opened. Onto the courtyard that separates the different blocks. Bigs will call out to the newcomer with insults, jeers and threats. They will try to make the newcomer sing a nursery rhyme. If the new inmate sings then the Bigs know they have won another slave. From then on, the newcomer, now a Bird, will be expected to hand over cash, food, cigarettes, weed, on demand. Or ordered to do chores and run errands.

If any targeted newcomer refuses to sing then that person can expect a penalty. Uncooperative newcomers are often stuck with a blade during Free Association.

There have been calls for Lewis to sing but he has ignored them. He's calculated the risk.

No one has tried to make Pow-Wow sing. But he understands why Lewis doesn't like to leave the cell.

Watching the TV screen is meditation for Pow-Wow; the long, noisy nights have made him tired and the random daytime programmes drain his thoughts. He is desperate to hit some weather. Would like to do some weights in the training area of the yard that is home to older boys. His adolescent muscle spindly compared to the build of the body-pumpers.

The horn sounds and Pow-Wow stretches up, out of the chair. He is comfortable in these surroundings now, and he struts to the door with a pretend limp.

The air outside is thin and he takes hurried breaths to fill up. Spots Coach over on the bench. Walks over, offers a hand to shake. Coach keeps his head and hands turned away. The few others sitting with Coach say nothing.

– Yo, wha's up, Coach? Pow-Wow says.

Coach refuses to offer an acknowledgement, looking at the fence, at the sky.

– Yo, wha's up, Coach? he repeats.

Coach takes a bite on his fingernail. Drops a gaze on a guy next to him. Flicks a stare at Pow-Wow. – Walk on, sucker.

– What's moving? Pow-Wow asks.

– We know you's the granny-killer.

Pow-Wow huffs. He knew it would come out. – Man, don't believe that.

Coach looks back at the fence. – I've heard the vine.

– Goddam, Coach. They snarled me. They mother-fucking snarled me.

Coach points at Pow-Wow. – Listen, you little baby-fucker, we rock NWL, we eat the beat, we do what we gotta do. But you do it all wrong. You hear me clear?

– I got stuck.

– Let me tell you, from the Daddies, you is out. You got me? Now walk on.

– But . . .

– Walk the fuck on or you gonna get a regret.

2

In the afternoon, Pow-Wow has visitors. Only two are allowed.

Naomi makes eyes at the other boys. Half-heartedly.

Brenda cries and asks questions.

Coach is talking to another Daddy, Reefer, on the other side of the room. Pow-Wow continually looks over for acknowledgement but they ignore him. One time he catches Reefer's casual glance but it goes straight through him and down onto Naomi's legs.

– We can deal with this, Brenda says.

– I'll be fine, Mom. Ain't nothing going to happen.

– When you get out of here you gonna change your ways.

– You know what, Mom. I think you're right.

Naomi and Brenda exchange suspicious stares.

– I'm serious.

– I hope you are, Tyrone. I really do.

– I'm tired of other people taking control of me.

– We'll be here for you, says Brenda brightly, for the first time in the visit.

– Papa's going out with Ileasha, Naomi says.

– That's shit, replies Pow-Wow.

– Real, Naomi replies.

– I got more things to fret about, Pow-Wow says.

Brenda gives Naomi a look that demands silence.

The table of three avoid eyes.

– Are you sharing a room?

– Cell, Mom, Naomi corrects.

– I got a nice, quiet guy. He studies all day.

– He sounds good.

– He's true. Giving me a lot of ideas.

– About what?

– Education.

Naomi lets out a smirk.

– Yeah, damn right. Why not? argues Pow-Wow.

– That'd be . . . great, Brenda beams.

– Not some sort of boring stuff, but real things. Expanding the mind, developing myself.

– You could go to college.

– One day everyone is going to be brown, he says.

– Is that so?

– It's like mixing paints.

Naomi snorts and adjusts her top.

Brenda nods, looking confused.

– I didn't kill no old lady, Mom, Pow-Wow says.

3

Sunday night is another slow grind, in which voices shout and echo outside the window.

Pow-Wow imagines the night in Willesden. Dense heat of the city and the rattle of trains running past the house. Out on the streets the packs will roam and the Daddies will be in air-conditioned cars and bars. Mister B among them, seeking a thrill and a future among the adults. Probably slamming a girl in one of the pimp houses. Initiated into the Game with a prostitute called Sashima or Devina or Shakila.

He will call Mister B from the payphone. Only fair to let him know the deal from his end; now that rumours are alive. Mister B will believe him, will remain on side. Ready to meet him at the gates when the mess is all cleared up. And they can go for a ped ride in the sun and take their tops off. Examine Mister B's new Daddy Crew tattoos that will cover his body. Pow-Wow will be able to explain the escort mistake to a sympathetic ear.

The courtyard security lights smear the room in orange. Pow-Wow recalls his arrest. He thinks about the arrest. Considers whether the murder rap isn't just a mistake. Maybe he's carrying the can for some crafted plan that had his name down as the mug?

Pow-Wow sits up in bed and stares his thoughts at the window. Never doubted that the real killer would be caught and truth would out. Never doubted that a little bit of detective work was going to send him back to Willesden in a week. Now the prospect of conviction enters the room and stands cold over Pow-Wow's rickety bed. In his head, things begin to conspire. The police questions that he thought were a formality suddenly take on greater import. The duty lawyer they gave him for the initial appearance did, with hindsight, not give a shit.

Free Association, the next day. Monday morning. Pow-Wow leaves Lewis and heads to the yard. He steers clear of the groups dotted on the benches and by the basketball hoop. Coach and crew peer over and return to chat.

The training bars are free and Pow-Wow hops up and begins a series of pull-ups. It has been a while since his last weights session and he feels the muscles burn as he digs deep. A bit of shadow-boxing and leg-stretches. Back onto the low bar for tricep dips.

– Hey, a voice says.

Pow-Wow stops and turns round.

– What's new, Coach?

Coach is frowning, keeping his distance. – I hear you're still on remand wing? he asks.

– No word of change.

– They'll probably put you on protection soon.

– Why's that?

– Word gets round. People don't like what you did.

– Man, I told you, it weren't like that.

Coach shakes away the plea. – Whatever, whatever.

– You gotta listen, Coach.

Coach screws up his face. – Why don't you mother-fucking listen to this. You want back in?

– Of course, man.

– Life could get rough if you're not down, you hear me?

– I know the state.

– You get back-up, you get respect.

– I'm ready for action, says Pow-Wow.

– Ain't you just the big bad wolf.

– The Daddies know that I can duel.

Unimpressed shrug from Coach. A quick glance back to the bench, where the other members of the crew wait.

– Do you know Robinson?

– You mean Lewis? Pow-Wow says, flicking up his chin to encourage more information.

– The rat that doesn't sing.

– He doesn't want to become a Bird, says Pow-Wow defensively.

– That's his decision, replies Coach, casting a watchful gaze about the yard. He dips into his strides, draws out a six-inch blade.

He hands the knife to Pow-Wow, who quickly grabs it and slides it into his pocket before security get a glimpse.

– If you want back in, you gotta slice the dude, says Coach. – Birds have to sing songs.

– You got him wrong, Coach. The guy's just trying to get by and do his thing.

– Well, now you gotta do yours.

– But I'm gonna be out of here in a bit, Pow-Wow protests.

– Either you slash or you get slashed. Up to you, bro.

– Man, this is loose.

Rolling Stones

1

Brighton is beaming beneath a thin layer of wispy cloud. The whites and blues of the buildings dazzle as Patricia and Clive walk down the hill from the station. The ambience is very European, with the huge open-fronted shops and rows of café tables lining the route to the beach.

They have made it to Brighton by lunchtime, which was good going considering Clive couldn't decide what to pack. Spent the entire Sunday evening looking for suitable shorts (that didn't show too much of his spindly legs), summer shoes (that he couldn't wear in Somers Town without looking daft), and suntan lotion (that wasn't at least three years out of date). And he had to choose T-shirts, trousers and then jerseys – the evenings were cool on the coast. There was no way the bed-full of clothes was going to fit into the Adidas holdall and so the process of elimination began. Hardly got any sleep but woke on the Monday full of excitement. Disbelieving that he and Patricia were actually going away together. Never had the opportunity to take a woman away.

Stanley and Clive used to dream of a holiday with a female. When the two of them spent a week in Swanage, over ten years ago, they couldn't help but envy the happy couples bouncing around the beach and walking arm in arm back to the hotel. In the evenings, when Clive and Stanley walked the streets with a bag of chips in hand, they would spot the same couples through the windows of restaurants, sitting satisfied among candlelight and empty wine bottles. 'Some day' both Stanley and Clive thought to themselves.

Clive takes Patricia's hand as they walk lazily. Gives it a

meaningful squeeze and feels ten feet tall. The passing pedestrians – most half-naked and eclectic in style – are invisible to Clive. They have become background, like the flocks of seagulls swooping above the promenade.

The bed and breakfast that Patricia booked is in a small, rather dingy street behind the seafront. From the outside the place looks closed, but inside the landlord is pleasant and welcoming, carrying Patricia's bag with him as he climbs the cramped stairway.

The two rooms are identical: soft bed, musty curtains and a chest of drawers. They share a bathroom on the opposite side of the corridor. Their windows look out onto the back yards of other hotels. Layers of pipes, fire escapes and discarded rags.

They quickly change into fresh clothes and leave the hotel for a chance to explore the town while it is still warm.

As a couple, they link arms and enjoy the cool breeze that blows off the Channel. The waves roll onto the stones. Swaths of the beach cackle and sigh as the tide retreats.

Clive smart in his favourite white T-shirt. Patricia clean in a green dress.

Patricia does not look that broken to Clive. She may seem a bit detached and a little glazed. But the warmth is still there, the softness intact. The sea air will blow away the pain of Mother.

– W-w-w-why is life so sad? Clive asks, hoping to get the morbid reasons for their trip out of the way early.

– Maybe it's all a test? Patricia replies.

– I d-d-d-don't ever want my parents to die.

– No, Patricia sighs, noticing how well he looks. How well the white top suits him. How his stutter acts like a little song at the start of each sentence.

– I sometimes l-l-l-look around at my flat and imagine it all without me. All those possessions and s-s-spaces left without me.

– Things would go on.

– Mum and Dad would miss me, but n-n-not all the spaces and stuff at the flat. They'd j-j-just wait for the next tenant.

– I'd miss you.

– Thanks, Clive smiles.

They both watch their knees as they stroll.

– I'm going to have to clear out the house. There's so much of Mother's stuff.

– I thought you'd d-d-d-done all that?

– It's not her possessions so much as the furniture, the curtains, the carpet.

– How come some p-p-people can throw out everything and some people can't chuck a thing?

– I think it'll give me some control over events.

– C-c-c-control, um, yeah.

Two rollerbladers come straight at them, swooshing along the promenade. At the last second the bladers split and go round Patricia and Clive.

Patricia holds her hands to her face.

Clive is aware of Patricia's shock and shouts at the bladers.
– There's n-n-n-n-n-n-n-n-n-n-n-n-n-n . . .

By the time he gets to the 'no rollerblading allowed' they are gone.

– Thanks, Patricia smiles, pulling him closer.

How comfortable Clive feels. Being able to remonstrate with others in public. She makes him feel so confident.

They stand by a rose garden and watch a fountain spray water. There is a café nearby and they agree to stop for a drink and a bite.

Patricia has a tea, Clive a carton of juice. They go back into the park and sit on one of the benches. They share an apple pastry, Clive offering her the centre bit with most of the fruit. They rest hands on each other's legs after they have finished eating.

– You're so good to me, Patricia says.

– People always say that I m-m-mean well.

– And to think that I had you down for a stud.

– B-b-but if they say that I mean well are they really saying that I don't actually do well?

– You do perfectly well, Clive. Don't worry what others say.

– My dad always told me to spend more time listening to others.

– It depends what they say, I suppose.

– My d-d-dad told me to 'look before you leap', but he'd also say, 'He who hesitates is lost.'

– I can't imagine a young, naughty Clive, Patricia says jocularly.

– M-m-many hands make light work.

– I'm sure you had a cheeky grin.

– T-t-too many cooks spoil the broth.

– Do you look like your mum or dad?

– It c-c-c-can be c-c-c-confusing listening to others.

After walking the beach, the main thoroughfares and streets full of jewellery shops and arts and craft stalls, they go back to the hotel. They go into Patricia's room to talk and have a coffee before considering the evening's choice of meal.

The kettle rumbles on the chest of drawers while Patricia fiddles with the sachets of sugar and powdered milk. When the two tiny white cups are prepared and ready for the hot water, Clive and Patricia are left to sit close on the bed and wait for the kettle to boil. Eyes on the orange light. A nervous grin or two. And slowly they edge nearer each other until their arms meet. And then they fold together like a greetings card and embrace. First with arms and neck and shoulders. Then with lips. The coffee is forgotten.

Beneath the white T-shirt is a slim, slight body.

Beneath the green dress is best underwear.

The bed smells of lavender.

His legs are skinny and wrap around her like string.

She is very big in the hips and haunches, but he doesn't mind.

2

Curtains shut. Stanley sits on bed with legs crossed. Lines of daylight dissect the room. His face is patchy with light and shade. Like a mask.

There are none of Sylvia's clients today and Stanley is left to stew alone to the melodic grooves of Patrice Rushen.

The police came round on the Saturday morning, having traced the mobile number to his address. They wanted to know about the escort business and Pow-Wow (or Tyrone Davenant, as they called him). Sylvia was concerned but Stanley just told them everything he knew, exactly the way it happened. He had nothing to hide. The detectives left happy enough. It seemed to Stanley that they'd already nailed the guy.

Clive came round in the afternoon, after the funeral, and spent an hour crying for Patricia in the lounge.

Later that evening Clive called him to say that he was going away to Brighton for a few days with Patricia. 'Charge her!' Stanley suggested but Clive wasn't having any of it.

Now it's Monday and with Clive gone to love it up on the south coast, Stanley feels the chill of loneliness. He can't face moping for an afternoon, so he decides to hit the road and walk some streets.

He heads up near Copenhagen Street. To see the drinking house. No cars outside. The FOR SALE sign leans.

Notices how desolate the area is. Broken walls line the pavement, weeds the size of small trees, patches of mud where grass used to be. And for a second there is no sound. The surrounding city falls silent. Just for a second. Before a train clatters and the spell is broken.

Stanley closes his eyes and breathes in a lung of summer soot. Turns around and makes for the Brewers.

Just two faces at the bar. He recognizes neither. Used to be filled with Sons at this time. Even Ron the landlord looks different and offers an ambivalent hello before collecting Stanley a drink from the cold shelf.

The back of the pub, where Stanley and Clive normally sit, gives a good view of the bar and the large floor area normally filled with Arsenal shirts.

It was never a lot to ask of ambition. Become a Son. For Stanley, the businesses and the money could take a back seat if Dean or Kenny came up to him and asked, 'How about it, Stan the man? You want to be a Son?' The words never came and now the Sons don't even come to the pub. Gone up to some place in Hertfordshire to live out a new chapter, while he's stuck in the city lagging behind in the book of achievement. Barely read the first few pages.

Everything is so peculiar. As if he's the only one left following a disaster. It's not survivor's guilt he feels but there is certainly a pull to be with those who have departed. What would life be without Clive to make him laugh, and to make him feel important? What would it all mean if he can't aspire to be a Son? Working seances and sitting alone in the pub are no future. Perhaps the tidal wave has hit and he wasn't even savvy enough to see it.

– Where did you say the Sons have gone, Ron? Stanley asks, returning to the bar.

– Radlett, replies Ron, hunched over the bar on a stool.

– Any particular addresses?

– Not yet. They said they'd be back down when they get settled.

– How long's that gonna take?

– A few weeks. Month, maybe. I dunno.

Too long, Stanley thinks. Beginning to formulate a plan.

He leaves the pub and goes to the flats and houses occupied by Sons or the families of Sons. From Phoenix Road and Polygon Road up to Pratt Street and over to Mornington Terrace. Tries every place, but not one sole remnant of the Sons left. Somers Town has become a ghost town. The only clue to their whereabouts is Ron's Radlett lead. And Barry Stainer's confirmation.

Stanley sees the rest of the week, like the rest of his life, laid out in front of him as a wasteland. He's got to do something. Now that Good Times has gone down the tubes, Clive's buggered off with a broad and the Sons have said the goodbyes. He's thirty-six years old. Too much time has gone. Too many years wasted waiting for the door to the Sons of Arsenal to open. No longer is he going to keep knocking, he's going kick the door down. He's going to be a Son. Smiles to himself when he feels the inspiration. No better time to leave London for a few days and track the lost tribe. That's what he'll do. That is it. He'll find them. If the mountain won't come to Mohammed.

Stanley tells Sylvia that he's taking a holiday. Doesn't mention the hunt for the Sons. She can manage the seances on her own for a few days. She even slips him a twenty-pound note as he bounces through the door carrying his rucksack with two-man tent strapped to the bottom. Camping equipment stolen from his

Boys Brigade days – managed to smuggle the kit out of the storeroom while the rest of the company paced about the hall being drilled.

Makes a mistake by catching a train in late afternoon. There are no seats and he stands squashed between commuters. His rucksack is cumbersome and as the train rocks and rolls Stanley finds himself thumping into other passengers, who tut and sigh and swerve to avoid the swinging bag. He tries to remain cool but his face drips perspiration and the crushing conditions make him too nervous to play it cool, to argue or apologize. There is something sad in his stance. His expression quivers as if he is about to cry. He forgets his age and feels like an infant among adults. Hears the bloke in the shop telling him that his legs are too short. He rides the train to Radlett imagining himself shrinking smaller and smaller amid the crush.

The town is like any suburb, like any town. And so Stanley walks up from the station without regard for the pedestrian crossing, tree-blurred housing, parking bays and bright shops squashed together along the length of the truncated high street.

He passes unhappy faces that make him think of the confident sneer, the well-groomed complexion that most of the Sons have developed. From pasty, blemished inner-city boys most of them transformed into sales-executive lookalikes with criminal records and violent instincts hidden beneath moisturized skin, plucked eyebrows, immaculate hair and sunbed tans. He thinks of their cars; big-name marques, the convertibles, the bold colours.

First, Stanley needs to make a camp. He's not going to rush things. Will enjoy a few days' break. Will plan a dramatic entrance when the Sons have been found. This can not be undertaken hastily. It could ruin everything.

He buys a map of the area and identifies possible sites. Plenty of fields to choose from, away from residential properties and farmyards. He follows the sign to Aldenham along a narrow pavement. Nosing into the gardens and at the façades of the detached houses en route, looking for Arsenal flags or banners posted inside windows. For the obligatory cannon emblem stuck to the front door. No luck. But finds an interesting footpath that leads from the main road towards a village called Letchmore

Heath. The path runs through a field that is sheltered by a row of trees on one side. The field is near enough to the town but far enough away to avoid interference. The ground is dry but sufficiently moist for tent pegs. A shrivelled stream runs through the trees, parallel to the path. Bushy branches laden with leaves will provide shelter from any recurrence of the recent rain.

Stanley enjoys the sense of escape, particularly after the fraught journey. Alone to pitch the tent (which is not as straightforward as he remembers), lay out bedding inside, test the small gas stove, rinse the billy cans with bottled water, boil a pan for a brew, rip open a bag of crisps, make a seat from a milk crate found by the stream, watch the stumbling clouds overhead, and decide whether to have a beef and onion pie now or later.

3

The single bed is hardly ideal but neither wants to tell the landlord about their change in circumstances.

Contentment mitigates the cramped arrangements, and Clive moves as close to the edge as possible to allow Patricia more space.

They lie next to each other naked. His long caramel body alongside her plump whiteness.

Fingers drift over skin trying to locate smoothness. Open hands slowly slide down legs and arms as if attempting to put the limb to sleep.

– You know what would make things perfect, Patricia says quietly. – A nice G and T to relax things.

– We can go out for a d-d-drink, he suggests. – But remember, I'm a b-b-bit of a lightweight.

– I'm not that much of a drinker myself.

There is a settled silence as they consider the prospect.

– W-w-will it help? asks Clive.

– Help what?

– You know, the Mother b-b-business.

– It might be nice.

– You're taking the whole thing so w-w-well.

Patricia pauses. – What else can I do?

– How d-do you stop yourself thinking about it?

– I don't know.

– I'm f-f-f-finding it hard and she wasn't even my mum.

– I don't want to talk about it, Patricia says, with a hint of tetchiness.

– Sorry, he whispers into her ear.

She puts her hand on his knee and caresses an apology.

They take it in turns to shower, and they change in their individual rooms. Clive wears his mauve jacket. Patricia puts on her blue dress. Both attired as for their first date. This coincidence is acknowledged privately, neither wanting to expose the other's lack of wardrobe.

Brighton is busy on the Monday, crowds flocking in and out of the bars and clubs.

The cosmopolitan nature of Brighton is evident during the hot evenings, when the full spectrum of population emerges onto the streets. The gay couples, the young trendies, the old swingers, the dancers, the pensioners with sticks, the transvestites and the holidaying families. There is a buzz in the air and Patricia and Clive can feel it. No one gives them a second glance as they strut the pavement. Not a look at the mauve jacket, the wonky eye, the mixed races, the age gap, the sheer awkwardness of them.

First pub is an old-fashioned affair with low ceiling and real ale. They each order a gin and tonic. Patricia and Clive are high on the atmosphere even without a drink.

The earlier intimacy has also relaxed them. They now know each other in a different way. The hands fit snug without the heat of unfulfilled desire. Body touches are no longer electric but reassuring. The silences contented not gaping.

The first drink is soon downed and Clive is up at the bar ordering the same again.

Patricia watches Clive approvingly as he stands straight and slim in his jacket.

Clive feels conscious of her eyes on him and finds his arms and head unable to move properly, wrapped in some kind of invisible binding.

Second bar is black and metallic, serving cocktails and bottled beers. They read the menu on one of the tables, choosing then changing their minds over what to drink. Eventually they brave the bustling bar and ask for a Blind Man's Fuck and One up the Arse. Patricia doesn't smile when she orders. Her serious expression and sober tone contrasted with the names of the cocktails make Clive laugh. Once the bartender goes to prepare the drinks, Patricia turns to Clive.

– What's so funny? she says innocently.

– D-d-d-don't you r-r-realize what you just asked for? he laughs.

– I got them right, didn't I? A Blind Man's Fuck and One up the Arse.

Clive bends over in hysterics.

– You silly mop, Patricia grins.

He then laughs even louder, bouncing against the bar with tears of laughter spilling all over his face.

– Stop it, chuckles Patricia.

After the stronger-than-expected cocktails, they walk across the road to a theme pub. Huge great theatre of drinking, complete with pillars, mirrors and several floor levels.

Tucked into a corner on the second tier of tables, they wrap in each other's arms, leaving a hand free for drinks. The music is loud and so conversation is reduced to a minimum. Their embracing bodies say everything.

Two more drinks later, she fondles the back of his hair, strokes the nape of his neck, pushes her mouth over his ear and says. – I love you.

Clive has never had a woman say that to him and he is stunned.
– D-d-d-do you r-r-really? he says over the music.

Patricia nods eagerly, mouthing the words 'I do, I really do.'

– Thanks, he replies, shaking his head with disbelief.

– Do you love me? she shouts back.

– Of c-c-course I do! he yells.

They both smile. They both want to kiss, but their positions are tricky to negotiate and the pull of the drinks too hard to resist.

This is the best pub by far. Not because of the beer or the music or the interior, but because of the intimacy. They are slightly reluctant to leave but Patricia wants another One up the Arse and so they help each other up from the seats and stagger towards the door.

Back in the cocktail bar, Clive is too drunk to stand and wait at the bar. He finds a seat, scans the menu and asks for a beer – the cocktails are too much.

Through drowsy eyes, Clive watches Patricia try to catch the attention of a bartender.

She is standing by a group of guys obviously on a night out, wearing smart shirts and slacks. They are swigging bottles and throwing shifty stares at Patricia's bottom. Clive is not comfortable observing from a seat by the front window.

One of the guys next to Patricia sees that she is not getting served and calls out for a barman. Almost instantly one appears and the guy points to Patricia.

Patricia smiles a thank-you and orders the drinks.

As she waits, the guy who got her the barman appears by her side.

– You've got to shout to get anything in here, he grins.

– I'm not much of a shouter, replies Patricia.

The guy can tell Patricia is drunk: one of her eyes is all over the show and her speech is stiff. He studies the blue dress and notices that the material is loose around her chest. If he peered down he would be able to see her tits. The guy is not interested in Patricia but he is up for a laugh, and up for the opportunity to flirt and maybe make her keen. He winks to a friend standing close.

– Can I tell you something secret? the guy says to Patricia.

Patricia puts the change in her purse. – What's that? she smiles.

– You'll have to come close, he grins, putting his finger on the neck of the dress and pulling her towards him so that the front of the frock stretches out. He stares down onto the exposed chest.

– You're wearing a white bra, he whispers conspiratorially.

Patricia pushes his hand away. – Get off, she says jokily. She is not offended, she is inebriated. Assumes these sorts of things happen in modern pubs.

The guy's friends become aware of the scene and they turn to see what's going on. They watch him drop to his knees in front of Patricia.

– Now what colour panties? he laughs, slipping his fingers to the hem of the dress.

– Don't you dare, Patricia says, still half-heartedly, shoving his head backwards.

– Spoilsport, the guy says, getting to his feet.

– I'm too old for you, Patricia adds.

– Can I at least get a kiss for getting you served? he says with a glint. – Just a peck, he continues, proffering his cheek.

– Go on then, you charmer.

As she goes to put a kiss on his cheek, the guy quickly turns his face so that she kisses him full on the lips.

– That wasn't the deal, Patricia jokingly protests.

– You know you liked it, he teases.

She takes hold of the drinks. – Well, I'd better leave you to chat up the next unsuspecting woman.

– You're a good sport, he smiles. – No offence.

– Bye, she smiles back, balancing her cocktail and Clive's bottle of beer.

Turning to the seats, there is no sign of Clive. Probably gone to the toilet, thinks Patricia. But then catching a glimpse of the mauve jacket flash past the window. She thumps the drinks on the table and runs for the door.

Clive is standing against the window of the neighbouring shop. Fidgeting with the buttons of his jacket. Looking agitated.

– What are you doing? Patricia asks as she approaches, taking hold of his arm.

Without looking at her, he pulls his arm away and turns to stare into the shop window.

– What's wrong? she says.

– I saw what was h-h-h-happening at the b-bar.

Patricia huffs. – He was only having a bit of fun. He wasn't being serious.

He shakes his head to deflect her excuse. – Why d-d-did you do that?

– I didn't do anything, she argues.

His jacket seems uncomfortable and he wriggles around trying to loosen its constraint. – You k-k-k-kissed him.

Resigned to the misunderstanding, Patricia drops her arms to her side and takes a deep breath. – He was being silly. Couldn't you see that?

Clive doesn't think. – I c-c-can't believe that with all that's happened, you act as if you haven't a c-c-c-care in the world.

She doesn't get sucked in. – Stop been ridiculous, Clive. We're having such a nice time together, don't ruin it by being all funny.

His reflection in the window is grey and obscure. It suits him. He turns around to face Patricia. She looks so nice in her blue dress. – After what happened b-b-between us this afternoon, how can you be like this?

– Like what?

– I g-g-guess you've finished with me now and are looking for the next man?

– Did you listen earlier when I told you that I love you? Her arms open and she waits for him to embrace her.

The drink has altered him and it is harder than usual for Clive to get a grip on things. – Maybe this is y-y-your way of d-dealing with things?

– Maybe it is. But anything that happened in the bar was harmless. The boy was playing around. He was being friendly. What would you have wanted me to do?

– I don't know.

Patricia can see the resistance weakening. – Clive, I would never hurt you.

– I'm not used to this sort of th-thing.

– We're both new to it. Let's enjoy it. Let's go back and have our drinks.

Clive raises a little grin.

– One up the Arse? she smiles.

The grin breaks into a smile.

– You look so handsome when you laugh.

– You m-m-must be drunk, he jokes.

184

Out of This World

1

The first night was colder than Stanley expected. Once the daylight went a dampness descended and the wind began to flap at the tent. He slept on the groundsheet under a sleeping bag, gradually folding himself up into a lump as the night progressed. Waking intermittently during the early-morning hours to shiver. At one point, out of desperation, he lit the gas fire and allowed its ferocious blue flame to heat the inside of the tent. He fell back to sleep, waking with a jolt half an hour later to cut the gas before the canvas ignited.

He is well organized considering it is his first camping expedition. Bags of supplies are stored in a nearby tree and at the foot of the tent. Matches, torch, string, lock-knife, hooks; he's seen the survival programmes on television. Though wasn't prepared for the strange and unnerving array of sounds that tormented him once it got dark. Rustles on the outside of the tent, snaps in the trees, splashes from the stream and growls from the middle of the field. Stanley slept with his knife.

Stanley wakes at around seven o'clock on the Tuesday morning. Famished. Eats a cereal bar, followed by bread toasted over the gas stove and smeared in peanut butter. Consumes a packet of Twiglets, a tin of baked beans, a handful of smoked ham from the plastic packet, a couple of tomatoes, and a cold sausage roll. He drinks a coffee. A tea. Cooks some more toast (this time with jam), eats a bag of peanuts, two apples, a banana, a chocolate bar, half a packet of ginger nuts. Finished off by a handful of wine gums.

The open-air lifestyle produces some hunger.

He takes a bottle of water and empties it over his head, rubbing it in and wiggling his fingers inside his ears. Runs a comb through his hair. Opens up the tent to allow fresh air to circulate. Sorts out the bedding, shaking out the sleeping bag. Assesses the grumpy sky. Cleans the cup and cans. Looks back in the box for more food. Demolishes the last of the ginger nuts, has a packet of bacon crisps, a second packet of bacon crisps. Munches a Scotch egg, a large slice of salami, two chunks of Cheddar cheese, a pickled onion, another pickled onion, five sesame seed breadsticks, four jam tarts, eight squares of white chocolate, six Starbursts, a bag of M&Ms. And an orange.

He uses the mobile phone to call Sylvia and touch base. Reluctant to turn it on in case it rings before he can dial home. Still not ready to deal with another escort situation.

Sylvia's voice is empty and faraway. The house echoes. A crackle on the line makes her sound even more hopeless.

– Mr Furtle is coming over as usual, she says.

– Don't forget the whisky, Stanley replies.

– I'm not sleeping.

– Maybe you should have the whisky?

Two timid laughs. The stilted conversation grasps for presence but distant voices fail.

– How long are you going to be up there? she asks.

– Won't be long.

– How long is that?

– When I've done what I've got to do.

– I don't know why you want to be up there.

– The houses have all got gardens.

– Can't waste time messing about in a garden.

– You'd like it on a summer's day.

– You better not be thinking about getting me up there.

– I'll be coming back, don't worry.

– Do you need any money?

– I'm OK for the moment.

– Food?

– They have got shops.

– You take care, boy.

– Mustn't run down the battery.

Radlett is a narrow town centred on the thin main road. Stanley decides to lurk near the shops, to spy on any known faces making an appearance. Finds a small Methodist church on the opposite side to the row of shops. A path runs down one side and affords Stanley a concealed view. He leans against the wall and tears apart a packet of Maltesers. Opens a tube of Smarties. He will phone Clive tonight.

Stanley runs across the road to the mini-market and replenishes the temporary tuck supply. Returns to the edge of the little church. Bites on a Walnut Whip. Hopes Sylvia will be OK. She does not like it when he's away. So protective of him since Sausage died. Licks the melted chocolate off the wrapper. She wants him to find a job he enjoys, to meet someone he likes, and stay at the flat. Mouthful of Jamaica ginger cake. Sylvia and Stanley don't talk a lot when they're at home. It's more about being there. A security. Work is a comfort and purpose for her. Stanley plays his part in his black suit and oiled hair. He splits a packet of chilled frankfurters.

Sitting by the church wall, as daylight dims and faces and figures become shadows, he eats three bags of dry-roasted peanuts, two chicken salad sandwiches, a packet of tortilla chips with salsa dip, a strawberry yoghurt, a Snickers, and a bar of Dairy Milk. Drinks a can of Lilt and a bottle of Lucozade. Becomes excited when a pub across the road lights up. The Dick and Turpin. Hunger ignored as the prospect of patrolling the local drinking dens motivates. Certain that the Sons will have established a regular spot for congregation and beverage. The Brewers transplanted to Radlett. Filled with the same shirts and shouts. Checks the watch and decides it's time to explore.

Peering into windows, catching glimpses through doors as people enter and exit. Three pubs along the main road and no sign of the Sons.

A disappointing day. Wanders slowly the mile back to tent. Perhaps they're not in Radlett?

Above the silhouetted trees London is a trembling corona.

2

Stanley wakes at ten on the Wednesday. Clammy. Gets dressed inside the tent. Clothes damp from touching the canvas condensation. Unzips and crawls through the opening. The morning air is flimsy. His bones crack as he stretches. Wipes lank hair out of his face. Looks at the food-bag tied to the tree.

He slept later than he thought. Surprised at eleven hours' sleep in such uncomfortable conditions. Kept waking up confused. The folded clothes for a pillow seemed to disintegrate into his fingers as the night went on. He kept trying to reinvigorate the pile with his hands but by morning the clump of clothing seemed no more than a handkerchief.

Cupping water in his hands, he throws it over his head. Losing breath with the shock of the cold. Shaking his head like a dog, soaking the neckline of his sweatshirt.

– I can see you from my bedroom window, a girl's voice calls out.

Stanley looks up through his bedraggled hair at a young girl coming towards him. She appears fifteen or sixteen, though Stanley can't tell any more, with girls developing so fast. Dark hair tied behind in a ponytail. White jeans tucked into muddy boots. A dog on a leash.

– Keep that dog away from me, Stanley says. – I ain't keen on mutts.

The girl smirks.

– I'll kick it if it comes near me, he threatens.

– I've only come to say hello.

Stanley stares at the dog.

– I can see you from my bedroom window, she repeats, pointing to a distant line of trees from behind which pokes a tiled roof.

Stanley's attention turns to the girl now that she stands still and the dog sniffs her boots. She's pretty. He doesn't know what to say.

– You shouldn't leave your tent up all day. You're lucky no one takes it, she says.

– People don't steal out here.

– And you shouldn't leave your food out like that.

– People have respect for other people's stuff in the countryside.

– Who told you that? she asks.

– Everyone knows.

The girl smirks again.

She stands taller than Stanley.

He can't read her pretty face.

– What's it like living in a tent? she asks.

– OK.

– I would just love the freedom. I've got plans to travel when I'm older.

– Oh yeah?

– I'm going to get out and see the world.

– You shouldn't waste your time with all that. You want to be getting work and making money, climbing the ladder.

– I thought you're meant to be the tramp, not me?

Stanley squirms. – I ain't no tramp. I'm camping.

– What's the difference?

– I've got a home to go back to.

– Where are you from?

– London.

– You've got your own place in town?

– Course I have.

– How big is it?

– Big enough.

– London's boring.

– Like excitement, do you? Stanley asks.

– Only boring people get bored.

– You're only young.

– How old do you think I am?

– I dunno. Sixteen?

– That'll do, she smiles.

Stanley feels shoddy next to her. His damp clothes and hair.

– I think people should enjoy themselves more, she says.

– Fair comment.

– You only get one life.

– I suppose.

– If you want something you've got to go for it, don't you think?

– Are you still at school? asks Stanley.

– Yes, she replies defensively.

– They teach you all this at school?

– We're taught to think.

– Different to my day.

– How old are you?

– A bit older than you.

– How old? Go on, tell me.

– Don't you worry, Stanley says, worried that she'll laugh if he told her.

– Older guys are much better than the arseholes my age.

– Eh? he says, taken aback.

– All my girlfriends go with older men.

Stanley has a rush of blood to the head. – What's your name? he croaks.

– Shannon, she says with a show of teeth.

– Stanley, he replies.

– I'm glad I came over.

– Yeah, Stanley nods.

– I'm not sure Mum would be too keen if I told her.

– Don't.

– I won't.

– So that's your house over there, is it?

– You can just about see my bedroom window.

– Bedroom?

– I'm often up there looking out. It's beautiful with all the fields. I never close my curtains, she grins.

– How often do you walk the mutt? Stanley says, changing the subject.

– I'm always having to do it, she says with an exaggerated groan.

– Might see you again, then?

– Maybe, she smirks, pulling the lead and dragging the dog back the way they came.

3

Stanley decides a new tack. Decides to walk every residential road of Radlett in an effort to find some evidence of the Sons. He cannot face sitting next to the church for another nine hours – even if it is near to the snack-filled mini-market.

Up avenues, down roads, along drives, through lanes, over bridges and into closes. Suspicious stares from the windows of houses and bungalows. Stanley keeps his notebook at the ready. Still no sign of the migrated Somers Town community.

By ten o'clock in the evening, following a hefty feed (cold pizza, ham in a baguette, a can of sweetcorn, three Mars bars), he is lying on the sleeping bag back in the tent. He thinks about Shannon. Never had too much luck with girls. He talked things up to Clive, gave an impression of man of the world.

The time on the school trip to Colchester when he went missing for an hour. Told Clive and the rest of the class he was shagging a girl from a south London comprehensive. Had really spent the time walking the shops.

The time he split from Clive on one of their rare nights out in the West End. Told Clive he had met a model from Maida Vale and spent the night at her penthouse pad. Had really ended up walking the city at night and standing alone on Westminster Bridge.

Stanley knew the stories smelt wrong but he told them none-theless.

Shannon liked him, he was certain. Something about her smirks, her references to older men, the mention of her bedroom window. She was attractive. Stanley imagines her. Then reconsi-ders the bedroom window. Maybe she is looking for him. The binoculars are to hand. It has been raining and the field will be muddy. Wide awake and bored, he cannot stop himself from lacing up his shoes and pushing out of the tent. To the house hidden behind branches.

From the middle of the field the bedroom is visible. The light is on. Stanley focuses the binoculars. There is no sign of Shannon. He walks nearer. Next to the hedge, the room is out of sight. A fir tree will provide a vantage point. He ignores the soaking from the wet needles as he pushes feet onto branches and hands into fronds. Arrives halfway up and dangles, gripping the trunk with his right hand. Uses the left hand to hold and focus the binoculars. He feels uncomfortable peeping into a bedroom window at night. And yet there is a thrill. And then she appears, walking to the window and pressing cupped hands against the glass to peer out. Stanley pulls the binoculars away with fright. Pushes himself deeper into the tree.

She pulls back, wipes away condensation. Wearing a vest. Her hair loose.

He repoints the binoculars.

She moves into the middle of the room under the light made mute by a blue shade.

His hands shake and in response he tightens the grip.

She grabs the sides of the vest and begins a slow undress. The top folds. Her stomach appears.

His foot slips. The right arm tries to hold the weight but needs help. The left hand automatically gropes for support, floundering into the tree without finding contact. He starts heading downwards. The rubbery branches bounce him from side to side until Stanley hits the soaked ground. Winded by the fall he bites for breath. Rolls onto his front and chews on grass. Gradually clambers to his feet just as the bedroom switches into black. Stanley hobbles back to the tent guiltily.

Within These Walls

1

Two nights have passed and Pow-Wow is yet to stick Lewis with the knife. The days have been spent on the wing, as usual; Lewis holed up in the cell while Pow-Wow sits in front of the box or beats the other kids at pool.

As the evenings approach Pow-Wow gets more uneasy, the thought of blading Lewis plays games inside his head. Turning the simple deal into something more sinister. Slotting a blade means nothing – he's done it before. But Lewis is not an anonymous face under a cap in Adidas apparel.

There is Free Association tomorrow, Thursday. When he will be back out to face Coach and crew. Tonight is the last opportunity to wet the blade and get himself back inside the folds of the gang. Pow-Wow knows how tricky life could get if he fails. He's watched Birds being battered in the yard. Heard about them being shafted. And these are just the muppets without a crew or status. Pow-Wow is an All-Star, more is expected from him. His betrayal would be bad business. When he's back on the streets things will get worse.

He tries to avoid interaction with Lewis as the cell balances a silence. Pow-Wow pretends to enjoy the music coming through his headphones but the beats are sour. The tea Lewis made, and Pow-Wow is loath to sip, is also foul. Tea made in the normal way, with the same tea bags, fresh milk, and usual good intentions. Yet it is the latter ingredients that make Pow-Wow grimace as he drinks.

The security lights ignite at nine thirty p.m. as the last hints of purple sky fade. The courtyard is quiet; the shouting won't really

193

begin until later. But Pow-Wow can feel a sadness. Sadness in the way Lewis keeps throwing over glances, hoping to catch his eye and share a smile or some kind of communication. But Pow-Wow is keeping his head straight and ignoring the desperate glares coming at him from across the room. He turns off his side-light and enjoys the screen of darkness. Tucked into the corner of the room with a knife hidden beneath the bedclothes.

Ten o'clock, lights out. Lewis lays down his book and switches the room into sleep. – Night, he whispers.

Pow-Wow tenses at the voice and doesn't reply.

Two a.m. Cold night from the breeze breathing through the window. Lewis a lump in the opposite sack. Sleeping face turned to wall.

Pow-Wow gently rises from his bed. The chill licks him. The floor freezes his feet. His track-suit bottoms sweep the ground as he inches towards the lump. The uncertain light seems to create movement on the bed. Pow-Wow waits by the table to assess the situation. The light plays tricks. Pow-Wow edges nearer.

Never rammed a friend before. And Lewis is a friend. A real nice guy who kept his distance but made the effort with the tea, the banter, his studies. Even though his parents had given up on him.

And for what? Pow-Wow thinks, his mind working fast. Save himself? Make things easier? He'll soon be back in Willesden and he won't be afraid of the gangsters. They've taken up too much of his life already.

– It ain't gonna happen, Pow-Wow says to himself.

The heap in the bed stirs.

– I ain't gonna do it, Pow-Wow confirms.

Lewis mumbles into the pillow and rolls onto his back.

Pow-Wow gradually steps back towards his bed.

– Is that you, Pow-Wow? Lewis yawns.

– It ain't nothing. Go back to sleep, man.

– You on the night watch? Lewis says.

– Something like that, bro.

2

The next day, Pow-Wow strolls towards Coach. The guys around Coach lean back with arms folded and watch Pow-Wow with tilted heads. Not one word. Coach puffs on a stick and blows clouds over the surface of the picnic bench.

Pow-Wow digs into his shirt and throws the knife, wrapped in a bag, onto the table in front of an uninterested Coach.

– I hope you ain't left no blood on the blade, Coach says.

– There ain't no blood, brother, Pow-Wow replies.

– You sure you rammed the kid?

– I did what I had to do.

Coach looks up to face Pow-Wow. – I didn't hear no alarm.

– No need for alarm.

– I didn't hear no wail-wagons.

– As I say, Coach. I did what I had to do.

– You better had ripped him good. You ain't the type of snake to go making things rough for yourself.

– Lewis isn't a problem, says Pow-Wow.

3

Pow-Wow chooses to spend the rest of the day in the cell. It's not that he's afraid to wander the wing, it's just that he wants to get some peace and take stock. Prepare for the changes that are bound to come.

More determined than ever to forget the pressures to conform and forge his own future. Things happen, lessons are learnt. Coach can't offer him anything any more.

Lewis shines at the table under his reading lamp, which is not really needed as daylight still floods the room.

Six p.m. Three officers in too-tight uniforms squeeze into the cell. One of them clutching a piece of paper.

– Davenant, the one holding the sheet says.

– Yo, Pow-Wow replies.

– You're moving.

– I don't need no mother-fucking Rule 43.

– Rule 43?

– I can rock my own parties.

The officers grin.

– You're not up for Protection, you're moving to D wing, the first one says.

– That can't be right, Lewis interrupts.

– Gather your crap. We'll wait on the walk.

The officers leave the cell.

Lewis doesn't know where to look. His stare flicks from the table to Pow-Wow. – They've got it wrong.

– Don't listen to those deadheads, they're taking me to Protection, Pow-Wow says confidently.

– Why would they do that? Lewis asks.

– It's a tale, home.

Lewis stands up from the table. – I don't want this to happen.

– You heard the fuckers. What can I do? he says, beginning to collect his things.

Lewis scans the floor for inspiration. – But we get on.

– I hear that, Pow-Wow nods, grabbing his toothbrush and paste.

– We've worked well together.

– You got it.

– Friends?

– Sure, man. Damn right we're friends.

Lewis tries to smile. It's faint, obscured by a fear. – I don't want this to happen.

Pow-Wow places the rest of his possessions on the bedding. Turns to Lewis and notices him twitching. – Ain't no big thing. I'll be back. You keep those books warm.

D wing is colder, brighter, than remand. The atmosphere is tight. More clinical. Which surprises Pow-Wow, who imagined the permanent wings to be more homely.

With his belongings wrapped in the blankets and draped over shoulder like Father Christmas, Pow-Wow walks along the corridor. Passing closed doors and spotless walls. Pushed inside an open cell. A single bed. Stainless-steel ablutions. Carpeted floor.

– This is Protection, right? Pow-Wow asks.

– I told you, it's D wing, the officer replies.

– But it is a 43 wing, yeah?

– You'll soon find out when the boys come back.

Pow-Wow busies about the cell, sorts out bed and toiletries. Tests the kettle. Lies back on the bed and watches the white ceiling turn grey. Hears breathing and turns to see a muscular white guy in the doorway, wearing a top that shows off the developed upper body.

Pow-Wow sits up, eager to leap into the guy invading his space without so much as a door knock. Keen to let people know that this black boy ain't going to take none. But decides to play things easy and work out the ways of D wing before jumping into conclusions and conflict.

– What's the throw, cousin? Pow-Wow asks.

The white guy sniffs and peers at Pow-Wow through the side of his eyes.

– I'm the new guy, I know the deal, says Pow-Wow.

Again, the guy offers only a sniff for response and swaps his weight onto his other leg.

– I'm not going to make all the effort round here, Pow-Wow says quietly. – How about a helping hand?

Nothing.

– I'm Pow-Wow.

– Kill old white ladies, the guy says coldly.

– Not me, man.

– Fold old white ladies into boxes.

– You got the wrong rat, man.

– That could've been my nan.

– Rest it, big gun. You ain't got your facts.

– You've got what's coming.

Pow-Wow is unable to ignore the provocation. Jumps into the guy's face. – No mother-fucker porcupine is going to make threats.

The white guy is unflinching, his eyes still leer lazily.

– Walk the plank, hank, before I do my stuff, Pow-Wow says.

The white guy casually turns his back and wanders into the corridor. – Catch you later.

That first night, Pow-Wow is woken by the sound of the door being unlocked. Half-asleep, Pow-Wow strains to make out a bundle of bodies emerging from the brightness of corridor. They are gibbering excitedly and pushing and feeling their way into the darkness of the cell.

Pow-Wow is swallowed up and dragged out of the sheets and onto the floor. Feet and fists begin to batter his body.

Within two minutes Pow-Wow is motionless.

An officer pokes his head into the cell. – Get back into bed, son, he says, closing the door and relocking the bolt.

Nowhere to Ride

1

Stanley wakes early on the Thursday and ensures an acceptable appearance in anticipation of Shannon's return. Stands around by the tent looking incongruous and pretending to tighten guy ropes and adjust loosened pegs. A dog barks and Stanley looks along the edge of the field to see Shannon approach. Contains his nerves by playing with the entrance zip as if it is caught. Gives up the pretence and stands to greet her.

– I came over to see you yesterday but you weren't here, she says.

– I was a bit busy.

– I thought of you when it was raining.

– Don't you go to school?

– Only when I feel like it.

– What do your parents say?

– Mum doesn't care.

– Dad?

– Gone.

– Oh.

– She's got a boyfriend.

Stanley nods slowly.

– They call you the tramp.

– I'm camping, Stanley protests.

– Ignore them, they've only seen the tent.

– Tell them I'm camping.

– Mum wants to call the police.

– Don't be stupid.

Shannon surveys the tent. – Are you enjoying your camp?

– Not bad.

– Maybe I should buy a tent?

– Is your mum strict?

– I can pretty much do my own thing. She doesn't let me smoke weed in the house.

Stanley steps back. – You're a bit young for all that, aren't you?

– I can get you stronger stuff if you like.

– You serious?

– What do you want?

– And you're sixteen?

– Man, I've been smoking blow since I was twelve.

Stanley stares, quizzical.

– I better not tell you what I was doing when I was thirteen, she laughs.

Stanley returns a frightened giggle.

Shannon throws her head back. – And I thought you were going to teach me lots of things.

Stanley fights his inferiority. – Don't get me wrong, I'm a geezer, I've played a few cards in my time.

– How much travelling have you done? she asks, with a sudden straight face.

– You name it I've been there, he shrugs, now playing the part, on the offensive.

– Spain?

– Loved it.

– Africa?

– Magic.

– The States?

– Superb.

– You've been out in the world and done it. That's so wacky.

– You've got to take the bull by the horns, that's what I say.

– I tried to see you from the window last night. I thought you might have a fire going or something.

Stanley gulps. Returns a strained smile.

– Maybe you'd like to come over for a bath? she suggests.

– Oh, I don't know . . .

– Mum's often out. You must want a nice bath.

– I, er . . .

– I could you make you some proper food?
– I can always eat, Stanley says.
– Well, do you want to come over?
– When are you talking?
– This afternoon?
– Bit soon, isn't it?
– You want to come or not?
– Could do, Stanley says, trying not to look petrified.
– I've got some weed tucked away, she winks.
– What time?
– Around three. Come round the back.

That morning, in Radlett, Stanley gets his first taste of success. Waiting by the church, he catches sight of Dean's mum. Stanley is excited. His head thumps. Things float like a dream. She is carrying a handbag and looking older than he remembered her. He used to fancy Dean's mum.

He follows her from the shops, along an avenue of semi-detached houses. Follows from a distance, pretending his note-book is a map and carefully considering each house and its number as if lost. She turns off the wide road and into a cul-de-sac. To a large bungalow in the corner.

Stanley notes the house number, the road, the time, the car in the drive – which isn't Dean's. But the Sons are near.

Rain smacks the tent. The weather changes so quickly. He ran all the way back from the town clutching carrier bags full of supplies.

Lying in the sleeping bag, hand propping up head, Stanley flicks through the notebook, pleased with his information on Dean's mum. Expertly compiled, he considers. Clandestine.

He fingers through the rest of the pad, stumbles across the Arsenal fixture list he brought with him and kicks himself for not thinking about it earlier. Tomorrow, Friday. Testimonial match against Real Madrid. In Spain. The Sons won't travel abroad any more – they don't even go to away games unless in London. Bound to be a local pub that will show the game for the group of twenty supporters. The match will be bait and Stanley will be ready to make the catch. He clenches his fist and punches the air.

But the exhilaration is short-lived. It is three p.m. and he has the bath date with Shannon. He heads for the house across the sodden field. Trudging over the mud, his shoes transform into sloppy bricks.

He taps on the back door. Waits longer than he expects. Taps again. Door opens.

– You made it, she says.

– Of course.

– You'd better leave your shoes on the step, she laughs.

He follows her into the kitchen. His damp socks leave prints on the floor. But he is not concerned, gazing at the short dressing gown that ends above her knees. Hair let loose to fall over her back.

She leads him upstairs and Stanley trembles.

At the top of the stairs she turns to Stanley. – You better have that bath first, she says.

– Yeah, sure, Stanley splutters, pricked by the word 'first'.

The bathroom is bright. Shannon pulls the shades and the room turns pink.

She stands there with her arms folded, looking Stanley up and down.

He looks at her shins. Shiny shins.

– Your hair could do with a wash, she says, breezing from the room.

Stanley hits the hot water and begins to fill the bath. As it flows he climbs out of the greasy clothes. Down to his pants. Reluctant to remove the underwear just yet; he'll wait until the bath is ready and bursting with the scents and oils dribbled from elegantly designed bottles resting on the bath rim.

Outside the room he can hear music: soft, soulful melodies. He imagines untying the knot to her gown. Pulling her open like a curtain.

Stanley lowers himself into the tub, scalding his feet but eager to get in and out and to the bedroom as soon as possible. The tell-tale waft of cannabis floats under the door. He plunges his head into the water and the music becomes a distant thump. The steady beat broken by a loud thud. Stanley pulls up quick, hears a voice calling out. A man's voice. He leaps from the water. Grabs large towel. Flicks open door and peers out onto the landing.

Shannon stares panic from her bedroom door.

– Shannon? the man shouts from downstairs. – Where are you?

– Quick, hide. In there, she says, pointing to a bedroom.

Stanley bundles his clothes and dashes into the empty room, climbing behind a curtain.

– Where are you? the voice calls again.

– Up here, having a bath, she calls back.

Stanley listens to the man coming up the stairs, then opening the bathroom door.

– There you are, the man says.

– Where's Mum? Shannon asks.

– I've left her there. I thought to myself, why miss such an opportunity? We don't get much time together.

– I'm not feeling too good.

– I'll soon sort that out.

– Not now.

– Come on, Shan. What a chance.

– I'm about to go out.

– You know how things are.

– I'm not up to it.

– Come on, let me make you feel better.

There is a splashing of water. A grunt. A sigh. Footsteps going from the bathroom to the bedroom. The sound of bedsprings. A rustle of clothing. A series of whispers.

Using the noises as cover, Stanley slips out from his hiding place. Dresses. Stands frozen in the doorway. Begins to move towards the stairs.

– Oh, Shannon, the man growls.

First foot on the top step.

– Yeah, the man grunts.

Stanley tiptoes a descent. Towards the back door. On with clodded shoes, through the hedge, away from house.

2

Friday morning is a smothering of light through the thin canvas tent. Warm and green-tinged. After a night of uncomfortable dreams and a nightmare of Clive getting married. The bad head is soon soothed by the thought that the Sons are in sight. Stanley rarely wakes up quickly, yet he is soon splashing water over his body and sparking the gas stove for tea. Whistling an Incognito tune from the *Best of British Jazz Funk*, Volume 1.

The business with Shannon is forgotten. A shame that it didn't happen. Maybe a blessing in disguise – he might have embarrassed himself. Perhaps there is still time for a sequel with Shannon. Once the more important matters are concluded.

Not very hungry – for a change. A cup of tea and a couple of Snickers suffice for breakfast. It is nearly eleven and he wants to be on the hunt by twelve – when the pubs open and when the Sons will congregate.

Looks across the field in case of an appearance by Shannon. Coming over to offer an apology and a rearranged time. There is no sign of her. Only the house is visible, peeping at him from behind its camouflage.

His clothes are a bit scraggy. Damp and creased from storage in the tent. Didn't bring much clobber with him. A few days was always going to be enough to track down his prey and then return home to regroup. The track-suit trousers are stretched at the knee and hang out in front. The sweatshirt is dotted with toothpaste stains. Not the best gear to impress the Sons. But his appearance is not important; he'll make his stamp with stories of business success. How many of them have been paid to play strip poker?

The walk to Radlett is a happy one, full of expectation. The town is smiling and Stanley smiles with it. Greeting people with a grin and a hello; largely ignored by the passers-by and pensioners working their gardens. Stanley doesn't notice their lack of response.

Strides into the cab office and beams at the man behind the glass screen. – I'm looking for a car to take me around all the local pubs, he says.

– Some kind of pub crawl? the man asks.

– No, I'm not stopping at the pubs to drink. I just want to nip in and out. I'm looking for some friends.

– You one of those Guns of Arsenal?

– Sons, Sons. How do you know about the Sons?

The man remains dour. – You'll want a car to the Wheelers then. That's where they live.

– Are you winding me up? Stanley says.

– I run a taxi firm. I know what's going on.

– You know the pub the Sons drink at?

– Do you want a car or not?

The days spent aimlessly wandering and waiting now seem a little wasteful. Never thought of asking. However, Stanley is not disappointed, the break has been better than he could have imagined. He's proved a few things to himself into the bargain.

The Wheelers is a large country pub set on its own. Garden and children's playground to one side, large shingle car park to the other.

Before he goes to the bar, Stanley scans the car park to name-check the motors. Dean's Porsche. Kenny's Merc. Darren's BMW. Martin's Audi. He stands among them smiling. Then walks with a strut towards the door.

The gathering of Sons turns and holds drinks still. A few mumbles, a few uncertain glares.

– All right, boys, Stanley smiles.

– What's going on? says Dean.

Stanley struts to the bar, through a stunned crowd. – Drinks on me, he calls out.

Orders for beers are shouted out from around the pub.

– Are you good for all this? the landlord asks Stanley.

– You take cards, yeah? Stanley asks with anxious eyes.

The landlord nods as he starts pulling pints.

Dean sidles up alongside Stanley. – What brings you up here?

– A bit of country air.

– Don't tell me Cl-cl-clive is up here and all? Dean teases.

– He's in Brighton with his woman.

– Clive with a woman?

– Things are changing, Deano. Things are changing, smiles Stanley.

Bottles and pints of premium lager are distributed about the group. Stanley is thanked with a couple of hair ruffles and a few slaps on the back. The hair-ruffling hands return to wipe themselves on Stanley's sweatshirt.

– Dressed for the occasion, I see, Dean says, looking him up and down.

– I save all my good clothes for work, nowadays.

Dean sips from a pint. – Work?

– I run my own male escort agency, he says casually, deciding to use the story even though the phone has been off for days.

– You what?

– You know, growing business, plenty of women with money.

– I assume you've got proper people working for you?

Stanley can see the line of enquiry. Best keep quiet about Clive and his own exploits. Dean has got a point. – I've got models, blokes with degrees, guys with the right equipment, if you get my meaning.

Dean is clearly taken aback. – And you're making nice loot from this?

Stanley plays it cool. He wrinkles his nose. – We do all right. We've no complaints.

– What about in a week? Are we talking tens, hundreds . . . thousands?

Again, Stanley refuses to commit himself. – We do all right, he winks, allowing his smugness to do the talking.

– Fuck, Dean swallows.

Stanley lets the silence between them increase his status. He can see himself becoming a man of few words.

– And we all had you down for a total loser, continues Dean.

A clearing of the throat and a reach for the drink give Stanley time to compose himself. He's playing the man who's about to make it, not a man about to lose it. – That's up to you, he croaks.

– If anyone was going to end up staying in Somers Town without a job or a future it was going to be you and Clive. Let's face it.

– Cheers, Stanley mumbles.

– I don't mean to be cruel, Stanley. But come on. You think of some of those shitty little schemes you kept trying to organize. Roping in poor old Clive to do your dirty work.

– What do you mean? says Stanley.

– Oh, I don't know. Your window cleaning and that.

– I was learning the basics of business. We've all got to start at the bottom.

– You never seemed to leave the bottom.

– And Clive enjoyed working with me.

– No use for him now, though, I guess. Not exactly prime male escort material, is he? How's he taking your success?

Stanley delays an answer by bringing out the mobile phone and pretending to check it for missed calls. – Clive's doing fine. I can afford to look after him.

The conversation slips away. Dean is thoughtful as he pours the pint into his mouth.

– We're not staying here to watch the match, says Dean.

– Where you off to? asks Stanley.

– Sports Bar in Watford. You bring your motor?

– Left the Jaguar in London, says Stanley.

– Jaguar, eh? How about coming to the bar in my wagon?

– Sounds spot on. One for the road?

After sinking three pints in the Wheelers the Sons make their way to the assortment of cars.

It has begun to rain and Dean and Stanley rush to the Porsche. Stanley sits in the front seat, beers lubricating thought. He looks through the windscreen at the convoy of motors trundling over gravel.

– How do you like Donald Byrd? Dean asks.

– Class.

The trail of cars parades along Radlett high street.

– I need to get some cash, Dean says. – Trouble is the machine ate my card yesterday. Can you sub me?

Stanley is a little edgy. Already put fifty pounds on his overdraft in the pub. Could probably spare a ten or twenty. – How much do you need? he drawls, still playing the part.

– Two hundred?

– Right, nods Stanley, putting his lower lip over his top.
– Where's the cash-point?

He leaves the car, walks across to the bank and withdraws the cash. His account flashes up a warning.

– There you go, Stanley grins, passing Dean the money in the motor.

– Got the cash, all we need is the girls, smiles Dean, pushing the cash into his wallet.

– That'd be nice, agrees Stanley.

– And here they come now, right on time.

Two girls appear out of the Wimpy, sheltering under jackets and umbrellas. All that is visible is two long pairs of bare legs.

– Right movers, I can tell you. Shag anything, Dean says, sliding down his window. – Shannon! he shouts out.

One hundred miles per hour along the M1. Cars indicate left and pull over as Dean drives up behind them. Shannon and her friend, Melanie, sit silently in the back. Stanley is not bothered by Shannon. In fact, he couldn't care less. At least she wanted him. And there is nothing she can say to Dean about the tent or the things he's told her that he wouldn't be able to explain away.

Stanley is smiling because he is in Dean's car, driving to watch the Arsenal. Part of a convoy. Part of something.

Despite the miserable sky, the clouded thoughts from the alcohol and the earlier derogatory comments from Dean, Stanley sees the world outside as a welcoming place in which there is a hell of a lot of life yet to live. There is still plenty of time to prove himself. Things are not so bad.

Revisiting Time

1

Following Tuesday's hangover – when the day was spent in bed and the room left only to collect fruit juices and packets of crisps – the Wednesday and Thursday were spent exploring the parts of town that Patricia knew as a child. The pier was boisterous. The Pavilion packed with day-trippers. The Lanes longer than expected.

The time in Brighton was the best of Clive's life. Wallowing in the days with Patricia, anticipating the nights in bed shunted into the sheets beside her. Watching her shower and brush her teeth in the morning. Things so normal yet so personal. Patricia perched on the loo.

Hand in hand, arm in arm, his narrow frame pressed into her soft embrace. Patricia, with her older ways, felt less at ease than Clive when they entered restaurants as a couple or kissed on the promenade. But it was no problem. The thrill of the relationship emancipated her and left them both floating about the town.

Patricia won twenty pounds on the bingo. Clive was unable to keep up with the caller; dropping his pencil, mishearing the numbers and trying to check Patricia's card for missed calls. He had barely put pencil to paper before Patricia called out 'House'.

He did better on the fruit machines, managing to lose a fiver less than her.

They watched jazz in a little square near the station. Stopped to have a drink in the pavement bistro alongside. Two coffees came to a lot more than Clive anticipated. He hid his surprise at the bill by coughing. This made the gathered jazz crowd throw disproving glares.

*

The journey home on the Friday is a morbid affair. Both of them feel like crying at having to leave their Utopia.

Brighton fades into the morning as the train peels itself away from the platform. The heavy metal wheels struggling to find rhythm and pace. Stuttering like Clive's speech. But Clive doesn't want to talk – he can't. Struck dumb by the departing sign, 'Welcome to Brighton', that says it all. Can't face looking at Patricia, afraid of what he may see. Doesn't want to witness her sadness. Noticed in the bathroom that morning that she appeared more agitated and distressed than she did at the funeral. A different kind of departure.

Clive reaches for Patricia's hands to compensate for the lack of eye contact. Her hand is chilled like a dead fish. And it flaps.

– W-w-w-what's wrong? Clive asks.

A stony silence greets the question. Her face seems to be throbbing.

– We c-c-can come back another t-t-time, Clive offers as balm.

It does not stop the shivering.

– Am I breathing too loud, Patricia asks.

– N-n-no, Clive replies, shaking his head.

– I can hear such loud breathing inside of my head.

– Shall I close the w-w-window? suggests Clive.

They get back to the house in the early afternoon. Patricia isn't right and her head aches.

Clive lies next to her on the bed as they try to grab a siesta. He sleeps like a baby. She shuts her eyes and thinks of Brighton.

2

The house on Fairfield Road breathes. It is a slight, shallow breath, but enough to keep Patricia from sleeping. A wheezing, cold inhalation and exhalation of air. Filling the bedroom on the Friday night with movement.

Clive is gone. He had to go back to the flat and sort things out.

He had to see his parents. His smell lies next to her on the pillow. The scent of apricots.

The darkness makes her feel lonely. Now that the house is hers, now that family has gone. The freedom is meaningless. The thoughts of Clive reassure. The size of the house intimidates.

Home has made things real again. She thinks about a new job. What will happen to Joan? Tries to concentrate on the practical aspects of life alone. Tries to stop her mind wandering back into Mother's room and the sight of the pillow pushed against a head.

Unable to calm herself down, and unable to stop the headache, Patricia descends the stairs. Without a light; she doesn't want to dazzle tired eyes. To the kitchen, which is cast in a dismal glow. Dissolves some aspirin in a glass. Stands by the sink staring out into the garden. Shapes flicker in the dark patches by the trees and shed. The breathing in her head is still loud, making clear thought difficult. Can't help but feel a tragic ambience around her. Senses someone standing in the hallway. She turns around to look. Nobody. The emptiness is a presence itself. She's never lived alone. Maybe Clive will move in. One night alone is already one night too many. No point delaying a new life. Especially one filled with such prospects. She will cook nice meals for Clive. Though he's not a big eater. Even these forced thoughts offer scant enthusiasm, for her head is filled with storm clouds.

Patricia retires upstairs once the pills begin to quieten things. Lies back down on the sticky bed, still hot from where she lay waiting for sleep. And then hears a noise. Coming from outside the room.

Tap-tap-tap. Mother's glass on the side-table.

Patricia stops still. Crushes her eyes shut to hear the unmistakable sound and resists the instinctive pull to climb up, grab slippers and gown, and go to Mother.

Then there is a silence. The tapping stops.

Patricia tries to recall the sound; to deduce whether it was real or not.

3

The actor walks straight past Clive without eye contact. Clive's polite smile is left hanging in the air above the pavement. His gait becomes more stilted as he heads towards his parents' house.

But he is not overly fazed. He is happy. In love. He has left Patricia back at the house in Bow to come and see his parents and tell them all about his break in Brighton.

Mum and Dad are in the lounge, reading quiz magazines. Clive takes a kiss from Mum and a big wink from Dad. He sits down next to Mum on the sofa and joins in the silence. His suggestion to make a pot of tea greeted with enthusiasm. Mum assures him that she will fry some potato bread a little later.

He brings in the drinks on a tray and puts them down on the coffee table.

Dad clutches the cup of tea contentedly. He almost drops it when Clive announces:

– I've m-met somebody.

The words are met with nothing, as Mum places her drink on her lap and Dad shakes spillage off his hand.

– I was actually in B-b-brighton with her, not on my own.

The initial silence that gave his parents time to adjust flowers into enthusiasm.

– That's wonderful news, Mum says.

– Good for you, son, Dad adds.

Clive can't hold back a proud smile.

– Tell me all about her, Mum says. – Who is she?

– She's c-c-c-called Patricia.

– Oh, Clive, I'm so thrilled.

Clive sits on the edge of the sofa, getting himself as close to Mum and Dad as he can.

Mum asks the questions, Clive tries his best to answer, though reluctant to give too much away about their first meeting and the age gap. Plays it vague. A lie here and there. Says they met through Stanley. Not so far from the truth. Doesn't mention the murder of Mother. Might sound bad.

– We've always been so worried for you, Mum says, making Clive feel uneasy.

– What do you m-m-mean?

– We worry, it's natural. You deserve a bit of happiness.

– Why?

– You've been through a lot. We understand, Mum says, trying to brush off further questions.

Clive sighs as Mum retraces the familiar steps of his past. More than twenty years ago when things began to dip. When he first went to speech therapy for his ever-worsening stammer. When he went to the hospital to see about his lack of muscular development. When he was moved classes at school because of bullying. Things that happened so long ago they have become part of a blurred, uncomfortable past which he no longer visits.

But for Mum it is still her baby boy sat on the sofa waiting for his potato bread and dating for the first time in years.

– Don't look at me like that, Mum says.

– Be h-h-happy for me.

Mum reaches for her tea. – I am. I really am.

Dad turns to the wall, faces a Post Office cap mounted in a frame.

– We've been seeing each other for a while now. I wanted to w-w-wait before I told you.

– That's best, Mum says softly.

– I'd like you to m-m-meet her.

Both parents stare surprise.

– Here? Mum asks nervously.

– Of course, Clive grins.

– Meet us?

– You'll l-l-like her.

– Oh, Clive.

4

Friday afternoon, Mister B arrives at Cheetham. Swaggers in front of the guards and sneers when searched. Open shirt to show off the huge gold chain slung round neck. Never had to do any time despite his record with the All-Stars. Whenever the police have snooped around the patch following a crime, the details are impossible to discover, the witnesses are nowhere to be found. Members of the public who see things outside their windows don't ever remember. The gangs aren't the enemy in NWL.

Pow-Wow and Mister B are allowed to embrace. Mister B pretends not to notice the bruises and cuts covering his friend's face.

They sit alongside each other in the open hall. No tables, and no sad pauses; they have spoken on the phone and Mister B knows all about the events.

– How's things? Mister B asks.

– I can take it, Pow-Wow replies.

– You should have taken the sucker out, argues Mister B, aware of the recent developments through Papa.

Pow-Wow snorts his disagreement. – Lewis is clean, bro.

– But what about yourself?

– Things have changed for me. You've cracked it, but I'm coming from a different angle nowadays.

– Nothing's changed. You're down if you want to be.

– I don't want to be down, you get me? There ain't no life left in me for taking orders and then hoping to make good.

– For your own safety, G. For your own safety.

– No point delaying. Once I'm out of here I'm planning a different route.

Mister B's despondency is spoken in his slouch, in the way he drags slowly on the cigarette. – You're going to make things rough-tough.

– No pain no gain, Pow-Wow replies.

That night, alone with insomniac adrenalin and his buzzing mind, Pow-Wow listens to the courtyard. Shouts for Lewis return; they still want him to sing. Now alone over the other side of the yard.

At one a.m. Pow-Wow hears the rattle at the door. A cluster of shadows sweep into the cell, along with urgent whispers.

Pow-Wow tries to fight back with a sock loaded with PP7s from the radio. He whips it out from under his pillow and tags a head as it rushes towards him. But then his arms are tangled in others and he is ripped from the bed. Stretched apart, Pow-Wow is whipped with plugs attached to electrical cable. His skin burns and throbs and then itches. And the blood dries into the swollen slits.

5

Lying on the bed, in agony, Pow-Wow listens to the approaching scream of an ambulance. He assumes that a guard has seen enough and finally decided to call emergency services to get him some treatment. He waits in the darkness of the room for the frantic running along the corridor and the clank of keys. He will spit at the screws as he is carried off on a stretcher – he's not that broken. He'll curse the wankers on the wing who are dishing out the punishment – they won't conquer him. But no stretcher arrives. No feet come thumping along the wing.

Fifteen minutes later he hears the news being shouted around the courtyard. The ambulance is for a boy on remand who tried to hang himself with a sheet. Found in the cell leaning from the window bars at forty-five degrees.

Pow-Wow knows it is Lewis.

Is That for Me?

1

Arriving early on Saturday morning at Fairfield Road, Clive is met by a tired-looking Patricia. She did not sleep much of last night; her thoughts were full of chaos, the room full of heat. Brighton had bought some time, but Bow was still waiting to wrap its dark cloak around her. By the time the first splashes of morning hit the curtain, Patricia had spent hours working herself into anger. Trying to erase the horror of hearing Mother's glass tapping downstairs. A sound she tries to dismiss. It has been an unsettling two weeks – the mind will play tricks. There was no sound. The glass, if her memory serves her correctly, is wrapped inside a box in the bedroom. That she filled with Mother's belongings. Years of hurrying to Mother's beck and call are bound to have an effect when the house is empty and she is left to sleep alone.

The day is still not quite clear for Patricia although the sky is bright and Clive enters the hallway with a dazzling smile. She is not ready for him. She is not ready for the hangover from last night that still fills her with dread.

– M-m-m-missed you, Clive says, leaning towards her to proffer a kiss.

She accepts, half-heartedly.

– Everything OK? Clive asks.

Patricia shrugs and leads him through to the kitchen, where she puts on the kettle and stares away from Clive, out of the window.

Following the experiences of Brighton, Clive is bewildered by Patricia's detachment. He expected their reunion to be one of relief and excitement. He's keen to tell her about the proposed visit to his parents. That can wait. He stands in the shadow of her silence.

– Tea? Patricia asks, opening the door to a cupboard. She wants to be normal, she wants to be enthusiastic, but her mind is dark and won't allow in any light.

– P-please, he answers, hesitant to say any more. He doesn't want to aggravate the situation with a careless word.

– How were your parents?

The question is flat.

– F-f-fine, really well, he replies cautiously. This is no time to take the parent plan any further.

They go into the lounge and sit on opposite sides of the room. The television is on with sound off. The picture distracts from the static between them.

Clive feels unwanted and his thoughts begin to blur. Things shouldn't be like this. What's happened? What have I done? Seeks answers in the tea that he sips despite its scalding temperature.

– I'm sorry to be so distant, she finally says.

He sighs relief. Not too loudly. – I d-d-don't mind.

– I've had a bad night, she says, shaking her head.

It begins to make sense for Clive. The return home has brought her back to the truth. It is not every week you have your mother murdered. The trip to the coast followed a period of shock. Only now is the enormity of the situation emerging. She will need time to come to terms with what has happened. – I'm here f-f-for you, he whispers.

– I know.

The truth is tougher than she thought. It is fighting through her guard, through the mental barriers that she has erected to deny her guilt. The house is more full of Mother than it has ever been, even though most of her possessions are cleared. The presence lingers in unexpected places. In the fridge, in the cupboard with the teapot, in front of the TV. Patricia stands up to turn the set off.

The house is empty of food and they agree to go shopping. Perhaps a walk outside in the wind will blow away some of her concerns.

To the Roman Road and into the world that Patricia knows so

well and has lived for fifty years. Yet she feels excluded from it as they enter the supermarket.

Clive attempts to put his arm around her but Patricia is not comfortable. Her stiff shoulder gives Clive the clue and he retreats.

There are pointed fingers aimed at Patricia. A few faces appear from behind shelves of bread and rows of cereal boxes to offer condolences. They know Patricia, they knew Mother. One lady takes hold of Patricia's trolley and pulls it towards her to force intimacy. – So sorry. So sorry, the lady spits into Patricia's face.

Clive can tell that Patricia is struggling. Her expression is laboured. The breathing is almost a pant.

Without any final straw, Patricia pushes the trolley away and walks for the automatic doors. – I can't do this, she says.

Clive jogs after her and tries to take her hand. She resists, offering an apology instead.

It is only early evening, but Patricia wants to go to bed. She is exhausted from the lack of sleep last night. She wants him to stay. Which confuses Clive, having considered himself an unwelcome presence throughout the day.

He watches her undress from the side of his eye. He is eager to hold her again and feel himself next to her. Yet he knows that tonight is a bad time. She needs to rest and he will have to satisfy himself with stroking her thighs.

The passion of Brighton seems an age ago. Before Patricia got herself entangled in some kind of mental cobweb.

– It's n-n-not me, is it? Clive asks, as he runs his fingers over her next to her in bed.

– Of course it's not, she replies, a trace of impatience.

– You w-w-want to be with me?

– Of course I do, she says, more meaningfully.

– I l-l-l-love you.

And within seconds Patricia is asleep. Her face sunk deep into the pillow.

As she dreams, Clive lies on his side, gliding his hand over her back. Soft and white like a bigger pillow. Gradually Clive is enticed into closed eyes by the sound of Patricia's rhythmic breath. Falling onto her shoulder.

Within an hour, Patricia is stirred by the sound. The sound of the glass tapping below. She jolts upright. Listens into the gloaming of the bedroom. It is Mother's glass.

She wakes Clive with an urgent shove. – Can you hear it? she hisses.

Tap-tap-tap. The sound is as clear as the glass.

– Isn't it outside? Clive mumbles, coming round.

Patricia fumbles for the lamp switch and heads downstairs, to where the tapping continues in the same tempo as Mother's.

At the bottom of the stairs the sound stops.

Mother's bedroom is hazy; from the streetlight, from Patricia's straining sight.

By the bed is the side-table, on the side-table is the glass. Mother's calling card. Patricia clearly remembers packing it away. Nevertheless, she takes the glass and returns it to the cardboard box by the door. Changes her mind and wraps it in newspaper before throwing it into the dustbin in the kitchen.

Back upstairs, Patricia immerses herself in the sheets and hides her anxiety by a dismissive shake of the head.

– What w-w-was it? asks Clive.

– Ah, it was nothing.

Before sleep returns, the tapping begins again.

Patricia holds the duvet over her face.

– Is that the n-n-noise again? says Clive.

– Oh, God, Patricia moans. – What's happening?

– Do you w-w-want me to go?

– Stay here, she says, getting up and going back downstairs.

The glass is back on the table.

Patricia grabs the tumbler and throws it across the room so that it shatters, leaving a carpet of diamonds. – No! she shouts.

2

As soon as Patricia wakes up she recalls the terror. Things are closing in and the house reeks of despair.

Clive is in the kitchen, preparing breakfast in bed.

When Patricia appears behind him in her dressing gown, he is disappointed. – Stay in b-b-bed. I'll bring it up.

– Don't worry. We'll eat here, she replies, sitting at the table.

She wants to mention the smashed glass but it is one more thing she wants to forget and so stays mute.

– There wasn't much to c-c-cook, Clive shrugs, offering a plate of toast and sliced smoked ham.

– That's fine, Patricia says, looking at the food rather disdainfully.

The silence is overwhelming.

Clive's embarrassment is complete when Patricia pushes away the half-eaten plate and pretends to be full. His stomach shrinks at her unhappiness and he, too, fails to finish his breakfast.

– I've got to clear the house once and for all, Patricia says.

– I'll h-h-help.

– You don't have to.

– Well, it's up t-t-to you. I will if you w-want.

The presence still breathes. She drowns it out with the hoover, the radio, the television, a manic humming. The curtains are dropped from each window, the last forgotten shelves of books and trinkets are swept into bin bags, the plates and cups used by Mother are thrown in too.

Patricia continually washes her hands. Whenever she touches a door, a light switch, a banister, a cupboard, she runs for the nearest sink. Her skin is drying out. It is flaking and cracking. Her fingers look like Mother's.

While Clive washes up in the kitchen, Patricia dusts and polishes around the hallway. Wearing an apron. A squirt from the polish can, a wipe of the cloth.

As they work, Patricia hears the water pipes coughing. She knows the sound of the running bath. A check on Clive ensures that he isn't the one with taps flowing. Returning to the hallway, Patricia thinks quick and runs over to Mother's room. She enters to find steam drifting from the en-suite and filling the bedroom. Patricia rushes to the bath to stop the flow. She burns her hands on the metal, grabbing a towel to wrap around the taps. The breathing is around her. It is louder, being exhaled in short machine-gun bursts. Sort of laughing.

– Get out! Patricia shouts.

Clive hears the shout and comes dashing into the room. He stares at Patricia, standing numb amid the sweating heat.

– What's happened? he asks.

– I think it's Mother.

– What?

– I can't stay here.

3

They arrive at Clive's flat by lunchtime. Patricia brought the first few things she saw and threw into a bag. Clive is happy to go back and collect anything she has forgotten. He is delighted to have her staying with him. She may unwind away from the memories of home. Time apart from Fairfield Road may release her from the strange distance that she has created.

– Don't shut m-m-me out, Clive says to Patricia, who sits shrivelled up in the armchair.

Patricia replies with a forced smile and returns to reticence. Her eyes are scared.

Clive goes over and rests a hand on her shoulder. She puts her hand over his.

– You're so c-c-cold.

– You're so warm.

– Do you w-w-want me to get you a blanket or something?

– I'm cold to the bone.

– Have a hot b-bath.

Clive perches on the arm of the chair, retaining a hand around her head. He uses a finger to caress the back of Patricia's neck. Running the digit up and down the bone. Over a nest of hairs. He looks at her healthy legs bulging through the dress. He wants to take her to the bedroom.

– I'll p-put some music on. It might help you r-r-relax.

Rummaging through a pile of cassettes, he pulls one out and holds it to the light to read the scrawled handwriting on the sticker.

'I Choose You' by Paris crackles through the speaker. A track Clive has played countless times, invariably accompanied by the fantasy of dancing with a woman.

He stands in front of Patricia and offers to pull her up. – Let's d-d-d-dance, he smiles nervously.

– I don't think so, she says.

– You c-c-can forget everything, he insists, taking her hands and wrenching her to her feet.

– Oh, Clive, she says tetchily.

He wraps himself around her and drags her to the middle of the small room. – I've n-n-never really danced with a girl properly.

She is stiff and unwilling.

– Relax, Clive urges.

– I'm not really in the mood.

– F-f-f-forget about everything.

Patricia closes her eyes and puts her head onto Clive's shoulder.

Clive pulls her in closer, allowing his hand to drop below the waist and just to the top of a buttock.

– I can't! Patricia says, untying herself from the clinch.

– I-i-it's OK, Clive says, keeping his arm round her to accompany her back to the chair.

Patricia falls into the seat and into the memory of the boy blamed for the murder. In all innocence, oblivious of the trap Patricia had set for him. So very young. Takes her back to when she worked at the bakery and dated Edward – 'love and it goes stiff on ya' (*Lavandula angustifiola*). Everything is going stiff and stale and shocking. She sniffs Clive and he smells of the aftershave that filled the house on that Tuesday afternoon.

4

Clive cooks, makes endless hot drinks, takes her on a tour of Somers Town, runs to the shops, allows her the single bed while he crashes on the floor.

But Patricia is not herself. She keeps crying. She calls out for help in the middle of the night. She sweats buckets. She continually washes her hands. Continually hears the sound of a hair-dryer.

Clive massages her at night with purple oil labelled 'Tranquillity'. Her skin pasty and vulnerable against his dark hands. His touch cautious and hesitant; still hungry for the intimacy that they have not shared since the bed and breakfast. Her body tense and jumpy, fighting other forces. His mouth salivating as he admires and desires her.

She won't talk about her problems. Tightening up as Clive's conversation hovers near.

He has stopped asking questions. Gives her the space to unwind and root out the trouble for herself. Serving up anodyne clichés such as, 'You'll soon get over it', or 'We'll soon have you right.' Phrases that don't even sound like him. Phrases that sound like her.

He wants to talk about their relationship. He wants to tell her how happy he is since they've been together. How nice it is with her staying. But he can't find the nerve to knock at Patricia's shell. His love for her is the same. He is unsure about her feelings.

The relationship is so new that nestling amid Patricia's silence still offers a degree of comfort. Watching her face chew on anxiety is less soothing. There is only so much tea he can make. None of which has washed away Patricia's bitterness.

– You know I'm in l-l-love with you? Clive says, with sad eyes, imploring her to be happy. Sidled next to her on the settee.

– I know, she replies.

– I've n-n-never been in love before.

– You're so sweet.

– Things I've always wanted to feel, I f-f-feel around you.

She tries to smile.

– Watching television, films, listening to records, reading stuff. Always l-l-love and I never knew what they meant.

Patricia wipes a hand down his face.

– It's a joy, a bright c-c-colour. Do you feel it, s-s-see it?

– Things have been hard, Clive. Go slow for me.

– And then I think about k-k-kids. Have you thought about k-k-kids?

– I'm past all that.

– But things h-h-have changed. I was r-reading in the paper about a w-woman who had IVF at sixty.

Patricia is keen to move back into silence. – We'll see, she murmurs.

– When we d-d-did it . . . Clive's voice fades into a wondrous shake of the head as he recalls the Brighton bed.

Her hand stops on his chin and fingers the light stubble around the jaw. – Ssshhh.

– I w-w-woke up this morning so happy.

– I can't sleep.

– Thinking of y-y-you.

5

Stanley is back from Radlett. The Thameslink from King's Cross makes the journey simple and he intends to visit once a week. Although he'll make sure that he travels off-peak.

Stanley is looking forward to seeing Clive. He has missed his friend while he has been away in Radlett. Not so enthusiastic about meeting Patricia. Clive told him that she is not having a good time. She is still suffering over Mother's death.

The Monday streets are quieter than usual. The humidity has sent many people to the park or into darkened rooms to sit in front of fans. Patches of wet spread under Stanley's faded shirt.

Seeing her for the first time curled on Clive's settee, Patricia is different from how Stanley imagined. She is older than he thought. More sour. But Stanley can excuse the manner in the light of circumstances.

– How are you? Stanley asks her.

– Getting there, she replies, trying her best to look him in the eye and be sociable.

– It'll take time, Stanley nods.

Clive brings in three mugs of coffee. Puts the tray on the side and takes a cup over to Patricia.

– I've put c-c-cream in yours.

She thanks Clive and stares into the mug.

– Clive's told me so much about you, Stanley continues.

– I've heard a lot about you, she replies.

Clive sits on the floor next to Patricia. He pats her leg. – Everything OK, d-d-darling?

Stanley raises an eyebrow.

Patricia appears slightly embarrassed.

The atmosphere is desolate. Gradually it fills with tension. There is something in the way Patricia sits, in the way Stanley stands, and the tragic huddle of Clive nestling against Patricia's legs.

– Right, Stanley says, swigging the coffee to the bottom of the mug without a concern for the temperature. – I've got to hit the road. Mum's got a job on this afternoon. Some bloke who lost his brother to cancer.

By the front door, Stanley and Clive are alone.

– Everything OK here? Stanley asks.

– As I s-s-said on the phone, she's struggling.

Stanley pulls Clive in and hisses at him. – She seems a bit loopy to me, Clivey-boy.

– She's the b-best thing that's ever happened to me.

– Just take it easy.

– We're thinking a-a-about having k-k-kids.

The mouth drops and eyes gaze huge. – Eh? Stanley says.

– We're n-n-not getting any younger.

– Is she right for you?

– I'm h-h-happy.

6

Pow-Wow is locked in twenty-four hours a day. He can hear the yelling in the corridor and in the courtyard. There is nothing he can do except sit and dream and dread the approaching night. Brenda came yesterday, on the Sunday. She seemed pleased with herself for no reason.

Pow-Wow did his best to maintain composure in front of his

mum. He didn't want to tell her about the change of circum-stances and his yearning to be at home. He wanted to ask about the trains running behind the house, but he couldn't think of a suitable question that didn't make him sound mad. After years of the rumbling track, the desert of noise during the day is painful. The trains made him part of things, almost as much as his All-Star affiliation. Now there is nothing save the screaming and singing of night. Like lunatics. And he can feel himself cracking up under the constant pressure of loneliness and the threat of violence. Beatings that have stopped over the past couple of nights. Although the verbal threats continue. They arrive with the three meals a day. When the guards bring the food, a voice or a group of voices taunts through the open door. Pow-Wow tells them to go fuck themselves and then scours his dinner for fingernails and glass. Yet at no point does he regret acquitting Lewis. No way could he harm a friend. That was a lesson the gang had taught him a thousand times previously. Do strangers, rivals, opponents, but never do a friend. What did they expect? And now all Pow-Wow can do is wait and expect the next battering. It comes that evening.

The gang use belts to tie Pow-Wow to the bed's steel frame.

– Killing grannies your buzz? one of them says.

– Old white ladies your ticket? another says.

– Did she beg for mercy?

– Did you want to fuck her?

– Did she snap as you folded her up?

– How many others have you zapped?

A wooden stump breaks across his face, causing the nose to collapse and feel comfortably warm.

7

Chapter Road is dusk. Ten-year-old Troy rides his bike up and down the street with a group of friends. Wearing a vest which shows off his arms and the words I AM THE FUTURE tattooed down the bicep. The friends throw bottles of Coke to each other to swig and pass on. Broken cars crouch along the kerb. Up above, blinking aircraft circle for Heathrow.

One of the kids notices two big boys turn out from the station underpass. They are strutting towards them with their hands jammed inside paper bags.

– Hey, Daddies, the kid shouts.

Troy looks up and panics. All week there have been phone calls to the house. Brenda has taken them and then immediately cut off. Threats, messages for Pow-Wow, warnings about a visit.

One of the other kids on a bike pedals towards the big boys, prepared to turn and hare off the other way if one of them so much as blinks. – Are you going to shoot someone? the kid asks.

The big boys don't reply and keep strolling towards Brenda's house.

Troy stands up on the pedals and sprints back home.

The house looks ill; like all the other houses along the street. Troy reaches through the metal grille to rap urgently on the wood.

Brenda pulls open the door to Troy's petrified face.

– Mom, Mom, they're coming to get us. They're coming to get us!

Brenda looks over at the big boys walking along the other side of the road. She pushes open the gate and lets Troy rush through into the house with his bike.

She stares at the big boys. Her pretty face is saturated with strain.

The two stand opposite the house and pretend to look nonchalant.

Brenda continues to gaze defiance. From behind her, Naomi and Emmanuel emerge. Poverty hangs from them.

– Shall we call the cops? Naomi asks.

Brenda doesn't reply. She continues to challenge the boys with her stare. – You want something? she calls out.

– Shall we call the cops? Naomi repeats.

Brenda's face begins to break into tears. She wipes her face with a hand decorated with cheap rings. The two children cling to her as if she is about to collapse.

Troy's friends watch from behind the safety of garden gates.

– Just looking, mama, one of the big boys shouts back across the road.

– My brother ain't done nothing wrong, Emmanuel says.

– Just looking, boy. Just looking.

Timber

1

The joys of Brighton seem another life; someone else's. When memory and guilt were contained within the passion for Clive and the release from the tortured routine. But the tapping of the glass has echoed further than she realized.

Clive's flat hasn't offered Patricia refuge. It hasn't really worked out. In many ways it has exacerbated her torment. The bedroom at Clive's is too small and the walls close in even more threateningly than home. At least at Fairfield Road she had the comfort of her own double bed rather than the too-soft single. She hasn't slept, the nightmares are bad, and the day is filled with frightened expectation. Made worse by the desperation of Clive's affection. He stares at her for hours. He harries her in his offers of another hot drink or another sandwich. He strokes her hair when she can bear his touch no longer. It is suffocating and serves only to aggravate an impending sense of horror. Like awaiting execution. Now in a different cell. The prospect of another night lying alert on the bed is impossible to bear.

– I need to go home, she says, on the Tuesday evening.

– Why? asks Clive.

– I've just got to.

– Isn't being here h-h-helping?

– It is helping, it really is. But it isn't healing.

– T-t-time. Takes t-t-time.

Patricia looks through Clive. – I can't go on like this.

– Like what?

Again, she avoids eye contact. – Waiting for something to happen.

– But I thought it was too s-s-scary?

– I can't run away from it.

– You w-w-wanted to leave.

– Please, Clive, don't pressure me on this.

– I'm t-trying to help.

– I wanted to leave and now I want to return.

– I think you're b-b-being very strong.

The face is expressionless. – I'm not strong.

Clive has not been immune to Patricia's problems. He has suffered her sad silence and tried his best to lift her spirits and keep her afloat. But he struggles to comprehend the vastness between them. – What's h-h-happening? he asks.

– What do you mean?

– What's g-g-going wrong with us?

Suddenly a burst of grief comes from her face. – Oh, Clive. It's not you, it's not you. I can't explain, though. Something inside. I think I'm becoming ill.

He nods sympathy. It would make sense. She has run herself into the ground following the death. – I just w-w-want to support you.

– I only want to go back to mine.

– You're sure you w-w-want me to come?

She wasn't planning on it, relishing an escape from his intensity. But she cannot hurt his feelings any more than she already has. – Of course. Of course, she lies.

2

The house is as cold as a tomb. The warmth of the day has failed to penetrate the walls and windows in the way it normally would. Patricia and Clive feel as though they are intruding on the house's meditation. Their feet sound so loud, as do their bodies shoving and huffing their way into the hall.

– G-g-g-good to be home? Clive asks.

– We'll see, she says.

– My flat was a bit s-s-small.

– It was fine.

– Probably not w-w-what you needed.

She leads him through to the kitchen. – I need to make a new start and remain calm.

– Are you still f-f-feeling ill?

– I'm not right. Not right in the head.

– Why don't you take s-s-some headache pills? he suggests, leaning against the door.

The gushing water from the tap fills a glass. – I'll take a sleeping pill or something. I really need to sleep. I think that's half the problem. I'm becoming delirious.

– Are you still hearing the breathing?

– I think it's part of the tiredness. Probably just tinnitus.

– I d-d-didn't know you suffered with that?

– Nor did I.

Reluctantly, Patricia allows Clive to sleep in her bed.

For Clive, the squeaky bed is not as uncomfortable as the twitching from Patricia's limbs. They keep kicking and nudging him, forcing him to retreat to the edge of the mattress. Sudden snorts and grunts as she implores herself to sleep. So hot to touch as Clive's circumspect hand reaches for her flesh. He draws with his finger on her legs. Her body burning.

– This is hopeless, she blurts out into the darkness.

They both sit up.

– Are you too hot t-t-to sleep?

– I'm freezing, she says.

– Maybe you should read for a b-b-bit?

– Don't you think the house is cold?

– No.

– Don't you think the house seems different?

– N-n-no.

Clive lies back on the pillows. Patricia remains bent upwards, leaning on an elbow.

– What's that noise? she says.

– I c-c-can't hear anything.

– Something's wrong.

– Is it to do w-w-with us?

– There's something here.

– Only us.

– Can you go to Mother's room?

– What do you w-w-w-want me to do?

– Just go and see if everything is all right.

Clive leaves the room. The sound of slight footfall on the carpeted stairs. Then a clunk of wood on wood.

He returns and walks through the darkness back to the bed. – Nothing.

– What was the bang?

– The laundry box was too close to the door.

– What do you mean, too close to the door? Patricia says quietly. – It was in the corner of the room.

– Well, s-s-someone moved it, Clive says dismissively.

– Get up, Patricia blurts.

– I am up, he says.

She grabs his hand and together they return downstairs. Into Mother's room. To switch on the light and stare at the box squatting by the door.

– It m-m-must be a terrible thing for you to look at? says Clive, attempting to help her through the ordeal written bold all over her face. – Your p-p-p-poor mother.

– Do you know what she used to make me do in that box?

– N-n-no? replies a puzzled Clive.

– Poor Mother, she sneers.

– What do you w-w-want to do?

– We're going to get rid of it. Help me lift, she says, bending over the box and reaching for grip underneath.

As they struggle with it through the hall and kitchen, Clive doesn't recognize Patricia's anguished expression. She is no longer Patricia. He has known it for the past few days, but the grim stare urging the box out of the back door is ultimate confirmation. But he loves her and is determined to help.

They lower the box onto the lawn and Patricia runs off to the garden shed. She returns holding a sledgehammer and a hand-axe. She hands the hammer to Clive and without a word she begins to chop at the wood with the axe. Grunting as she does, mouth snarled.

Moonlight casts the two woodcutters in blue. White bullets fly off the disintegrating box.

Run for Your Lives

1

On the Wednesday morning, the kitchen is cold and even Clive can feel the chill penetrating his pullover. He waves his hands in the steam as the kettle boils. Digs his fingers into his eyes to remove sleep. Shattered from the troubled night and Patricia's constant crying. She won't talk to him, choosing to curl up in the corner of the bed to sob and sniff until dawn.

He hears a scream. Runs upstairs to Patricia.

She is standing on the landing. Every part of her is shuddering. Eyes ablaze. Her shivering arms are wrapped around her body as if holding herself up.

– What is it? Clive shouts.

His voice goes straight through her.

– W-w-what is it, Patricia?

– There's someone in there, she trembles.

– Where?

– Standing in the corner, under a blanket.

– In the bedroom?

Clive runs past her to check. – There's no one here, he says, turning from the doorway back to Patricia.

– I think it's gone to Mother's room, Patricia says, moving away from Clive and down the stairs.

– There's no one here! Clive insists.

Patricia doesn't listen, still shaking as if overcome with fever. She thumps down the stairs to stand in the hall. The white door to Mother's room appears bigger than it has ever done. Patricia shrinks before it.

Clive leaps down the steps and between the door and Patricia. Compelled to halt the madness.

– Let's l-l-leave it.

– Let me go in.

– Who's d-doing this?

– Please, Clive. This is my house.

– Is it M-m-m-mother?

Patricia begins to cry and fall to the floor. – What have I done? she shouts.

– You haven't d-d-done anything, Clive says. – It's n-n-not you.

– It's me. It's me, she moans.

2

Patricia won't go back into the house. She stands in the back garden gazing up at the windows. Hoping, dreading, to see something looking back at her. Something that will actually confront her.

Clive is at a loss to help. All he can do is hold her in his long arms and hope that she will stop crying and start loving him again. Not that his desires are purely selfish, but he is getting to the stage where he is crippled by her madness. If it is not sounds, it is moving boxes and figures in corners.

The sky is a mixed palette of white and grey. In swirls. The house looms over them with its dank walls and flaking window frames.

– What w-w-was it? Clive asks, now that the initial shock wanes.

– It was just waiting there. In the room.

– D-d-did it speak?

She shakes her head.

– Could you s-s-see anything under the blanket?

– I don't know, she says.

He sneaks back into silence. To stare at the house.

She pulls out of his grip, his breathing is too close as it fans her neck. It is too much in rhythm with the internal breath that continues its persecution. Now a minor distraction compared to the unfurling events.

– I can't go back in, she says.

– Do you think you're b-b-being haunted?

– I can't face it, whatever it is. She begins to cry softly.

– Do you want me to go in and check e-e-every room? Give it the all-clear?

– There's nothing you can do.

His helplessness saturates him. Drags down his shoulders and his solid stance. He seems smaller than her as they stand together on the dried-out lawn with its crusty yellow grass and patches of mud. – Stanley's m-m-mum can speak to ghosts, he says, with a sudden burst of resolution. – She c-can help.

– Stanley's mum?

– She's a m-medium, psychic thingy. She can d-d-deal with these sorts of things.

– I want the house to be normal, Patricia replies. – I want to be left alone.

– She can do that, Clive says. – She can m-m-make things leave, she can t-t-tell them to go away.

Turning to Clive, Patricia's eyes are alight with expectation. – This could change everything.

– I know, I know, Clive answers eagerly. – We c-c-can return to how things were.

An expression of calm momentarily spreads over Patricia. Clive catches it and smiles.

– This could change everything, she repeats.

3

Clive calls Stanley from the living room while Patricia waits outside on the lawn. Clive recounts the background to Patricia's problem. Stanley cannot help but snigger when Clive talks about the blanketed being in the bedroom. The laugh is cut short by Clive's urgency.

Patricia can't stop herself from crying as she sits alone on the grass. She heard the glass, she turned off the tap. Putting her head into her hands, she feels the pull of Mother enticing her towards the house. Despite her tight lips to Clive, she knows the meaning behind the haunting. Only she knows the truth of that Tuesday afternoon. It is torture to recall. Keeping it shut away behind the present and behind denial has made life acceptable. But now it is coming for her.

Her head was once full of lightness and relief, now it is stuffed with nightmares. She is awake but her mind is cloaked like night. Can no one see how evil Mother was? Her death was good. It was good. Why is it coming for her? Why is it beginning to shout in her head? It is a deafening roar that screams guilt. Patricia wants to rip it out of her skull. She wants to wrench off her head and stamp the cries into the earth.

Clive watches Patricia from the kitchen door. He watches terrified as she sways and spits and tears at her black hair.

– What are you d-d-doing? Clive shouts, running over the patio to Patricia. He grabs her hands and lifts her from the grass into his arms.

She throws her head onto his chest, soaking it with tears and smothering it in the bedraggled hair. – It's inside of me, she sobs.

– It's OK, he shouts over her frenzy.

– If only you knew.

Sylvia and Stanley arrive by mini-cab.

Clive hears the knock and he goes through the house to receive them.

Sylvia has never seen Clive look so ravaged, so torn.

Stanley takes a handshake, then ignores Clive, as he pushes his way into the house to see what Patricia looks like. His curiosity has been ignited by his friend's urgent call. He couldn't get Sylvia into the cab quick enough.

He finds Patricia standing on the patio with her hair falling over her face and her body shaking with terror. She is a frightening sight and Stanley gulps before calling through Sylvia.

When Clive appears in the back door, Stanley throws him a gobsmacked stare. 'What the hell is all of this?' it says, before he turns his gaze back onto Patricia.

Sylvia edges towards Patricia cautiously, as if approaching a wild animal. She recognizes the ghostly torture of Patricia's eyes. The expression behind the chaotic hair is sheer torment. It is not the first time Sylvia has witnessed haunting.

– You think it's your mother? asks Sylvia.

– I don't know what it is, Patricia sighs. – I just want it to go.

Clive and Stanley stand open-mouthed at the scene. They have forgotten the presence of each other, enraptured by the two women.

– Look at me, Patricia. Look at me, Sylvia says, gently pushing Patricia's hands away from her scratched face.

Patricia finds it difficult to look at Sylvia. Too much going on internally. Too much shame.

– We have to do this together, urges Sylvia. – As one.

The swollen eyelids mask bloodshot eyes. Patricia gradually moves her face towards Sylvia and latches on to Sylvia's comforting stare. That holds her.

Taking Patricia's still-shaking arm, Sylvia pulls Patricia closer. So she can feel the problem. Sense it. Sylvia runs her hand over the elbow and up to the shoulder. – Shall we talk to Mother?

The name of Mother causes Patricia to momentarily lose composure and the shuddering erupts into spasm. – I . . . just . . . want . . . things . . . to . . . stop, she stutters, as if freezing cold.

With Sylvia escorting her by tucking arms around the waist, Patricia is able to return into the house. Only as far as the kitchen. It smells rotten, as if the bin needs emptying.

Clive and Stanley tread carefully into the room behind them and dare not make any kind of noise.

Accompanying Patricia to the table, Sylvia pulls out a chair and gently presses her onto it. Sylvia then gestures to Stanley to join them at the table. Stanley in turn winks the message to Clive.

– Is it your mother? Sylvia whispers, lowering herself onto the neighbouring seat. – Do you think it's your mother?

Calmed by the chair, Patricia looks about the table and watches Clive and Stanley sit down. There is some kind of smile at Clive but it is hard to distinguish. Hard to decipher.

– I know it's Mother, Patricia whispers back.

Sylvia nods knowingly, as if she is being proved right. – Shall we get her to explain herself?

Patricia shrugs and seems to fight off an internal enquiry.

– Everything will be OK, Sylvia says softly. – We can do it if we just trust each other.

The kitchen feels cramped, the four bodies nestled together around the wooden table. The air is delicate, and the breaths quick and shallow.

There is the tiniest of grunts from Patricia. It is acceptance. Agreement. It is a willingness to try anything that may bring a remedy.

Sylvia smiles at the ceiling, closes her eyes, smiles again. – Let's try. Let's try, she says.

Bringing her hands onto the table, the fingers decked with heavy silver rings, she strokes the surface. She sighs. Lifts a hand into the air.

Stanley, Clive and Patricia bow their heads automatically as if in prayer.

– Mother? We know you've been trying to get through. We're here now, says Sylvia loudly, clearly, a sudden burst of voice after the whispers.

Patricia feels nauseous. Her mouth fills with rancid saliva in preparation for vomit. She swallows continually to keep the problem at bay.

– Come and speak to us, Sylvia says, in the tones of compromise.

Footsteps can be heard coming down the stairs. Soft, steady steps.

Clive peeks up and meets Stanley's raised eyebrow across the table. He is next to Patricia and he reaches for Patricia's knee to offer a comforting squeeze. The leg is rigid and Clive can see that she is swaying, almost ready to collapse. He puts his hand against her side as support.

The footsteps finish their descent and move slowly along the hallway to the kitchen door.

– Hello, Mother, Sylvia grins. – You're here.

Patricia retches.

– I hope you're going to tell us what this is all about?

Tears trundle down Patricia's cheeks. She can sense Mother: the smell of cardigans and wet afternoons in front of the radiator. She can see her face, looking up from the bath with her blotchy skin. Can feel the bones as she pushes her into the box.

– We're here to listen, Sylvia says. – Whatever it is you want to tell us.

The room fills with a tingle. Static sparking against bodies and causing hairs on head to hover.

Patricia wobbles, Clive bolsters. She sighs 'I can't' but Clive ignores her, bending himself forward almost to the middle of the table to listen to Sylvia.

Patricia slowly sinks onto Clive, grabbing at him to stay on her seat.

– It's about the day you died? Sylvia asks.

– Make her stop haunting me! Patricia suddenly shouts.

– She wants to talk about the day she died.

Patricia's vision fades into a fog. A cold claw runs down her neck; it is Clive's hands trying to stroke her. But she does not want to be stroked.

– Who did? Sylvia says. – While you were in bed?

Patricia goes to scream a halt to the proceedings but the stomach catches the shout and refuses to let it go.

– Patricia? Sylvia questions. – Patricia?

Stanley and Clive look to Patricia, who is beginning to struggle for breath. The lungs heave and the throat gulps. Then the stomach relents and the room shakes with the sound of Patricia's scream.

Sylvia breaks from her trance and stares evil at Patricia.

Breaking out of Clive's clutch, Patricia staggers to her feet.

– P-p-patricia? Clive says helplessly.

Her face is full of blood. Her jaw hangs loosely as if broken. Patricia trembles furiously as she shuffles towards the sink. She appears shrunken and thinner as she stoops and hobbles like an old woman. And opens a cupboard, automaton-like, climbing into the minute space. She knocks over bottles and cans, treads on Brillo Pads and brushes, before pulling the door behind her.

– Box! Patricia barks from inside the hole, sounding strikingly, eerily, like Mother.

Home-boy

1

Pow-Wow always believed that it was only a matter of time before someone in authority got hold of the case and shook out the deceit and threw open the cage door. Never doubted. But never imagined that it would take so long and would lead to so much. Even as they led him through the gate to the waiting wagon to return to court, the guards could not offer an apology or a regretful silence. No, they gloated in the usual way.

The wing was at lunch and so he didn't get to see the faces of his night-time visitors. Who hid behind the veil of lights-out and would certainly hold no remorse for beating an innocent. They enjoyed it. Apart from the one who got the batteries in the face.

Brenda was waiting in the public gallery for Pow-Wow's appearance. Her happiness had never been so real. Nor had his. Especially when the judge moved away from discussing the 'systematic brutality' and 'sickening injuries' of his imprisonment and moved on to the topic of 'substantial compensation'. Pow-Wow knew it was going to work out better than he could ever have expected.

Mother and son travelled home on the train. Past the backs of houses that line the route like beggars. Pow-Wow looked at his bedroom window. Saw his tag sprayed on the outside wall.

Brenda and Pow-Wow walk arm in arm from the station towards home. A few kids on the street run across to exchange high-fives and a slip of skin. Some race their bikes up and down the cracked road. Life has gone on without him. Pow-Wow can feel the shape of things now that the future is in his hands. Along with the compensation cash that's going to come his way in the next few weeks – once a figure is agreed. Money towards a drop-top. Perhaps too many gangster connotations in a drop-top. Maybe something more sophisticated will be better. He enjoys the dilemma. Forgets the pain of the beatings. Remembers Lewis. Heard he was OK. He will visit and keep in touch. Give him a bit of support. Use him as an incentive to enrol for an education. There's a big college on Dudden Hill Lane. Only ever used it as a landmark. It could be a start. Mister B will piss himself when he tells him about going back to school.

A car horn blurts. A black Mercedes swings to the kerb. Brenda pulls Pow-Wow back, like an infant being pulled away from a stranger.

Pimp Papa gleams from the lowered window. The All-Star Chapter Crew, the Daddy-Boy Homing Crew, are still running things in NWL. But without Pow-Wow. Still killing each other, still sticking each other.

– Hey, smooth-thing, Papa winks, offering a thumb.

Pow-Wow bends over and presses the thumb with his.

– How's it cooking? asks Papa.

– I'm back, Pow-Wow grins.

– You back down?

– No more gang-banging.

Pimp Papa nods. – You've had it hard. You might think things over.

– I'm out, Papa. Leave more for you and Mister B.

There is no sense of betrayal. Papa knows about Pow-Wow's Cheetham treatment. The kid has taken enough. – You're lucky we're giving you the choice.

A half-nod. A shrug. – I guess.

Papa sits back and a girl's face peers from the passenger seat.

– You gonna say hello, bitch? Papa snarls at the girl.

– Yes, Papa, she replies quietly.

– You gonna show some respect?

– Yes, Papa, she repeats.

The girl pushes forward and Pow-Wow squints into the shaded interior.

– Hey, Pow-Wow, she says, with a brittle smile.

Ileasha's face is haggard, hair scraped over her head.
The protruding set of gold teeth makes smiling difficult.

2

Since Patricia's confession things have stabilized. Things have begun to settle and the breathing in the house has stopped. Her state of mind has levelled off and the horror of those final days before Sylvia's arrival is now over.

The solicitor was unperturbed and encouraging. There were plenty of things for him to work with: the history of abuse, the glowing references, the lack of previous convictions, the remorse. The elements of Patricia's case that concern him – the delay in coming forward, the ruthless plot to frame an innocent boy – can be mitigated by the duress and mental condition of the client. Diminished Responsibility may be a defence. He hasn't promised Patricia anything but is quietly confident that the sentence will be sensible.

Patricia is just happy to have the truth exposed. Where it can be examined, discussed and conclusions drawn. She is prepared for whatever.

The solicitor got her bail. In time for the weekend. Not that the Bank Holiday is going to be a ball. But at least she is able to sleep in her own bed, sit in her own chair and look out of the kitchen window onto the summer garden.

She stands in the hallway, staring into Mother's room. A stream of sunlight burns through the front-door window and emblazons her in white. The bedroom is empty – she even got rid of the dressing table and the bed. Just the carpet remains. Yet without the furniture it does not appear the same. It is surprising to notice the patches that have seen such little wear. Places where the fibres are still lush and vibrant. That make the large thread-bare sections seem even more desperate.

There is nothing left to see in the room. There is nothing left to hear. For the house is dead and the haunting has stopped. All that remains are four walls and a variously shaded carpet. Patricia allows herself one final smile before closing the door.

It is two in the afternoon and the heat of the day is baking the house. Maybe the clearance of clouds and the outbreak of sun will enliven Clive. He is due over in half an hour. They still have things to discuss.

At least they are talking. She wasn't sure if they'd ever reconcile after her confession. Clive was cut up. Took it to heart. Put down the phone on her – that was something. She had never seen that from Clive. But, of course, she could understand. It was good of him to listen the following day when she called. With her begging and her excuses and her plea for compassion and understanding. And for the chance to meet.

3

Clive walks the slow trek from Bow Road station to 26 Fairfield Road. Unsure about coming. Stanley certainly wasn't happy about it ('You should stay well away, Clivey-boy'). But it seems the least he can do. To perhaps salvage something from the relationship. He doesn't want to lose her. Yet at the same time he doesn't want to be used by her. As if she can do anything and he will accept anything. That is not love.

The final days of Patricia's ordeal were a strain, he acknowledges that. He was pushed to the limit himself. In the light of events her behaviour can be explained away, but the explanation wasn't what he wanted. Her answer wasn't really an answer. It was much more of a question.

He trusted her and believed in her and didn't want to be told that she was actually a murderer. Didn't want anything to jeopardize what he had found with her. Certainly not this. Though how can he forget the things they had together? Brighton will always be Brighton, regardless of what came before or comes after. No one will stop him laughing at One up the Arse. Or recalling the first time he touched her on the bed as the kettle boiled and spat water all over the cups and sachets.

Of course he must come and see her to discuss things. Mother was a nasty piece of work. Patricia lived a life from hell. He mustn't forget that. But why do what she did to the boy? Maybe he'll come to understand it all. Things take time. Everyone knows things take time.

He knows that if she goes to kiss him he will not be able to resist.

4

Under the flaming sun, Victoria Park has never looked so irresistible. The grass sparkles, the leaves are drenched with life, the water in the lake reflects the flawless sky. And the gentle, distant sounds of a football being kicked and a duck flapping its wet wings are all the noises Patricia and Clive need. Speech is worthless when the hot pavement warms the shoes and hands brush as they walk.

Clive doesn't want Patricia to cry – he hates it when she cries – but there is nothing to stop the tears dripping down her face.

He swallows and swallows again to contain his own emotion.

They turn off the path and stroll over the neat grass. Cut short enough to act as a rug. Wander beneath a canopy of trees. Through a collection of bushes. Past a bed of shrubs; bushy brown, long streaks of yellow and jagged green leaves. With the slightest of pushes Patricia steers Clive into the protruding yellow strands. That stroke his legs. That belong to the plant called *Iellabe yeffurah* ('I'll be there for ya').

Acknowledgements

Anna Davis – for all her hard work and ceaseless support. Also, David Burrows, Alice Chasey, The College of North West London, Martin Keyland, Nick McDowell and all at London Arts, Richard Milner and Barry Seymour.